PRELUDE
TO
DISCLOSURE

NIRVAN

ACKNOWLEDGEMENTS

I would like to dedicate this book to Osho, my beloved master and inspiration who was formerly known as Bhagwan Shree Rajneesh. Osho's own self-discovery enabled him to help many others find their own inner being. For this I am most grateful. Without his guidance this work of art would have not been possible to write.

A book is written by one individual, but it is produced by a tribe. In that spirit there are others to thank. My editor, Prakriti, comes first to mind for her continuous encouragement and hard work that gave this book its polish. She is in this book as much as I am.

My gratitude also goes out to those who read a very rough draft of this work and encouraged me to craft it and see it to its conclusion, they include: Leena, Stacey, Susan, Myuri, Chitta, Jayapal, Crystal, Simon and Vinaya.

Finally, I extend my love and appreciation to my beloved wife, Nirmal, who was the first to urge me to pursue this creative journey. Without her support and enthusiasm this manuscript would have not seen the light of day.

FOREWORD

You probably have never read a book like *Prelude to Disclosure*. It combines different stories, scenarios, and times, and never stops being a page-turner.

Nirvan writes with fluency that is both engaging and interesting. He postulates scenarios so familiar and completely his own. The stories involve Boston, Milan, Athens, Dharamsala, and the mountains of the Himalayas. And these places change often with different people in different times and relationships.

The plot spans mysticism, and spirituality, delves into Buddhism and the distant past, addresses the complexities of writing, and somehow easily brings it all together in a cohesive story.

Basically, it is a quest for meaning and understanding and eloquently wraps the different threads as an adventure story, that spans continents and cultures.

Prelude to Disclosure is a strange, wonderful, and multi-layered book. It is completely engrossing and never stops building on the tensions and beliefs of the characters who attempt to discover long-held secrets and travel across continents to attempt to unravel these mysteries. At the same time, we are introduced to a non-fictional Indian mystic, a sunny stoop located in one of Boston's city districts, Athenian hotels, and inside Buddhist temples. This novel seems partially to describe Nirvan's search for himself and an engrossing adventure of mammoth proportions.

We travel from modern-day America to spiritual adventures, through long-held family mysteries to strange and ruthless cloak-and-dagger societies, to places we can only imagine, always searching for a truth that seems often to be elusive.

You get the feeling that Nirvan is describing his personal experiences and uses his personal search as a guide to what is revealed.

The levels of intrigue in this book are extraordinary as we follow several convergent stories through tantalizing dimensions, learning of seekers, of universal wisdom, ancient civilizations, and mysteries.

A gripping and engrossing yarn!

John Feld

Perhaps the answer lies in the interconnectedness of all things; then again, it might just be due to mere happenstance. Regardless, the world needs to know what is about to unfold. Thus, the story begins.

1

Sparkling lights shimmered on sunlit waves that mirrored the twinkling stars on a moonless night. This is what I saw from the stairs upon which I was sitting in my hometown of East Boston. I, a rather slim, six-foot man of Italian descent have lived in this neighborhood off and on for most of my life. My ethnicity is shared by most of the neighbors that surround me, which makes for a very insulated community.

Having a disposition that avoids being a leader as well as a follower I consider myself a soloist treading his own path to whatever end it may reach. As this trait of mine has progressed with age I found myself attracted to some rather unusual directions in life. The thoroughfares I have taken led me to an East Indian guru, and a mystical view of existence.

At times my predilection toward a more etheric view of the world disturbed my more conventional family and friends which had the side-effect of disrupting my own emotional well-being. Regardless, I intended, as Joseph Campbell directed, "to follow my bliss."

While sitting on this stoop, my bliss was calling me to write a novel, and although my temperament was not conducive to enjoying long hours sitting alone writing I committed to doing just that.

The stairs offered the magnificent view of the dancing lights on Chelsea Bay that I already mentioned. Losing myself in the awe that arose from that sight I melted into a memory of another encounter I had with the mystical.

On a similar sunny day twenty or so years ago, I was sitting on this same stoop when a friend walked by who called himself Amrit Bodhi. Amrit was a young man of my age who had a boyishly good-looking face, and exhibited a fine sense of humor with his lively smile and outrageous laugh. Although I've known him for only a few months, he had lived in East Boston for several years.

"Hi Amrit, what's going on?"

"Just out for a walk on this beautiful day, my man."

"Going anywhere special?" I queried.

"Eventually," he said. "Right now, I am going to the center to run Dynamic Meditation. It starts about 8:00a.m. Come join us?"

As a follower of Bhagwan Shree Rajneesh, Amrit called himself a 'neo-sannyasin'. He was dressed from head to toe in one shade of orange or another, and wore a string of beads around his neck. Attached to the end of the beads lying in the center of his chest was a framed picture of his guru – the Bhagwan. Whenever Amrit would talk about Bhagwan, he would light up, even though he had not yet met him.

Later he would go to India and fulfill his dream of sitting with the master, but at this time he was running Bhagwan's meditation center located in Cambridge.

"You have any more converts coming to the guru *via* that crazy meditation you run?" I asked.

"Of course!" he gleamed. "Are you coming this morning?" he asked again.

Truth be told, I had been tempted to become part of his group for some time. About a month before my remembrance, I went for the first time to his center, and experienced what he called "Dynamic Meditation." It really blew my socks off.

The meditation consisted of five parts. Each segment was fifteen minutes long, and all segments were done with eyes closed or blindfolded. The technique started with a fast and furious breathing through the nose creating lightheadedness and an abundance of energy. After that phase a gong went off, and everyone started seriously emoting in whatever way they were moved to express themselves. During this segment I heard screaming, shouting, crying, laughing, floor slapping and more - much of which was coming from me. From that somewhat disquieting, but exhilarating time another gong went off ushering in the third phase. During this part of the meditation, we all jumped up and down with arms over our heads shouting what I was told was a Sufi mantra HOO! HOO! We continued this to the point of exhaustion. Gong, we entered into a fifteen-minute long period of pure silence. In that silence I reveled in a relaxation I had never known before that day.

Lost in a deep peace, a final gong rang and I was directed to open my eyes and celebrate the wonderful feeling I had just experienced by singing and dancing to Indian music. What bliss!

After such an experience I was, to say the least, captivated. Indeed, over the following month I continued to do Dynamic Meditation another eight or nine times. Amrit had often led the meditations, although he would be substituted from time to time by another guy dressed in orange.

Responding to Amrit, I told him that I was not quite ready to join the cult.

That was my introduction to Bhagwan Shree Rajneesh.

Coming back to myself I started thinking about what I was about to begin. I knew it would be a story starting in Milan, Italy during World War I. The story centered on a woman, her family, and an ancient secret the family protects.

As I was thinking these thoughts, I noticed a woman staring at me through the blinds of the first-floor apartment. I could see her standing at the living room window looking at me.

Hopefully, she didn't find me too invasive. Anyway, shrugging my shoulders I went back to my pen and notebook.

Just as I was about to put pen to paper the first-floor apartment door opens and out walks a very pretty woman about my age. She had dirty blonde hair with a bit of a wave to it that hung just below her shoulders. Being a woman of light complexion, I immediately assumed that she was of northern Italian descent. At first, I thought she might be German or Scandinavian, but guessed she was Italian, because just about everyone in Eastie was ethnically Italian.

She gave me an awkward smile that made me feel that maybe I was doing something wrong.

"Oh, I didn't know anyone was out here!" she exclaimed. "May I ask what you are doing sitting on my steps?"

"Hi, my name is Prem. I live about five houses away, and your steps have a much better view of Chelsea Bay than mine. I didn't think I would disturb anyone by sitting here?"

"Well, it is a little startling to see a stranger sitting here, but I guess it's okay, as long as you're quiet and respectable."

"I assure you that my intentions are of the utmost genteel nature. I simply want to spend some time writing my new story while sitting in the sun."

"You plan on writing a story here on my stairs?" she quickly caught herself. "It really doesn't matter, just so long as you are not noisy, and you don't litter up the place. Anyway, have a good time in the sun." Her voice trailed as she turned and strolled toward town center.

I watched as she took off down the street heading for who knows where.

Wow, I thought, that was a little strange. For such a nice-looking woman she had a rather abrupt way about her. I always did somehow attract feisty people. This trait of mine seems to be working even while quietly sitting alone.

I justified to myself that I had picked this particular spot to write, because twenty years ago I had lived in the very house attached to these stairs.

I then turned to the blank page and started writing.

2

Juliana was sitting in her living room staring at the mantel over the fireplace. It was quite an ornate piece of construction with strange faces carved into both ends, faces that looked out toward anyone in the room. The room was full of leather seating, a sofa, loveseat, and two plush chairs all turned toward the fireplace and its mantel.

The mantel had two very decorative vases with assorted flowers in them. The vases had some unusual Asian designs painted on them. Often Juliana would wonder what those designs were all about, but now she was focused on the empty area that bracketed the two vases. At one time they had served as the borders of a finely carved wooden box also of some West Asian design. That box, the same box she recalled her father talking about had not been there for a very many years. It had disappeared sometime between her sixth and seventh birthday.

At five years old Juliana distinctly recalled that her father told her oldest brother Thomas that he would soon explain to him the secret connected to the box. They were alone in the living room and were unaware of her eavesdropping as she was playing just outside of the room's entrance.

She was sure that her father had eventually told her brother whatever secret the box contained. As a matter of fact, she was sitting in that living room feeling some apprehension from the fact that her brother could die in this bloody war before ever being able to pass on that secret. Lately, this concern was occupying a good deal of her time.

After the death of her father, her brother was the only secret holder. Her father died in an unexplained explosion while sitting in the Milano library reading his newspaper. His death was devastating for her and the rest of the family. Stoically silent about the whole thing, her mother wore only black ever since that day six months ago. Her two older brothers were away at the war when it happened, and she had only minimal correspondence with them. She wrote them and received one response from Thomas and two from Guido. The tears she saw on her brothers' letters showed the depth of their grief. "How much more trouble can they take?" she thought while reading those letters.

If Juliana let herself, she could go back into the sorrow she felt upon hearing the news. She was Papa's favorite, of that, she was sure. Being the only daughter had a lot to do with that, but more than being his little girl, she and her father always seemed to be connected in some special way. They both liked opera, which her brothers hated. They both loved sitting in the library reading, and having coffee with cinnamon. In so many ways they were like two peas in a pod and she missed him terribly.

Her father always seemed to radiate a loving warmth and infinite patience toward her and her brothers. She was very impressed that his presence attracted many friends who would often come to the house asking his advice on just about anything. She missed his hugs and especially his smile and laughter.

Right now, however, she wasn't drawn to her remorse, but rather, to the secret her very vulnerable brother alone was entrusted with. What was it, and what would happen if he died before passing it on, and where the hell did that box go so long ago?

"Enough," she thought, "I will have to somehow contact my brother, and get him to tell me whatever it was my father told him." It would be difficult doing so, and would undoubtedly take *time, but she would worry about that later. Now she needed to raise herself up from her chair and go about the day.*

She took herself to the kitchen where her mother was sitting. The kitchen was large enough to fit a wooden table able to seat eight people. It was a warm room with a yellow motif that brought out its coziness even more. Her mother was sipping on her morning cappuccino, a daily ritual.

"I'm worried about Georgio," her mother said with a concerned look. "He wants to go into this damn war like his brothers, and I'm sure they will take him now that he's turned seventeen. He's too young to go, you know. Juliana, you need to tell him that he's needed here, and to forget about running off to this madness!"

Juliana had the same concern, but knew it would be to no avail to tell her headstrong younger brother to stay. With her other brothers and her husband already in the army, Georgio was the only male in the family still at home besides her small son. It would be unbearable to see him go, too.

Flushed with anger, she began to ruminate about who would help her with her mother? Was it always left up to the daughter to take care of the household?

I looked up from my notebook to watch a very old woman feebly walking by. The scene made me think that life never really ends without tragedy being felt – either the tragedy of old age, illness, or disability and, always the tragedy of death at the end. It reminded me of the Buddha's great supposition, 'Life Is Suffering.'

For sure, suffering was what my characters were going through during WWI. Suffering is what, in one way or another, we all go through while walking this path of life.

As was foreseen Georgio went into the infantry soon after that kitchen conversation leaving Juliana alone with Mama and her two kids to fend for themselves. This was a time of rationing in Italy, and the only blessing that came with losing her younger brother was the fact that there was one less mouth to feed.

Juliana would spend a good part of her day standing in line. If available she would get small amounts of vegetables, fish, chicken, and potatoes to last for four or five days; this was the routine. She would leave the kids with her mother or at school, while she waited a good part of the day for their allotted sustenance. She was grateful that the schools were still open and hoped the day would never come when they had to close because of the war.

It was after standing in line on one of these rationing sojourns, that she arrived home to find her mother occupying her usual seat at the kitchen table. She had been still thinking about the secret box over the past several weeks and had been pondering whether to bring the subject up with her mother. The one time she did so in the past she nearly got her head torn off. Evidently, there was some friction her mother had with her father about that box, and in no uncertain terms did her mother want to talk about it.

"Mama," Juliana began, "I know that you don't want to talk about the box that used to sit on the mantel. My curiosity is becoming too much, and I need to ask you about it."

"Please Juliana, don't start with that cursed box again. Your father always acted strange around that thing, and I never understood why. He would never tell me anything about it," Mama replied. "Why do you want to know anyway?"

"I don't really know, but for some reason I feel it is important for me to know," Juliana responded. "I just want to find out what happened to it. One day it was there and the next day it was gone, and nothing was ever said about its disappearance that I'm able to remember. I just recall that Papa looked horrible for some time after it went missing, and that he was in such an unusually bad mood for a long time afterwards."

"That he was, but he refused to confide in me about it, and I am still angry and hurt about that," said Mama. "Nothing was said because your father never said anything about that damn box even though we all knew it was important to him."

"So, you know nothing about what happened to it?"

"I didn't say that!" her mother yelled. "The box was stolen right from under our noses."

"What, how?" Juliana queried in shock.

"I don't know, and to this day the event freaks me out. Can you imagine, someone broke into the apartment while we were all asleep? Anything could have happened – we could have been murdered, for Chrissake!" her mother said, raising her voice.

"You mean you have no idea who did it?" Juliana continued.

Her mother looked deep into her eyes, then looked down at the floor as if she was trying to find words to respond. "No, I have no idea, but I believe your father knew, or at least I'm sure he had a suspicion."

Her mother, Sophia, continued, "I was in the room when he told your brother that he should have been more careful with the box. He said that his grandfather repeatedly warned him that this would happen if he wasn't vigilant. That was all I was allowed to hear, because your father asked me to leave the living room and then shut the door, while he told your brother to stay. They continued with the conversation, but I was unable to make out what they said. Can you imagine that my own husband kicked me out of the room, and my son said nothing to him! Men, sometimes, I cannot abide by them!"

Life became very hectic after this scene, and Juliana had neither the time nor inclination to pursue learning any more about the box or its secret. She had all she could do to take care of her mother, her children, and herself. The war was raging on and getting closer to the western border of Italy.

Italy was on the side of the Triple Entente of Britain, France, and Russia; although for most of the period leading up to the war, she supported the views of the Triple Alliance made up of Germany, Austria, and Hungary. Italy did not enter the war until late 1914 after it was already raging, thinking to assess first who had the edge. She picked the Triple Entente, and although

Italy ended up on the winning side, her experience of the war was disastrous, both during and after it.

The Italian military was advancing into Austria near its border, but got bogged down in what the Italians called Caporetto and the Serbs called Kobarid. Here they fought against not only the Austrian army, but seven divisions of the German army, as well. They were overrun and retreated over their northwest border close to Venice. They managed to stem the Triple Alliance's advance so that Milano along with the rest of northern Italy was spared a destructive horror.

They were not unable to avoid great loss of life during the war, however and the battle of Caporetto is still considered to be the greatest single defeat for the Italian army in its entire history.

It is no wonder then, that Juliana received the horrible news that her youngest brother had died during that battle and then shortly after receiving that letter her brother, Guido, came home missing his right leg, and much of his mental health. Today we would call it PTSD, but in those days, it was referred to as 'shell-shocked'.

With another loved one to take care of, Juliana was traumatized herself. There was no time to deal with her emotions, so she collapsed into survival mode and was indeed a survivor, as the crisis brought out the best in her.

Boy, that was a good start for the novel. I didn't think I had that much in me in one sitting. It was growing late, however, and there would be many more days to continue. As I got up and packed my notebook into my satchel, I looked up to see the feisty lady who had left me a few hours ago coming up the stairs.

"You're still here?"

"Yep, but I'm just about to leave. By the way, thanks for letting me write on your steps. It is such a pleasant place to do so and I got a lot done," I was being diplomatic.

She smiled at my attempt at diplomacy.

"You're welcome," she sounded ambivalent.

"You know, I told you my name when you were leaving the house, but you didn't tell me yours?"

"Let's leave that for now," was her retort as she opened her front door and disappeared into the house.

All I could think was, "Wow!"

3

Shanti and I had been lovers for a brief period in Poona, India. Our affair was short, but very sweet. She left me for another, although the parting was actually a mutual agreement.

I still have a great love for Shanti although it does not include sex. Love in my experience never deserts lovers, however, it often changes form as to its expression. I would argue that those couples that ended hating each other after parting either never loved each other in the first place, or were just protecting themselves from the deep sadness their ongoing love generates.

At this time in our lives Shanti and I had transitioned that love we shared into being roommates. We occupied the middle apartment of a three-story tenement at 23 Bremen Street just a few houses down from my favorite stoop. We also had front stairs, but they had no view of the water, and I was never drawn to hang out on them.

Our apartment was a cute three-bedroom affair with us each having one bedroom, while the third bedroom became a TV room. The living room was left to entertain company, or to sit and read, or meditate. The room was large enough to include a sofa and lounge chair at one end while on the other end it had zafus for sitting meditations, and an altar dedicated to our spiritual practice.

The two of us were sitting in the living room reminiscing about our lives as sannyasins. I was retelling her the story of meeting Amrit and how I came to take initiation with Bhagwan.

"I had done a month of Dynamic meditation," as I recalled. "After that I got further into the scene at the center and became good friends with Amrit and Soma, the other meditation leader. They turned me onto Kundalini and Nadabrahma meditations. I really loved these along with Dynamic and started doing one, two, or sometimes all three of them daily."

"I reveled in all the meditating I was doing, but I was not drawn toward the group even though Amrit and Soma kept on suggesting that I get more involved. It wasn't until another woman devotee named Gautami, lent me a taped discourse that she had of Bhagwan speaking that I became hooked. I decided to ask my friend, Jimmy, to listen to the borrowed tape with me."

After a dinner of wine and cheese sausages with broccoli that we had prepared, we retired into the living-room to listen to Bhagwan.

From the beginning sentence I was caught up in the overwhelming feeling that for the first time in my life someone really knew me. Bhagwan spoke as if he knew my personal life intimately. He talked about the fear and isolation that I felt, about my very personal quest to discover what love really was. He talked about going deep into the human condition to discover a more authentic self. Somehow, I could almost feel this authentic self even though I never until that moment thought I had one to miss.

Bhagwan spoke about the need for humans to become enlightened to who they were, and at the same time exalted Socrates' understanding that 'not knowing' was a superior state of being. Sounds contradictory, but when unlocked it is anything but. Mind with its constant chatter was simply mimicking what it had been programmed to learn by society, and that society included parents, teachers, relatives, friends and the general consensus at large. Enlightenment was remembering one's original self before any conditioning – what Zen practitioners meant by saying, "Find the face you had before you were born."

Anyway, I was striking two for two with this guru. First, his meditations were taking me to levels of relaxation never felt before, and now his message was resonating with my deeper core. Was it any wonder that I became enamored with the idea of following my sannyasin friends into becoming a disciple and calling Bhagwan "Master." Disciple, master, all terms foreign to my understanding of the world, but what the heck, sometimes it's just right to dive in. Of course, Shanti already knew all this.

I continued recounting to Shanti that the 'diving in' happened very quickly without much rumination about what I was diving into. This became my first lesson on the path. Namely, I discovered the satisfaction of spontaneously following my heart.

Taking 'sannyas' is a very old tradition in India and the term is used when an individual, usually after living the life as a householder, dons orange clothing and begins wandering through the countryside seeking enlightenment. These original sannyasins become celibate, homeless beggars who walk all over India meditating and at times pontificating the spiritual insights they may or may not have experienced. Bhagwan's sannyas was anything but old-style sannyas. Sex, material abundance and no begging were its tenets. Any resemblance to old-style sannyas consisted mainly of wearing all orange clothing and hanging a 108-bead mala around our necks. Our mala differed from the old traditional mala only by having a picture of Bhagwan at the end of it instead of ending in a simple knot.

The sannyas I became initiated into was all about experiencing just about anything, but with the stipulation of doing it with awareness. Old-style sannyas was repressive, whereas Bhagwan's new style is expressive.

Anyway, talking to Shanti, I said, "I took discipleship by mail, and I took it piecemeal. I started out dressing in half orange rather than the mandatory full regalia. I had to wait for a name and the required mala to wear, and when I received these through the mail, I called myself by my first name rather than the customary last. Such was my auspicious beginning."

She laughed and relayed to me a bizarre story that initiated her sannyas beginnings. It seems that one night, living in Manhattan, she had a dream in which she saw a guy who was behind a wall of fire. He was beckoning her to come through the fire to join him. She was hesitant and refused. Several nights later the dream repeated itself only this time she took the bait and walked unscathed through the flames to him.

Now the story really gets strange, because a week later she is walking by a bookstore in Soho, and on the cover of one of the display books, who does she see, but the same man who came to her in her dreams.

"Now, how can you refuse an invitation like that?" She smiled at me. "I immediately ran into that bookstore and grabbed that book just to discover who he was. He was Bhagwan of course, and then just like you I was mesmerized by the feeling that this person knew me in depth after reading just the first chapter."

Yup, we were part of the admiration society of Bhagwan Shree Rajneesh.

Naturally, the story continues, but that will have to wait until another time.

4

*A*t first upon seeing her brother Guido hobbling around on a wooden leg brought tears to Juliana's eyes and a queasiness to her stomach. Still with all her sorrow she tried to cheer him up, but he was not having any of it. His shock lingered while Juliana and her mother did their best to support and care for him. The household took on an air of depression as all of them shared in the horror of a life cut short, and another crippled.

If it wasn't for Juliana's daughter Lisa, the heaviness of the situation would have been even more unbearable. Lisa was a lot like her grandmother. She was gregarious and open, and adventurous with a can-do personality. At the age of seven she brought light into the darker corners looking continuously at the brighter side of life.

"Uncle Guido, please play with me and Sal. We can wheel you out and play with the ball Mama gave me."

"I can't do that," Guido sighed.

"Yes, you can," she would insist. "You don't need your leg to throw us the ball, and anyway we can run and get it for you if it gets away. We'll stay right in the backyard. Please!"

Every day it was the same scenario. Lisa would ask and Guido would refuse. This went on for many a day, and Guido in exasperation would shout at his niece to stop being a pest. She would not stop, however, and eventually got him to come out of the house-cave and throw the ball to her and her brother Sal.

Lisa was that type of a person even at a very young age to be able to walk into a room and bring with her a breath of fresh air. Almost everyone who met her would instantly like her, although in later years her exuberant energy would help foster jealousy in a few insecure souls.

She and her five-year old brother, Sal, were tight as a new jar of pickles. He would follow her everywhere; and she for her part was extremely protective of him.

Sal was quite different from his over vivacious sister. He had all the indications of growing up to be a nerd. Though outspoken with his sister, he was shy and reclusive with others. He tended to play alone when not playing with his sister and appeared to look at whatever he was involved in with more of a pensive attitude.

He would grow up with an intellectual bent and a scientific mind. The two of them were all and everything to their mother and grandmother, but even more to each other.

The war was dragging on and riots were breaking out in Milan making it at times one scary place to be. The family took to huddling together during this time anxiously waiting for some word from the front about the status of the other two men.

Sadly, oh so sadly, tragedy began repeating itself when another letter came to Juliana that declared the death of her husband. Her younger brother, and now her husband died in what was implied to be the glorious line of duty – for country and friends! A final letter arrived that informed them that Thomas was missing in action, and although they held on to some hope of his return it did not look good.

How does one deal with such loss? To Juliana looking at the rest of her family it was incomprehensible. The grief was overbearing, indescribable, and beyond painful. Juliana, and especially Sophia often felt that they could not go on living. If either of *them was left completely alone the chances of not continuing to live would have been more probable than not.*

If it wasn't for Guido and the kids to care for, their will to go on would have been shattered. Love and sadness walked hand in hand aiding and abetting each other.

Over the course of the next ten years life was difficult, but they all survived, and to some of those looking on they seemed to even thrive through the difficulty.

That night, before going to sleep I pondered the extreme loss my characters had to endure. That kind of loss either broke you or drove you into a search for real meaning in life. When you realize that you cannot hang onto anything you are often driven over the cliff that yearns to discover what is beyond change.

Since change is a constant, the search for the changeless becomes a Zen Koan. Perhaps there is no answer to what is changeless, but then again perhaps there is.

In the morning after breakfast, I gravitated to my favorite stoop to continue my story. Unfortunately, or perhaps fortunately I was not able to immediately start writing, because I discovered a rather depressed ten-year old boy sitting there.

"Hey, how's it going?" I asked.

"Not very well," he responded.

"That sounds ominous. What's wrong?"

"Nothing."

"Don't sound like nothing," I insisted.

"I don't want to talk about it, and anyway who are you?"

"My name is Prem. What's yours?"

"I'm Joseph."

Our conversation was simple to the max.

"Are you related to the pretty lady that I saw here yesterday?" I asked.

"Yeah, she is my mom."

"Now we're getting somewhere," I said. "Are you having problems with her, has she grounded you or something? I mean I know how it can be with parents sometimes, they can be a bit grouchy!"

"No, no, I'm okay with her and my grandma."

A pregnant silence pursued this statement and continued between us for many minutes when he began describing what had happened.

"I was walking by the school on Trenton Street, when Ralphie and his friends stopped me. They grabbed me and held me down, pulled down my pants and pointed to my penis. It was horrible," he said looking down.

Having grown up in the inner city I knew what it was like to be troubled by a street gang. This was a sexual assault whether he knew it not, and that could leave scars.

"Anything else happened?" I asked.

"There were several girls there, and one of them laughed and said that it was so small, and then they all laughed," he continued.

I knew that I was in a very delicate situation here. What could I say to help this kid out? I heard both shame and embarrassment within his sentences, and then to think of the powerlessness he must have felt. A simple event taking mere minutes of time to occur could have such an overwhelming effect on a life.

"Joey, may I call you Joey?" I asked. "Don't let those idiots get you down. What could you do? There were a lot of them and only one of you, and that girl probably never saw a penis in her entire life, and has no idea what is big or small. Anyway, you are only a kid and things get a lot bigger when you grow up."

I hoped that would help, but who knows?

Joseph was not doing too well, but I knew that he would get over it, hopefully without much trauma. At this point the feisty, pretty lady from yesterday came out of a car that she had just paralleled parked. She ascended the stairs, and seeing the young boy immediately intuited his dejected posture.

"What's the matter Joey?" she queried.

He did not tell her all that he told me, but simply relayed that he had a fight with someone. She glanced over at me before consoling him.

"Come on. Forget about it. Come into the house. I have a pumpkin pie, your favorite." She went inside expecting Joey to follow.

"Please don't tell her what I told you", he pleaded.

I nodded my assurance, and he went into the house.

I was not long in my solitude before she returned, coming out of the apartment to sit down on the stoop beside me. Pulling out a cigarette she offered me one, and although tempted, I refused having just given up the habit.

"So, what's going on with Joseph?" Maria was staring at me.

"Honestly, I cannot tell you anything. It is up to him to share the details."

"Oh, come on. What's your name, again? Prime?" she said off-handedly. "He is my son and I have a right to know what went down here. He is only ten and I'm his mother."

"My name is Prem. I agree with you, but he asked me not to say anything to you and in this case, I believe that it is not life or death whether I tell you or not, so it is up to him to tell you, and not up to me. He is your son."

"What are you doing back on my stairs, anyway, and what gives you the right to interfere in my family's life? Honestly, I didn't give you permission to be here, or do so."

"I'm sorry that you are so upset," I sighed. "I wasn't expecting to converse with your son, although I think it was really fate that had me arrive here when I did. Joseph needed to share his angst with someone, so I don't regret that I was here. I also hope that he shares his feelings with you as well, but maybe you should leave that up to him, and not take it out on me."

At that moment, she was at the point of tears and seemed frustrated with herself. She took a puff of smoke, then turned to face me. Oh my god, she was pretty. No, beautiful. Why does sex rear its persistent head even at times like this? I could feel it welling up in me as I took in her face and figure.

"You're right," she acknowledged. "I am just worried about him and want to protect him. It is not your fault that he is hurting."

"You know," I said, "the streets can be a tough place sometimes and other kids can be cruel. Your son just ran into life not being so nice to him. I am sure that when he is ready, he will tell you, and I'm also sure that he is stronger than you think and that he will get over this."

"Anyway, thanks for being there for him," she said with some doubt in her voice. "He told me that you're pretty cool, so whatever you said to him must have been good. When I came out here, I was so distraught that I was going to ask you to leave, but truth be told that was just my frustration speaking. Are you here to write more?" she said with an earnest expression.

"That was my intention," I contributed. "Not sure if I can write now, after all this sharing with you and your son."

"Well, if you can't write, will you let me invite you inside and offer you a piece of my mom's wonderful pumpkin pie? Perhaps Joey will talk to me if you're there."

Joey was not ready to tell his mother about his embarrassment, but the situation I walked into in the pretty lady's kitchen was warmer and less distressed than it was moments earlier.

"By the way," I asked. "Now, can you share your name with me?

"My name is Maria."

"Maria, I just met a girl named Maria." West Side Story's soundtrack invaded my inner mind – I couldn't help myself.

Making coffee and offering me some pumpkin pie, Maria asked inquisitively, "So, tell me about yourself."

"Me? Where do I begin?" I proceeded to tell her that I had lived in East Boston many years ago although I was not originally from here. I told her that I was born in the North End and spent my early youth there. Of course, she knew of the North End as the other Italian section of Boston, the one with all the fine cafes and restaurants, and the Italians right off the boat.

"My parents moved to Eastie when I was in second grade. I went to public school all the way through East Boston High," I continued. We exchanged some high school stories as she also went to Eastie High although some three or four years after I did. We both took French class with Mrs. Mable and science with Mr. Alfonso.

We talked about crazy Ms. Frances who could never control her class. How she maintained her position stumped us both, but she did.

I told her that after high school I went to Bentley College of Accounting and got a degree there, and how I finally ended up in Suffolk University where I got a Master's degree in Psychology.

"How did you go from accounting to psychology?" she asked.

This question I got a lot, so I had my ready-made answer and quickly expressed it. "I hated working for International Harvester and thought it would be better working with people rather than chained to a desk working with paper."

My switch over was far more complicated than that, but I wasn't about to go into that whole story at that time. At this point I stopped in my narrative and turned the tables on her by asking her to tell me about her own story.

Maria informed me that she originally lived in the Jeffries Point section of the town. Growing up with two sisters in a three-story house that her parents owned she had both fond and uncomfortable memories attached to it.

Most of the houses in Eastie, as the city district was called, were three-story dwellings with an apartment for each floor. She said that she was one of many kids growing up in a neighborhood of sameness. That sameness could be seen in the almost identical dwellings on the outside and the similar lives on the inside.

Maria lived in her childhood house until she was twenty-two, and only left it when she married Mario. When she moved, it was only to go about a block away from her parent's home to Spencer Avenue where she found herself in the only two-story apartment building in the whole of Jeffries Point.

Their lovely apartment was very airy and gave them more room than they ever had in their lives. Living in a five-room apartment with four other people did not lend itself to living in spaciousness, but the four-room apartment with Mario seemed indeed grandiose. Furthermore, the flat overlooked Boston Harbor with a spectacular view of Boston proper.

The first few years of the honeymooners living in their own flat were happy ones. They found that they both enjoyed a similar lifestyle: walking along the bay especially on full-moon nights, going to movies, and jazz clubs. Most importantly, they were two Italians who loved Italian food and wine. Maria reminisced, "It was the best two years of my life."

All this wonderfulness came to an end she said after Joseph came into their lives. At first, their small six-pound, two-ounce, baby brought even more brightness to their Spencer Avenue apartment. It was hard work caring for him, but very rewarding. Mario and Maria grew closer caring for Joseph.

Unfortunately, the bliss did not last for long. Mario lost his job five months after the birth, and trouble began. Try as he might Mario could not find any replacement work. The burden of not being able to provide for his family quickly, some say too quickly, brought out the worst in him.

Funny, how survival brings out either the best or the worst in a person. With Mario it brought out the worst, and in that way, he followed the behavior of several members of his family. He began drinking, and then drinking too much. At one point, Maria had to go out to work leaving Mario at home to tend to Joseph, and that created an additional impetus for him to spiral down into even more self-destructive behavior. Pride, one of those seven deadly sins, took its grip.

Finally, after three years of fighting, crying, tension and exhaustion Maria had enough. She left him. "From bliss to despair," she said.

Meanwhile, a similar tragic scenario was playing out between her parents. Maria's eldest sister, she relayed, often said, "Our parents had an ongoing war for all the time we've known them." During Maria's time with Mario this war continued unabated, and eventually took its toll on her father's heart. He died of a massive heart attack while taking a stress test at the Massachusetts General Hospital.

Maria lamented that her mother, Isabella, was not one to be shy about her anger. She was a hard-nosed daughter of immigrant workers who grew up in the inner city of Boston. This did not make for a meek and mild-mannered personality, no, on the contrary, she could mix it up with the best of them. She was not about to forgive the doctors at 'Mass General' and would carry a caustic opinion of their worth until her death.

Isabella was, however, a woman with a large heart who cared and protected her family with a zeal that rivaled a mother jaguar. She loved her three daughters and adored her one grandchild, Joseph, beyond imagining. She loved her husband Roberto as well, but often fought with him.

She moved in with Maria about a year after Roberto died. Everyone in the family was on the same page with this decision as it would help Maria with Joseph and would alleviate her mother's loneliness.

Her story was all too familiar to me as my other friends had similar sagas living in provincial and insulated East Boston.

All in all, I had a great time sitting in Maria's kitchen relaying stories with her. Her son had left us toward the beginning of the conversation and her mother must have been out, because I did not see her there at all. Anyway, after this time I looked at my watch and realized it was creeping deeper into the afternoon, and that I hadn't written a thing.

"Maria, would you mind if I sit on your stairs and write for an hour or two?" I asked, "I really must write something."

"Oh, I'm sorry," she quipped. "I didn't mean to take up all your time."

"No, no," I didn't want her to feel that she had been an interference. "Please, you did not take all my time. I thoroughly enjoyed our connection."

"I did too." She smiled and said, "Sure, it's okay to do your thing on my stairs."

5

Her oldest brother had died over ten years ago and with him whatever secret he held pertaining to the now twenty-year missing box. Juliana had often thought about that secret, but had long ago given up any hope of discovering it.

Both her children were now in their mid to late teens, her mother was still very vibrant, and her brother Guido was still hobbling around. He had taken to woodworking, creating some of the finest finished furniture she had seen around the city. He was somewhat of a master with applying precious and semi-precious inlays to his tables, chairs, beds and sofas. Even the wooden leg Guido was fitted with after the war, was decorated with his fine inlays and craftsmanship.

The kids were still in school although Lisa was just about to graduate Scuola Media Superiore (high school), while Sal still had two years to graduate.

Lisa had grown to be quite the headstrong beauty, and her handsome brother turned out to be the studious and quiet boy his younger self seemed to predict.

The glue that held this group together was Juliana. She worked as a cleaner for the Italian government in the downtown area of Milan, while being the chief cook and bottle washer for everyone at home. Her mother helped with the cooking and caring of the house, and her brother helped with money whenever he could sell his furniture. With both of their incomes the family was able to live a comfortable if not lavish lifestyle.

Life for this family had settled into a usual and comfortable daily affair. No grand adventures were on the horizon, although Lisa's graduation foretold of something new to begin, but this was expected to be a rather mundane change as changes go.

It happened, however, that the graduation was more of a prelude to a much greater change that came abruptly on a Sunday in 1927. That day a message arrived via the Italian postal service. It was very unusual, to say the least, that a postman should knock on the door to bring a message of any kind to the family. In all the years since before the war never was a package or special letter sent to anyone at the family's address. Yet, that Sunday in November a knock did come, and a postman did stand just outside the door holding a letter addressed to Juliana.

The postman had a sheepish expression on his face when he asked for Juliana and presented her with an ordinary looking letter. She looked down at the letter and then back up at the postman who was beginning to speak.

"It is with great regret that this got lost in the mail for so long. Your government wants you to know that this was found in the vast postal system and is sorry for the delay." With that said, the postman abruptly turned and left Juliana wide-mouthed and speechless.

After a moment of surprise, she looked down at the letter in her hand to realize that it was indeed addressed to her from her missing brother Thomas, and that it was postmarked January 15, 1917.

"What the hell?" shaking internally. "This is over ten years old," her breath was short and uneven with her hands slightly trembling.

It was the following night that the whole family was sitting in the living room awaiting something that Juliana had cryptically informed them they would all need to hear about. While Guido and his mother were seated on the sofa, Sal was in one of the chairs while his sister was in the other. Juliana stood in front of them and steeled her gaze.

"So, what is all the fuss?" Guido started.

"Yah, what are we all doing here? I have some schoolwork to finish and so does Sal."

Sophia just sat with a serene, but puzzled look.

Juliana still had her apron on having just finished with the dishes. She must have been thinking some very deep thoughts, because the expression on her face was closer to a frown than a smile, although to be truthful it seemed to be something in between the two.

She reached into her apron pocket and pulled out a letter. She looked at it with deep penetrating eyes and sighed. Her hands would not stop shaking.

"What is it?" her mother questioned with concern.

"Mama," Juliana started, "this is a letter that I just received from Thomas."

"What!" Everyone, but Sal exclaimed.

"What are you talking about? Thomas has been dead forever. What are you saying Juliana, he's alive?" Guido shouted excitedly.

"The postman came by yesterday and handed me this" as she raised her hand with the letter in it. "He apologized to me, because he said that it was lost in the system for so long. It is dated 15/1/1917 just before the Battle of Caporetto."

"What does it say, Ma?" Lisa quietly asked.

"I don't know, because I have not read it yet," her mother explained. "I wanted to read it together with all of you."

They all looked at each other apprehensively. As Juliana broke the seal, she pulled out the enclosed letter and began to slowly open it. She began reading out loud her brother's words.

Dear Juliana,

 I am not sure if this will be my last day on the planet. We have been taking many casualties, and I am told that this may be all leading to some culmination in this war.

 I want you to know that I think of you, Mama and the rest of the family often, and wish that somehow, I could fly home on a magic carpet and get out of this hell. This fantasy is not to happen however, and I have a horrible feeling I may not get to see you again.

 Hopefully I am wrong, and I can return and see your lovely face again, but if it is not to be, I want you to give mama and Guido, Lisa and Sal my love. Tell them I am thinking of all of them.

 I am thinking mostly of you little sister. You, who was always under my feet. You, who always had a beautiful smile, and you, who had the most inquisitive nature.

 You were always trying to find out about that box Papa lost long ago, and it is about that box that I need to share something with you. It is important that you find it and bring it back to its proper place in the family.

 It would not be good for me to tell you all that was relayed to me from Papa. If this letter were to get into the wrong hands it might be dangerous for all of you.

 Just know that the flowers hold the key to the secret you covet.

 With all my love.

Your Brother,
Thomas

6

Several months before my first visit to India I was sitting on my bed reading one of Bhagwan's books. In it he was saying, *everything is perfect just as it is.*

This one statement had such a profound effect on my life. In fact, it could be said that this utterance so completely changed my life that I would differentiate between Prem before everything is perfect, and Prem after everything is perfect - kind of like B.C. and A.D. They represent two completely different universes, but not really.

The very concept was startling to me. Later, when I would tell others about this understanding it never ceased to amaze me that most didn't even understand what was being said in this short sentence. The majority of those that did understand couldn't feel the overwhelming indication of its power.

I saw myself as most imperfect. I looked at myself as either right or wrong, but not perfect. I felt myself lacking in great thoughts, feelings, and deeds, anything but perfect. To grasp the idea that everything could be perfect just the way it is, was mind blowing. The idea was outrageous, but so damn freeing.

It was the free feeling that I became focused on. Through that feeling that nothing could be wrong came the essence of freedom itself. I really felt that I got the message.

This was my first inkling of non-dual reality. After all, if nothing could be wrong, then nothing could be right.

After imbibing these words, I took a walk, and it was as if I was walking in mid-air. Normally, the concrete and city buildings could be somewhat oppressive, but I remember walking down that street only feeling the freedom of the slight breeze blowing from the bay.

Shortly after this experience I was on my way to India, and specifically to Poona, India. I went with a small group of fellow seekers. My close friend Govind was there as well as Debbie and Chandra. I, of course, by this time had taken sannyas by mail as had Govind and Chandra. Debbie had decided to take initiation when she found herself in the presence of the master.

It was a rather long trip taken on Air India Airlines. We stopped in Rome where the airport looked like a fortified enclosure. To my great surprise Italian troops with automatic weapons were everywhere. It was the first time I was out of the country, and my first venture off the plane looked like a war zone. We landed next in Dubai, a place I had never heard of in Arabia. We were not even allowed to de-board the plane in Dubai, once again bringing up a sense of paranoia. Finally, after some thirty-two hours we touched down in Bombay, India.

As the plane's door opened to start de-boarding procedures, the smell of Bombay assaulted my nostrils. It was a sensory experience I will never forget. The smell of waste material wafted in the air from what looked to be the seaside. With that rather unpleasant exposure I felt a most amazing feeling of coming home.

"Oh boy," Govind said. "We are in for quite an adventure."

Govind was older than I by about 5 years. We had met at the meditation center where he also became enamored with Bhagwan. A native of Boston, he lived in the multicultural neighborhood of the Fens near Fenway Park in Boston. Studying to be an architect he was an intellectual with a lively imagination. We spent hours together over coffee in Harvard Square discussing philosophy and life in general.

"You can say that again," our friend Debbie added as we went to find a downtown hotel via taxi.

Govind and I ended up rooming together in the Laxmi Hotel, which was a small mid-range hotel next to the luxurious Taj Mahal Hotel. Across the street from our dwelling was a boat dock that moored the ferry that motored to the island of Elephanta.

Chandra and Debbie had taken the room next to ours, and the four of us planned to visit Elephanta the next day before taking the hundred-mile taxi ride to Poona.

Having secured our room and parked our bags, Govind and I stepped out of the hotel to walk around our new surroundings. On the way to the hotel from the airport we were met with a colorful variety of living arrangements along the roads we traversed. First, there were mud huts, then corrugated metal shacks, and in between these were a multitude of people sitting, eating, and lying by the side of the road and in the passing fields. Every smell from onions cooking, to manure, and human shit accompanied all this. The four of us kept looking at each other as if to say, "What did we get into?"

Anyway, we ended up at our hotel where apartment buildings, hotels, and other beautiful housing were the norm. Wanting to see this area Govind and I began our stroll only to be taken aback at the sidewalk right outside our hotel. There in the gutter was a man who looked to be about fifty years old in a loincloth, dead. Flies were hovering over his body as we were stopped in our tracks.

Some years later, Govind informed me it was at that moment of seeing the dead Indian on the street that he first decided that this place was not for him. He was later to have an experience with Bhagwan that sealed the deal to this notion.

Bombay was a complete assault of the normalcy of our life in the USA. Somehow, we managed to continue our way weaving through streets all filled with countless vehicles driving all over the place without regard for any traffic lanes. Such a mess, but what a scene to take in on our first day. We ended up at a juice bar where we ordered what was called a 'mango pulp'. This was puree mango with crème on top, and to say it was delicious would be an understatement.

At this point, I suggested we go get some sleep, but to my utter surprise Govind told me that he wanted to get some hashish. Govind loved grass and hashish and we were told by friends back in the West that it was very easy to get hashish anywhere in India.

We had this street urchin following us around from the time we entered the street. He begged for some alms that we provided. After receiving his gift, he continued to follow us with what appeared to be just curiosity. Govind turned to him as we came out of the fruit place and putting his hands up to his mouth, mimicking smoking, he said to the kid,

"Hashish?"

The urchin looked puzzled for only a moment and then lit up with a smile and shook his head in understanding. He waved Govind on, and Govind started to follow him. I stopped Govind and told him that I was not interested in chasing after the weed. He insisted that he was, and so I departed for our hotel room, and he hightailed it with our little friend to parts unknown.

I have to give Govind credit. He really must have wanted his hashish to go boldly down unknown streets only with a foreign child guide he just met off the street.

I may have been only twenty-two years old at the time, but a 32-hour flight was still exhausting, so I went back to my hotel to get some needed shuteye. Indeed, I was asleep almost before my head hit the rather too soft pillow and stayed that way until I heard rummaging noises within the room.

Sure enough, it was Govind back from his adventure. Looking at my watch I noted that four hours had passed since I left him. I was still very groggy, but also very curious to know about his recent adventure.

"So, tell me, what the hell happened?"

"You're never going to believe this," Govind started. "I followed the kid through all these back alleys into a whole other world within the bowels of Bombay. We took so many lefts and rights that I couldn't tell you where I actually went. He took me past many people sitting out in inner courtyards and alleyways. We went into tunnels under buildings and over several small bridges crossing open sewer trenches. Finally, we ended up in a courtyard where three old guys were sitting cross legged in a circle smoking what I knew was ganja. I was so totally lost - there was no way I could get back by myself."

"The kid stayed with me all that time. He said something to the old guys and then they invited me to sit with them and have a smoke. I just took two tokes, boy, was it strong! We did some short negotiating, and I bought a bag of the stuff for 50 rupees. They lifted a colored plastic bag that I inspected. The smell was by itself intoxicating," Govind continued. "My little friend was so far out, really, I couldn't believe what he did."

"Tell me," I waited with some anticipation.

"He started taking me back through all the twists and turns we had previously traversed, and as we did, I started getting very dizzy with the ganja and the heat. I passed out in the middle of that labyrinth. Shit man, I had my money pouch and my passport on me, and I was completely out of it. Do you know what that kid did? He crouched down and watched over me until I was conscious enough to get up and follow him, and he brought me back here. Can you imagine?"

"You are one hell of a lucky son of a bitch to have come out of that alive," I exclaimed with a little bit of awe. "Just goes to show you that India is mind-blowing in so many different ways. I am so glad you made it back here intact," I finished with such relief.

I would have hated to have tried to find him by myself, or to have had to inform his mother, whom I knew, that her son was either dead or lost in India. It was really a selfish thought, but shit…this was a bit over my head.

We both went to our beds and slept through the night. In the morning we picked up Debbie and Chandra for breakfast and went on an excursion to Elephanta.

What I loved and was grateful to India for was the fact that most of the shop and hotel people spoke great English due to the fact that they had been under English rule for many years.

We found a great breakfast place for eggs in the Taj, and then started on our island adventure.

Chandra and Debbie had been a couple for quite some years. Over the past year they were going through a bit of a rough patch together, but interesting enough, becoming enthralled with Bhagwan together seemed to smooth out the difficulties their relationship was going through.

They were the impetus for us going to the Elephanta Caves as they had at one time both been very interested in the Hindu religion and history.

Elephanta is an island just six to seven miles off the coast of Bombay, and it was an ancient Hindu place of retreat and reflection. Although it has two Buddhist cave temples carved out of stone, it originally was a Shiva temple as five older caves are adorned with the images of Shiva and the Hindu cosmology of Shiva. One of the great temple caves occupies a good deal of the island, and it is obvious that this was a major place of worship during its time. Now, it is a well-visited tourist destination.

Walking up to the caves the narrow road was lined with vendors selling all manner of wares from small statuettes, to scarfs and wooden flutes. Also lining the road were a hoard of overactive monkeys. One of these little fellows stole Chandra's pineapple slices that he was enjoying on the hike. Chandra's face turned beet red as we all laughed at his misfortune.

The caves, and what was left of the stone sculptures were magnificent to quietly take in. The highlight of the place is a gigantic carved rendition of Shiva's three faces as the centerpiece of the main Hindu temple.

Unfortunately, many of the island's carved statues were destroyed by the Portuguese when they took over the island by force in the 1500s. These same Portuguese as they tried to carry away a large sculpture of an Elephant dropped it in the ocean. Hence, the name "Island of Elephanta".

It was while we were visiting the main temple cave complex that Govind and I became briefly separated from Chandra and Debbie. During this short interlude a fakir approached both of us and stopped us with a piercing look. He then proceeded to tell us not to try to leave Poona and go sightseeing to other parts of India because it would not happen.

"Stay in Poona," the fakir commanded. "You will not be able to go elsewhere from Bombay as what you seek is in Poona and nowhere else." With that utterance he left us with our eyes glazed.

"What was that all about?" I asked Govind. He simply shrugged his shoulders and gave a look of complete ignorance.

"Did you know that guy?" I said this as I came out of my awe and started looking for the fakir among the crowd, but of course, I could not see him anywhere. I knew that Govind could not have possibly known a fakir who was only wearing a lungi and badly worn sandals.

Govind finally found his tongue uttering, "How could he possibly know we are going to Poona?" India could be a mysteriously weird place.

The whole vibe of the country was one of mystery and strangeness. It was a bit confusing to me just why I felt so at home here, and how I felt that way from the first moment of my arrival.

Later that same day we were off to Poona in one of the most harrowing taxi drives any of the four of us had ever taken. We almost collided head on with four cars and a truck while nearly slipping over a cliff. Somehow, we all made it.

7

It has been several weeks since I have done any writing, but this was not the result of not trying. It seems that those times I took my position on my favorite stoop I was interrupted by Maria and/or her son.

At first, I thought this was just a coincidence, but after the third time realized they wanted my attention. First, it was Joey who needed to share more of the trauma of the incident with his pants. He was able to share the shame he felt during the violation. I found myself absorbed with his process. There was a delight in being there for someone who was in need.

Joey, I could see, was a thoughtful kid and rather timid. He reminded me of myself and of Sal, the character I created in my novel. He spent a great deal of time with himself preoccupied with his own activities. Being very sensitive, he could have easily tried to destructively bury it. I thought this would have happened without encouragement to explore his feelings.

While he was talking to me, I tried to get him to feel his anger, rather than his feeling of being a victim. I spent a considerable amount of time with Joey listening and helping him to vent his feelings.

Anyway, no writing happened that day; then about 3 days later I again was on the stairs pondering the direction that

Juliana and her family were going in when Maria stepped out to interrupt my revelry.

She started by asking me about her son, and I related to her that I had a very good talk with him. I told her about how sensitive I saw him to be; she nodded. From there we went on to other things. She talked to me about the difficulty of living with her mother. I shared with her the problems I had with my father. I told her that thankfully, he didn't live with me, but there were times when I felt guilty for being glad about that. He was often lonely, and although I hooked him up with adult day programs so he could find friends and activity, I still would question myself about leaving him alone in his apartment.

In turn Maria went on about her mother:

"Don't get me wrong and, you know, she is a great help with Joey, but sometimes she just gets on my nerves. Especially, when she tries to tell me how to treat him, or when she talks to me about going out more. I wish sometimes that I never agreed to have her come live with me. When I feel like that, I know what you mean when you say you feel guilty for not having your father live with you. I share the same guilt."

I asked her if she was okay with feeling that way or did it really get her down. She told me that she gets depressed about it quite often. I shared with her that it was very human to feel this kind of guilt, but that there was no need to hold onto it. I told her that she should watch it as if she was watching a landscape while moving in a car – it was just part of the ride.

She gave me a weird look as if I was talking Greek. I knew that she didn't understand what I was getting at, but she didn't want to challenge me about it. At this point I went into what I call a 'sannyas spiel'. One of the main tenets of being a sannyasin was spending a good deal of time meditating, and the most important tenet of meditating is becoming a witness to whatever is happening inside and outside oneself. Sharing this with her, someone who has never meditated before, must have sounded like gobbledygook. The weird look did not go away. We spent an extensive time talking away on her steps, so much so, that my writing went south that day as well.

Over the next few days, I tried writing at home but found no inspiration there, so I decided to let it go for a time. The following week on another glorious warm sunny day I ventured toward my favorite stairs with some great thoughts to put on paper. I started to write.

"What kind of cryptic message was that?" thought Juliana after reading her brother's letter?

She looked up from the paper she held.

Just then, as you might have already surmised Maria came out of her apartment and invited me in for tea.

"How can I refuse an invitation such as this," I shared with a smile.

I was finding myself attracted to her friendliness. It was a welcome change from her previous cautious reaction towards me.

"Tea would be wonderful."

Once again, I was ushered into her kitchen.

Sitting there was an older woman who looked a lot like Maria. She had a spry smile and a great figure for her age. Although I could tell she was significantly older than Maria, I still could have taken them for sisters.

"This is my mother, Isabella. This is Prem." We were introduced.

"So, this is the mysterious man sitting on our steps. The one my daughter was so suspicious about!" Looking at Maria she continued, "He doesn't look so bad to me, as a matter of fact, he's kind of cute."

"Mother! Cut it out." Maria said, turning red and raising her voice just a little.

"It is wonderful to make your acquaintance," I said with just a bit of redness going into my cheeks as well.

Maria warned me about her mother's forwardness, and I kind of liked it, but at the same time I must admit that I was taken aback for just a moment.

"Well, young man Maria said something about you writing a book here on our steps in East Boston. Can you imagine that! Don't think I have ever had an occasion of knowing someone who wrote novels, never mind having someone on my own doorstep doing so."

I began to explain to her and Maria that this was a new venture for me.

"I have never written fiction before," I explained.

"What made you pick our stairs to do such a thing?" Isabella asked.

I went into a long explanation of how I had lived in their house many years ago. I told them I lived in the top apartment, not the one they currently occupy. "I have fond memories sitting on these stairs, especially on summer nights when it was hot and the twinkling of the not so starry sky gave it just enough of a mystical feel to fill me with a sense of delight."

As our conversation moved along it turned to becoming something of a history of their Agosti family.

Seems that they came from northern Italy, Milan to be precise.

Funny, I thought, my novel begins in Milan.

Just about all the Italians in East Boston come from southern Italy. Most of them came from Naples or south of Naples, including Sicily. It was very unusual to have a family from northern Italy. I thought it such a coincidence that Maria was that rare bird from northern Italy.

Anyway, her grandfather and grandmother came from Milan to Boston in the early 1920s after already having been married for quite a few years. This also was somewhat out of the ordinary as most Italian immigrants in the neighborhood came when they were very young either just married, or they married here.

I told Maria and her mother that I had researched what Milan was like during World War I, and that I read that there were great riots on the streets to end Italy's involvement in it. They concurred and told me that many of their relatives took part in the marches and rioting.

I told them that I placed my fictional characters in the Rozzano region of Milan near the Parco Agricolo Sud Milano not far from the center of town. With some curiosity, Isabella shared that her parents had lived near the same park only on the opposite side of it in the Rosate area.

Somehow, I got a chill down my spine on hearing this. The closeness of these people in front of me to the characters I was creating was kind of eerie.

8

'What kind of cryptic message was that?' thought Juliana after reading her brother's letter.

She looked up from the paper she held. The rest of her family were all sitting there silently. What did her brother mean at the end of his letter when he said, "If the letter was to get into the wrong hands it would be dangerous and also what was he saying about the flowers holding the key."

It didn't make sense, although her brother's last thoughts about her and the rest of the family were precious to hear. It brought back the sorrow and nostalgia for her youth.

Her brother's mention of her father's box also brought back the memories she had put aside a long time ago thinking that there was no way to follow through with her desire to discover the secret she had at one time so desired to know.

Now, she held in her hand the words of her brother requesting that she not only discover the secret, but find the stolen box. But, how was she to do this after so many years?

Guido was the first to break the silence. "Just like our brother to be so cryptic. He was always like Papa in that regard. Do you have any idea what the hell he meant by that ominous warning at the end, Mama?"

"None whatsoever." Sophia with a tear in her eye looked at her granddaughter with a faraway stare. Then she turned toward Juliana and asked the same question of her.

"He obviously was concerned about the missing box and the secret that was left him by Papa. It must have meant a lot to him if he was thinking of it at the end before he died," Juliana said to the whole group.

"Yea!" Lisa contributed. "I think that he was telling us something about how we could go about finding it, and that whoever took it could be dangerous. I don't have the slightest idea, though, what his hint might mean. Do any of you?"

Silence.

"It made no sense to me," Sal chimed in.

"Mama, you were around that box longer than any of us. Concerning the flowers, do they mean anything to you?" asked Guido.

"The only thing I can think of is that I always saw it on the mantel in between those two beautiful vases and from time to time your father would put flowers in the vases, but most of the time they were empty."

"Have you ever looked inside the vases, Grandma?" Lisa exclaimed.

"No, I haven't. Have any of you?"

They all looked at each other realizing that none of them had. Immediately, Juliana jumped up and grabbed the vase on the left while Lisa picked up the vase on the right. They both reached into their respective vases at the same time, and at the same time they both exhibited disappointing frowns as they removed their empty hands.

Juliana looked at the vase she held very closely. It was made of porcelain with a wide neck tapered in at the top and then bulging out from the neck only to taper gradually down to a base that was as small as the opening at the top. It appeared to have painted bands up and down the whole of its surface. The top band was about two inches wide and decorated with a rather irregular design within its borders going all around the vase. A smaller one-inch band was below it with what looked to be a ringlet or overlapping wave drawn within the enclosed section again all around the vase. Below that another two inches in width that had similar irregular designs within the area, and below that another one inch in width band with an identical ringlet of wavy decoration within it. This continued down the whole of the surface of the vase until it ended in a one and half inch base painted antique red. The vases stood approximately 1.5 feet high each.

There was no way the vase she held could hold some secret compartment or contain anything inside its walls, and the two vases were identical.

Juliana looked at Lisa "You see anything at all?"

"Niente!" was the response.

'Where do we go from here?' It was a thought the whole family participated in simultaneously.

I looked up from my writing remembering another vase; the one that inspired the vases of my writing.

Across the way from the Poona hotel where we had reservations was a shrine to Meher Baba. I had never heard of Meher Baba before seeing his shrine on that overcast day of our arrival in a place that was called Guru Purnima – gift of the guru.

The vase was sitting on a pedestal that made up part of an altar enclosed within a small wooden shrine, the door to which was a locked iron gate. A beautiful assortment of flowers was arranged in the vase – always fresh and always with a heavenly aroma.

I learned *via* Bhagwan that he considered Meher Baba to be what he called the Avatar of the Ages. This avatar came every so often down into incarnation to usher in a collective rise in consciousness for the planet as a whole. Jesus was an avatar and so was Buddha. These advanced souls brought in a new spiritual revolution to humanity.

We are not separate. We are all one. That was and is their basic message to us. Each expressed the message with their own twist. For Buddha it is going beyond our suffering and pointing out very specific states to be rediscovered within the human condition. For Jesus it is finding love as the antidote for selfish concerns and giving to overcome our obsessive focus on self-centeredness. For Meher Baba it is opening humanity to seeing these insights in greater numbers than ever before.

He arrived just before the advent of our technological explosion when the internet and social media would become commonplace and instantaneous communication would be the norm.

Not many of my peers would know whom I was talking about if I mentioned Meher Baba, but Bhagwan considered him to be the most important spiritual leader in the past 2000 years. I marveled at the things that go on around the planet that we have no idea are occurring. Since I believed Bhagwan's understanding in this matter, I consider this one of them.

Now as I look around the world in the 21st century, I see just how far humanity has opened to a new spiritual world that wasn't so evident when I was a kid.

To be sure, I think there is still a hell of a lot of insanity on the planet, but the amount of spiritual insight has increased tenfold since I was young.

There indeed was nowhere to go for this stunned group of people as none of them had an answer as to what to do with Thomas' cryptic hint.

The whole inquiry lay there for close to four years before a new chapter would start the journey again.

9

East Boston had become gentrified over the past twenty years. It really was only a matter of time that this would happen as it was only a ten-minute trip by train to downtown Boston. It had a waterfront that when built up could rival views that one found only in a few other affluent cities such as Sausalito found next to San Francisco.

However, when I was growing up, Eastie was nothing but a semi-ghetto. A place where a person had to watch one's back when going too far afield of one's home ground. It wasn't as bad as I am making it sound, but it could pose problems if you wandered into another gang's territory or met up with the wrong people.

This made myself, and my friends somewhat on guard. The town was developing into a hotbed for drugs, especially opiates during my youth. I cannot tell you how many times I watched some of my friends shooting up heroin or something akin to it. While I had no taste for the experience, I did try synthetic heroin, or what we called 'dollies' once or twice *via* ingestion. I spent hours floating above the sidewalk and became acutely aware why several of my friends became junkies; although I was just too conservative to go down that path.

Why I'm telling you all this is to enlighten you about the background that Maria and I shared in our connection. We both experienced similar scenarios growing up in the same neighborhood, and this became a basis for conversations whenever we got together. We met more often as we would spend some time over coffee or tea at her apartment whenever I went there to continue with my fiction. I insisted that I had to have time to write so that I could not spend all day exchanging memories and more with her, but at the same time we had a great time together so often we would spend an hour or so just talking. Sometimes her mother was there and sometimes Joseph would wander in as well. To be sure life in East Boston was not all about being wary, it also was a great place to bond deeply with your friends who were more like a family than anything else. Those in your gang would watch your back. We had a close fellowship.

After a very short time I began to realize that I was modeling Juliana after Maria. They both were strong willed, but somewhat cautious. They both had father issues although Maria felt distance from hers and Juliana felt close to hers, but with a sense of distrust from him. They were both very attached to their families and were content with helping their families grow. Both had husbands that left them, although in Maria's case he got up and went for personal reasons, whereas Mario went off to war and died.

They were different for sure, but they also had the same temperament. Both ended up caring for their mothers and both had some resentment about it, but at the same time would not relinquish their responsibilities. They were not going to run off to parts unknown to fulfill their sense of self for that sense of self was rooted in their family.

Juliana was disappointed in the dead end she found herself in concerning the discovery of the secret. At the same time, she was not going to travel far and wide to go looking for the missing box. She had to admit to herself that what she had really wanted whenever her mind wandered to her father and his box was the deep connection she would have felt if her father had trusted her with his secret.

She became increasingly aware that she felt a sort of abandonment by him, because he did not include her in something he had held near and dear to himself. With this realization she became less interested in the drama of the secret box and became a little angry with Papa. In this way she began to align herself with her mother's point of view on the subject.

During the four years after reading the letter, Juliana met a carpenter coincidentally named Salvatore. They grew close together and eventually he asked for her hand in marriage. Sometime after he moved in Julianna's son Sal, returned home from university.

It was when Sal finished university and came home that the mystery of the vase took a turn. One day shortly after Sal had returned, he was visited by one of his university friends named Carlo. Carlo attended university with the interest of becoming an archaeologist. He in fact had spent some time with one of his professors in a dig in India uncovering some ancient Vedic ruins.

As the hostess, Juliana told Sal and his friend to go sit in the living room. She would make some coffee and serve it with biscotti.

"I've been looking for work ever since I got here," Sal lamented to Carlo. "No luck yet, how about you?"

Carlo told Sal that he wasn't interested in working yet, and just wanted to take some time for himself. He thought it would be difficult to find paying work in his field, unless he went off as a volunteer on some project to get his foot in the door. He was not interested in teaching, because he really liked the hands-on work of the excavation that he had been involved in.

Just as Juliana came into the room with the coffee Carlo looking up noticed the vases on the mantel. Juliana was asking him what life was like now that he left school, but he did not take her question in, rather he stared at the vase that sat on the left side of the shelf.

"Sal, you never told me that your family had some interesting antiques from India." Carlo exclaimed.

"What are you talking about Carlo?"

"Your family's vases, they have ancient Sanskrit writing on them, and they look very old. How long have they been in your family?"

"Those vases were my father's," informed Juliana as she stared lingeringly on the vase that Carlo's eyes had rested on. "We had no idea anything was written on them. As a matter of fact, I don't know anything about what Sanskrit is."

Sal immediately informed her that it was an ancient language that he had only heard about once or twice in his university history class.

They both looked at Carlo for more of an explanation.

"Sanskrit is one of the most ancient languages, and it came from India." He explained that much of the various Western languages such as Latin had their roots in this tongue, but that it was not used since long ago, although it is still understood by some Vedic scholars and religious Hindu groups.

"How did you get two such artifacts without having any idea what they were?" Carlo wanted to know.

Sal was the one who went into the story and told Carlo the long and short of the missing box and his grandfather's obsession with it. Juliana added some needed details about her father having a secret that was lost with her brother's death. They told him about the letter with the, oh so subtle, hint. They told him that they inspected the vases but found nothing in them and that they pretty much gave up on ever discovering more about the issue.

Now, Juliana feeling her heart beating rapidly found her lost interest returning with a vengeance. "What does the Sanskrit say?"

Just as Carlo was about to say something, Lisa walked into the room.

As the light was fading I decided to pause. Besides, I was supposed to go to the sannyasin center and lead a Kundalini meditation.

Since I arrived back from Poona the center was getting more people coming to the meditations.

Arriving at the meditation hall I found at least 20 people in the room waiting for me. I recognized most of them, although there were a few who were new to me. After some connecting with old and new friends, I began the session by describing the meditation.

"Like Dynamic meditation Kundalini is a technique developed by Bhagwan, especially for Western minds to relax by exhausting the body. It uses bioenergetics along with ancient Eastern methods. The meditation is done in four parts. It has three segments done to various music scores and ends in a silent 4th period. The first part is shaking that can be either done gently or vigorously, or both. This builds the energy in the body. The 2nd part is expressing that energy by dancing in whatever way one desires. The 3rd part is simply listening to the music being played. This leads into the 4th segment of lying silently watching the internal/external world of your being.

"Notice how the meditation gradually slows you down from being super-energetic to being still. Remember all of it is the meditation not just the silent part and remember there is a gong that separates each of the parts. Enjoy!"

I always love leading people into these meditations. I love seeing the glow on their faces when they return from their inner journey.

When the session was over, I had a couple come up to me and say that they decided to go to Poona to meet Bhagwan. They asked me what it was like in India, and this question brought me back to the first time I was in Poona.

"India was amazing," I told them. "In India all of life is right in front of you. The good with the bad is on display.

Unlike here in the West where much of the ugly side of life is hidden from view, India presented everything without censure. You will see beautiful landscapes, housing with ancient ruins and magnificent art. You will view many smiling faces, and gorgeous looking people. You will also see people with deformities and others living in mud huts or worse. There will be whole families living on the street or under bridges. Cows and buffalo, chickens and elephants will all be right there in front of you. All the smells, sights and sounds will confront your senses. Whenever I go to India I feel as if I have come into a life that is vibrant and raw."

As my mind went back to my times in India, I went on to tell them that, "Walking down the roads in Poona I sometimes thought of being in a surreal world bombarded by vibrant and bold colors as well as sounds of honking rickshaws and barking dogs. Of course, there were the smells of flowers, food and urine and so many more smells that it was hard to even reimagine them."

Yes, India was amazing.

India is a very dirty place. I often thought that the Indian sense of cleanliness compared to where I came from was other-worldly. I can see a chai *walla* (walla is the equivalent of a merchant) or a juice walla cleaning used glasses by simply dipping them in already used water to rinse them off for the next customer.

A Westerner going to India opened herself to a spiritual process simply by the fact that India broke down the traveler's sense of how things should be from her conditioned mental structure.

Since the whole process of spiritual growth is to help the seeker see beyond his or her judgments and conditioning into a new way of perceiving self, existence in India for the Western mind was indeed a growth group unto itself.

The young couple took in my narrative with wide eyes and exhilarating expectations. I shut off the lights and went home.

10

*L*isa saw her brother and mother with a strange young man in the living room. The young man was standing by the mantel holding one of her father's vases. Before he could answer Juliana and Sal's excited queries, he noticed Lisa's entrance. To even his surprise he could only stand there staring at Lisa.

"Lisa, what are you doing home so early?" Juliana started.

"They let us out of the bakery early today. What are you all doing here?" she asked, looking intently at Carlo. For a moment the two of them just held that stare for each other.

Sal spoke up, "This is my friend Carlo, and he has just informed us that Papa's vases have writing on them. Carlo, this is my sister Lisa."

"Enchanted to meet you," Carlo said, finding his voice.

She was taken aback when he put down the vase to take her hand that he subsequently kissed so lightly. "Thank you." There was a pause for just a moment, but then she became stern of face and inquired as to what writing was on the vases. She was sure the designs on the rows of the vase were only decorative in nature.

"Lisa, Carlo tells us this is Sanskrit" Juliana informed her as she pointed to every other decoration going down the vase.

As to be expected Lisa took up the query, "Well, what does it say?"

Every one of them was looking at Carlo with such intensity at which point he began to sweat. He looked at the vase and then back to his audience and then back to the vase. "I don't know what it says." Disappointment was thick in the air.

"What!" Lisa shouted. "How do you know it's a language anyway? Are you kidding us?"

Sal jumped up "Give him a break, Lisa. Don't jump down his throat." Turning toward Carlo he said, "You have an explanation, don't you Carlo!"

Juliana looked down with exasperation written all over her posture.

"I don't know what it says, but I know that it is Sanskrit. I have seen many of these symbols while working in India. We were digging up an old Hindu temple and writing just like this was all over some of its walls. I'm not able to translate this. I bet there are very few people in the whole of Italy that could do so. If there is someone who could translate, I would guess they could be found only in Rome."

That night Carlo stayed for dinner. Around that dinner table sat Juliana, Sal, Lisa, Carlo, Sophia, Guido and Salvatore. They all discussed what to do with this new information. Now, Juliana was certain that her brother must have meant that the writing held a clue to discover the missing box and its contents. Sophia thought the whole thing should be forgotten. Guido was torn between letting it all go and seeking to pursue the clue. As for the rest of them, including Salvatore, they were all convinced that, at the very least, they should find a translator to decipher what was said on both vases.

Thus, it was decided that Sal and Lisa should go to Rome and see if they could find someone who could read what was inscribed, and or find out where they needed to go to do so. Carlo chimed in that he wanted to go with Sal and Lisa as this was right up his alley as an archaeologist. He insisted that he go, and would not take no for an answer, even though several at the table expressed their reservations.

It did not take very long for a decision to be made. They decided that they needed to take some time to prepare for the trip. Lisa needed to take time off from work, but had to make a little more money before departing. Sal was ready to go at any time, while Carlo had some family obligations to attend to before he could leave.

Later, Lisa was sitting with her mother at a Café at the Piazza G Missori discussing the trip and the possible ramification of it. They concluded that it was a good thing that Carlo was going along as he probably could lend more expertise to the venture. Juliana mentioned that she noticed Lisa looking at Carlo with interest and cautioned her to be careful traveling with him.

"Don't get wild on me," Juliana joked. "And remember what you are going to Rome to do."

"We'll see!" was all that Lisa would retort.

11

Over the next week my schedule became busy with no time to write or do much of anything but earn money. I am a tax practitioner, and this was my season to make a living. I always thought it unfortunate that I was not born wealthy, because I prided myself in being able to enjoy a great deal of leisure time.

I did see Maria once during that week by accident. We happened to both be in downtown East Boston at the same time and bumped into each other in the convenience store. Naturally I invited her for coffee, and of course I noticed she looked wonderful in a short skirt and colorful blouse. I found myself looking at her legs while she was turned away and indeed was aroused.

With all this I was inclined not to pursue a sexual relationship with her. After all, my friendship with her was going along famously, and I really felt I needed to continue being able to use her steps while I worked on my novel. I felt that the stoop at her front door was a place of inspiration for my writing, and I didn't want anything to mess with it. I thought perhaps later, after the novel was finished I would attempt seeking something more than friendship. Anyway, I was still having trouble reading her and wasn't sure she would be interested in sexual intimacy.

During coffee we again reminisced over our childhood memories. She was telling me what it was like to grow up in Jeffries Point near the water. She said that she and her friends often played down by the old docks and when she got older it turned out to be a great make-out place. Although I was aware of Jeffries Point when I grew up it was not the part of Eastie I frequented.

As our conversation continued, she told me that she still had family in Milan. Maria had an aunt and uncle that her mother was still very close to, but she had little to no contact with them. Mentioning that they were the keepers of the family's heritage, I asked her what she meant by that. She said she had no idea, only that was what her mother repeatedly said over the years.

Joey had finally confided in his mother what happened in the schoolyard, and we discussed the cruelty of kids. She asked me for the best way to deal with the issue. I said that I thought he was coping with it in the best possible way, especially since he was able to share it with her. I admired her ability to stand aside and not push her son into sharing or giving him some immediate advice. I thought, perhaps arrogantly, that she was very mature for a non-meditator.

I can't tell you how pleasant it was to talk with her. We really did have a rapport. It made me start to think that I should not be so concerned about keeping things less complicated. But then again, sex can and often does, create complications.

It was Friday when we had met by accident, and it wasn't until the next Tuesday that I found myself on my favorite stairs peering down at my manuscript.

"This is going to be so exciting," Lisa thought. It was right up her alley to thrive on adventure, besides it might be interesting to get to know Carlo more. She was attracted to him, but also

felt wary of being alone with him in a strange city without any restraints.

They all had decided to leave by train to Roma on March 1st. The year was 1932, and Mussolini had worked magic getting the Italian trains to run on time. It would take the better part of twenty hours to reach Rome with the number of stops to be made so they took a sleeper compartment with two bunks.

They had to pack the vases very carefully as they were indeed a precious cargo. When they arrived in Rome it might take some time to discover where to go to translate these vases. As a matter of fact, they weren't even sure if they could find anyone in Rome that could translate them.

Both Lisa and her brother were thankful that Carlo was with them since he had several ideas of how to pursue their quest. They were sure they could manage on their own, but not nearly as well as with their friend.

March 1st came and the family, with the exception of Guido, went down to the train station to send them off on their venture. With adieu and wishes of luck the trio departed.

They arrived exactly on time at Roma Termini in Piazza dei Cinquecento. This was the first time Lisa was away from Milan and she was beyond excited to be in Rome.

Upon their arrival and after lunch at a small restaurant the three friends looked all afternoon for a small apartment to share. They hoped not to linger too long in Rome, but expected that they needed to stay at least a month to be able to hunt down the person they wanted to find. With a little luck they were able to secure a small flat at a very reasonable rate on a tiny street in the area of Portuense.

Now, they began to seek what they hoped to find. Carlo's plan was to first look in the libraries of Rome and ask the curators if they had any East Indian sections where they might discover experts in Vedic languages living in Rome. If that search failed, they would go to the universities in Rome. Surely, Carlo thought there must be one or two universities that had Hindu studies. In the event of not finding anything from these two sources it became a matter of trying to locate any part of the city that might have immigrants from India.

Every day the trio would spend the morning going to libraries throughout the city, and wherever they would end up in the city they would also sightsee the wonders of ancient and modern Rome. In this way they cemented a bond that was already there in seed form. Sal and Carlo had a mild friendship while at school, but here in Rome they shared more intimate aspects of their life. They compared their upbringings and the differences between their parents. Sal's home life was spent with very reserved parents who were quite conservative in nature, while Carlo came from a much more chaotic and liberal background. Of course, Lisa shared Sal's background, but shared it from an older sister and feminine point of view.

Carlo came to see just how close Lisa and Sal were to each other. They had relied on each other especially after all the family deaths due to the war. Carlo had three brothers, two of whom entered the war. Both came back and his father was home throughout the campaign. He did not suffer the same kind of trauma as his friends did, and that allowed him to be more optimistic than they were.

Sal noticed that Carlo and Lisa seemed to be getting along more than very well, but also was aware that his sister was not always comfortable with the close living arrangement they found themselves in. When he asked his sister if everything was all right, he only got back an automatic nod.

After one week of this schedule, they all came to admit that the libraries were not very helpful in their quest. Sadly, there was no information in the books or from the staff about anyone who could translate Sanskrit.

They proceeded onward to the universities. Again, they would start in the mornings and try their luck at finding anything that might lead them to a translator, while enjoying being tourists the rest of the time. The universities were more interesting and took longer to wander through. They did come across some departments that were connected to East Indian studies, but again found no one who could direct them to someone that could help them. There was one Professor Marconi who did know of a Vedic scholar living in Athens a few years ago. He told them this man was fluent in Sanskrit and that was as close as they got to their answer.

At this point the vases had not come out of their wrappings and our friends were experiencing frustration.

Sal had gone out to walk the streets of Rome sometime after finishing with the universities. He said that he needed to think about things so he left Carlo and his sister alone for a while. These two had not had much time alone together over the past two and a half weeks. They seemed to be a little nervous without Sal there.

"I am going up to the roof to watch the sunset," Carlo exclaimed. "I need the air," he continued.

"May I join you?" asked Lisa.

"Of course," Carlo said with a smile.

They climbed two flights of stairs to the flat roof just in time to see the sun dip between several buildings in the distance. It was an exceptionally warm day for March, and both had only a light sweater on while viewing the sky as it turned from blue to yellow and orange with a hint of red.

"Wow, Bellissimo!" Carlo couldn't help himself.

"It is so magical Carlo," Lisa added as she gazed at him.

"It is kind of like you," Carlo said, turning toward her. They turned toward each other and looked deeply into each other's eyes – the sky above melting into a partial rainbow.

"Oh Carlo, I am not sure we should be going there," Lisa interrupted. Despite this outburst she somehow found herself kissing him and being passionately kissed in return. They shared

a long embrace. Lisa suddenly disengaged and left the roof only saying, "we have work to do!" She took the stairs down to the apartment and went into her room.

Carlo came in a very short time later and knocked on her door. She opened it just about the same time that Sal turned the key to the apartment and walked in. "Let's go for supper," he declared.

At supper they brainstormed their next move. Sal noticed that he sat between Lisa and Carlo, and they often looked down, especially when talking to each other.

The gist of their conclusion as to the direction they now needed to go was that they had to try to find some East Indian immigrants in the city. This was their last chance, and it wasn't a very probable one. If this failed, their only lead was to go to Athens to find the Vedic scholar Professor Marconi alluded to.

While traversing Rome, they discovered that there were not very many people from India in the city. If they were to find any their only chance at doing so was to visit the Esquilino rione area of the city. That was the part of the city that held the most immigrant populace.

The next day they found Esquilino rione and roamed that part of the city to no avail. Unfortunately, the following days reaped the same results.

This was it, and they all communicated that thought in unison. Either they find a lead to a translator, or they give up and go back to Milan. The one other option was to travel to Athens if they could finance it.

"Have you noticed that we are being followed?" Sal said to Carlo. He pointed with his eyes to a man in a leather jacket across the street from the café where they were having breakfast.

"I hadn't noticed anything, but now that you mention it, I believe I have seen that man several times before. At least one other time this last week and possibly before at the train station when we first got here." Carlo added.

"Lisa, have you noticed the guy in the leather jacket before?" Carlo was concerned to see if she had.

"Yes," she said, "but I didn't think anything of it. Should I worry?"

"Let's not worry yet," Sal said looking at his sister. "I have an idea. You and Carlo leave the café and go down the street to our left while I go straight up the street. We will circle around and meet each other five blocks up on the street we're currently on. Let's see if either of us can spot him following."

Sure enough, Carlo and Lisa spotted him trailing their pathway. However, when they met up with her brother they noticed that the strange man had disappeared.

While standing on the corner they discussed the situation; concluding that there was nothing they could do, except be very watchful going forward.

As they were about to move from the corner to continue their search, they spotted an Indian couple walking right toward them. This was only the third time they had discovered anyone from India while searching the whole city of Rome.

"Pardon me, we are looking for someone who can translate Sanskrit," Sal almost jokingly said, stopping the couple.

The couple looked at him for a stunned moment, and finally the man said, "It just so happens that I can translate Sanskrit. Why?"

<h1 style="text-align:center">12</h1>

Sitting in a café on Newbury Street in downtown Boston with my good friend Paul, I am having a *caprese* sandwich and a chai. Paul is from Cambridge and is interested in his latte that he holds with both hands. For many years, he was intrigued with sannyas and sannyasins, but only from afar. As an engineer who has recently taken up quantum physics as a hobby he peppered me with questions about Bhagwan's path.

"I just can't believe you study quantum physics now. My brain cannot wrap itself around such a crazy topic. It is like seeing the world in mathematics and a kind of math that makes no sense to me. All I can do is marvel at the understanding that these math geeks can make of the universe after translating all that math into English. What I keep reading from these scientists sounded like the mysticism I had learned about over the past twenty years.

"Actually, Paul, I admire you and am somewhat jealous of your ability to understand how you do all that." I realized I was rambling, but being impressed with him and his world of quantum physics I couldn't help myself.

Paul took a sip of his latte while taking in my compliment without much fanfare.

"It comes easy for me, and I love it," he said. I also see how much it seems to corroborate mysticism, but I know you must leave soon, and I want you to tell me more about Bhagwan and your time with him."

"Again, you want me to share what I've tried to tell you before," I responded.

I began by telling him that I remember the first time I listened to Bhagwan's lectures in person. There were about two thousand disciples sitting in Buddha Hall waiting for him to come in. It was so quiet in that hall that you could hear the buzz of a bee across the hall fifty yards away. Then he arrived and believe it or not, the silence got even deeper. The silence alone would be enough for me to go into an altered state of consciousness. Being from the inner city and from a large Italian family, I had no idea silence could be so profound, because I never had to listen to it before.

When he began to speak the silence did not go away, but rather intensified again. He would lecture in Hindi and English, and when he talked in English, he would give a series of lectures about past enlightened masters of the world. These were people like Lao-Tzu or his disciple Chuang-Tsu, Jesus, Buddha, various Sufi masters, Hasidic masters, and more.

On the first day I sat with him he spoke on Lao-Tzu. He told a story about when Confucius went to see Lao-Tzu and found him to be a dangerous man. I quote word for word the later published book of this discourse, TAO: The Threes Treasures Volume One, by Bhagwan Shree Rajneesh:

And about Lao Tzu he (Confucius) said to his disciples: I have heard about animals like elephants, and I know how they walk. And I have heard about hidden animals in the sea, and I know how they swim. And I have heard about great birds who fly thousands of miles away from the earth, and I know how they fly. But this man (Lao-Tzu) is a dragon. Nobody knows how he walks. Nobody knows how he lives. Nobody knows how he flies. Never go near him. He is like an abyss. He is like a death.

And that is the definition of a master: a master is like death. If you come near him, too close, you will feel afraid, trembling will take over. You will be possessed by an unknown fear, as if you are going to die. It is said that Confucius never came again to see this old man.

Lao-Tzu was ordinary in a way. And in another way, he was the most extraordinary man. He was not extraordinary like Buddha; he was extraordinary in a totally different way. His extraordinariness was not so obvious – it was a hidden treasure. He was not miraculous like Krishna, he did not do any miracles, but his whole being was a miracle – the way he walked, the way he looked, the way he was. His whole being was a miracle.

He is not sad like Jesus; he could laugh, he could laugh a belly laugh. It is said that he was born laughing. Children are born crying, weeping, it is said about him that he was born laughing. I also feel it must be true; a man like Lao Tzu must be born laughing. He is not sad like Jesus. He can laugh, and laugh tremendously, but deep down in his laughter there is a sadness, a compassion – a sadness about you, about the whole existence. His laughter is not superficial. Zarathustra laughs but his laughter is different, there is no sadness in it.

Lao Tzu is sad like Jesus and not sad like Jesus; Lao Tzu laughs like Zarathustra and doesn't laugh like Zarathustra. His sadness has a laughter to it and his laughter has a sadness to it. He is a meeting of opposites. He is a harmony, a symphony.

Remember this. I am not commenting on him. There exists no distance between me and him. He is talking to you through me - different body, a different name, a different incarnation, but the same spirit."

Quote, unquote.

"That was what it was like being with Bhagwan. Whenever he would talk about a master I would feel that he became that master. He became Buddha when discoursing on Buddha. He became Jesus when discoursing on Jesus. He became Krishna when discoursing on Krishna. He became these individuals and their expressions because as I was to learn they all were expressing the same thing through different filters."

"What that thing was is about dying, but I have already told you that Paul. However, I am sure you will ask me again… so until next time. I need to leave now."

We said our goodbyes and I strolled off to the library.

Sitting in the library the silence reminded me of what I was trying to convey to Paul an hour ago. I closed my eyes and was transported into meditation and the inner space that I became aware of in Buddha Hall. The mind was still chattering, but at this point in my meditation I experienced those thoughts as mere white clouds moving within a deep blue sky not disturbing the space in any way. In truth, the clouds (thoughts) were simply part of the sky itself, not different from it.

I remember that when I first started to meditate I was distracted by those same thoughts following their meaning and judgment. At that time, they were indeed different from the sky. The sky was not noticed in my watching. Now, I thought, this is the difference between feeling separate and knowing unity.

Enough, I need to bring myself back to my story and find out what exactly was written on those vases for our Italian characters to get excited about.

The man's name was Anand Prakash, and his wife was called Sita. After listening to Carlo and his friend's explanation of what they needed, the couple became intrigued, and agreed to their request. Unfortunately, they were in Italy to study Italian artifacts and had lectures and viewings for several days. With these commitments they would not be available until the following Wednesday which was four days hence.

They all made plans to meet at Anand's house at that time. The Italian group would bring the vases, and Anand would attempt to translate them.

"This is very exciting, and I can't wait to find out what those flower holders say," remarked Sal.

He got nothing but nods from his two comrades, although Lisa began to wonder out loud just what they would do with themselves from now until Wednesday morning. They had done enough sightseeing, and coffee drinking. She was a little concerned with having all that free time with Carlo, and maybe she was a little excited too.

It was Carlo, however, who came up with an idea that proved to evaporate most of that free time when he said, "We need to discover just who is following us!"

13

aolo had been contacted by the group who would on occasion call him in to perform special projects. He didn't know who they were or what their agenda was, and he didn't care either. Clandestine operations of any kind, was work he enjoyed. Short of hiring out as a killer he was available to get involved in spying, stealing, snaring, and stomping. He called them the four S's and he excelled in them learning the S's by living in a tough Barcelona neighborhood most of his young life.

The group reached out to him six days ago and asked him to follow three young Italians — two guys and a girl. He was to only report their activities and was not to have any contact with them. He was told that these three people would probably not even notice him, because they were quote unquote, "innocents".

It was amazingly synchronistic that he had arrived at the train station the same day they arrived there two and half weeks before he was given his spying task. "What were the odds of that happening," he thought. Now that they had spotted him which he was told would be most unlikely he needed to first contact the group and tell them. In the future he would have to be extra careful.

Paolo did not like to fuck up and rarely did. His job would be that more difficult now, and he was beginning to dislike these young Italians for it.

He left a message at the phone number he was given whenever he needed to get a message to the group, and now awaited to be contacted with further instructions.

At that very moment Paolo was conveying his message, Carlo was sharing his idea to Lisa and Sal.

"We must spend the next four days discovering who is following us. We cannot go on with this unknown threat," warned Carlo.

Both his listeners remained silent.

"Well, don't you agree with me?"

Sal looked at his sister and told Carlo that of course they agreed with him, but neither of them had any idea of what to do about someone following them and the danger it imposed on them.

"Look Carlo, we are not spies or detectives, or even soldiers. How are we going to catch this guy and even if we could, what are we going to do with him?" Naively, Lisa was hoping that this problem would just go away by itself. "Maybe he was just someone who was looking to steal from us and once he discovered that we became aware of him he left for good."

Carlo, was feeling apprehensive, but knew in his gut that this was not the case. "Didn't you tell me that your uncle said that there was a threat or danger associated with the box we are seeking? We would be crazy to think that everything is okay when we know that someone is watching us."

Biting her lip, Lisa asked, "What do you propose we do?"

"All I know is that we need to spend the time we have to wait for Anand to help us with trying to find who this guy is. I don't have any idea exactly how to go about doing that, but we must think of something."

Sal listened as he sat somewhat away from the pair. Putting up his hands he stated emphatically: "Let me think, I may get an inkling of an idea." And with that he left his two companions alone and went outside for a walk.

Walking was Sal's most cherished thing to do whenever he had a problem to solve, and he thought he would need a rather long walk to tackle a solution to what Carlo insisted they needed to do.

"I hate to break your bubble, Lisa, but are you really up for this adventure?" Carlo asked Lisa right after her brother left the apartment.

"What do you mean by that?" she countered.

"I mean that this discovery we are on may be more and more dangerous, and I am not sure you are ready for it. Heck, I am not sure I am ready for you to be ready for it. I really would be devastated if anything were to happen to any of us, and especially to you."

"Don't be so chauvinistic with me, Carlo. You're not my father. Anyway, are you ready to face danger for somebody else's family's missing box? I can do whatever you can, Carlo, and probably even better." She went into her bedroom and closed the door wondering why she was so infuriated with him. This was not in her character, and besides he really didn't do anything that bad, yet she was feeling upset.

At this point I stopped writing, becoming overly aware of my own annoyance with Maria recently. There were little things while we were sharing that triggered some negative emotional responses in me. We have been hanging out together for about two and half months now mostly in her kitchen, but at times in shops around town. Occasionally, we would meet here and there by accident. Once I asked her if she would like to go with me to the theater at a local playhouse in Winthrop.

The actions that seemed to annoy me were expressions of endearment like pushing some hair away from my face or taking my reading glasses off. "I want to see your face better," she would say. As I said they were little things of familiarity, and I am not quite sure why they irritated me. Perhaps they were my way of keeping some distance between us, and perhaps, I am using this experience to project on my character Lisa because she wants to keep some distance from Carlo. This is just a yarn, yet everything in fiction comes out of something real. Reality informs what is made up, so is anything really made up?

I wonder!

The library is closing, and I need to think about this story line. How can the trio become super sleuths? I will have to wait for another day or two to find out. Goodnight.

14

arlo's plan was quite simple. Every morning one of the three would leave the apartment at around 8am. From upstairs in their apartment one of them would scan the street below for any indications of spying happening on the one who left. He or she would have a long-range camera to get the guy on film. The third person would carry a smaller camera. He or she would sneak out the back of the apartment building, and after a while would follow along the path the first person was to take. Of course, they would all be aware of the path the person who left the apartment would go on so a considerable distance could be maintained while they were trying to uncover any spies. The individual who left would invariably end up at a café sometimes right near the apartment, some days a bit further away. He/she would remain there for an hour or so; as an hour seemed to be more than enough time to draw out their nemesis. In this way they planned on capturing their follower on one of the two cameras, or perhaps both.

After getting this information they thought it best to go to the police and have them handle it. After all none of them was experienced enough to deal with a real-life spy, and who knew what the man was capable of.

The first day of implementing the plan nothing seemed to happen. Sal, the first decoy, was never followed, nor was anyone suspicious hanging around the café he stopped at.

The second day was a reenactment of the first day. Nothing at all happened. This made for some nervousness on all three of the search party. Lisa even mentioned the idea that perhaps they were mistaken about their original idea. Sal and Carlo, however, nicked that supposition.

Sal said that he was 100% sure they were being followed and Carlo backed him up 1000%. They both were puzzled and somewhat alarmed that they appeared to have lost their spy. This in fact seemed more ominous than if they had rediscovered him. Where did he go?

Meanwhile, right after contacting the group Paolo was told to keep surveillance on the three friends, but was further informed that the group thought it unlikely that they would do anything individually. With that in mind he entered the apartment located across the street from the one that Lisa and company occupied. He had acquired the apartment right after getting his original mission from the group, but up until now only used it occasionally for surveillance. Now he lived in it and kept constant vigil on his targets.

He had his own long-range camera set up in the bathroom looking in on the living room of his targets. He spent most of his day looking through the lens of that camera although he could see the occupants from his own living room without the need of a lens.

That first day he almost went for the bait when Sal left the apartment, but he could see quite clearly Lisa sitting in her bedroom intently looking out the window with a binocular camera in her hand. After seeing this he decided to wait just a little bit which was enough time to see Carlo come out of the back of the building following the same route as Sal.

"Clever," he thought. "They think they are setting a trap, but little do they know. Such amateurs."

Later he did follow them when all three left the building at the same time, but they didn't seem to be going anywhere of interest. Usually, they went shopping or out to eat. However, he would keep vigilant, since the cabal thought they might be up to something. They would not tell him what that something was, but that was to be expected. For right now this was a routine surveillance job, nothing else.

The next day was the day Lisa and company were to meet Anand and Sita, and they had not had any luck in tracking down whoever was following them which meant that they would have to be super careful when going to their meeting. Whoever was tracking them was obviously a professional, or hopefully he simply had stopped. They swore to each other to be on their toes continuously.

It was very lucky that our searchers even found the Indian couple the day that they did. The couple was not actually living in the area of Esquillino rione. They were just tourists and were only visiting that part of the city that day. They were staying in a luxury hotel quite some distance from where they met the trio. The Hotel Majestic was a beautiful establishment that overlooked the Piazza Barberini. The hotel was built in 1889 and during the twenties had been the place to be for the rich and famous. At this time the hotel was still quite popular although its stylish antique décor was less sought after then it was in its heyday.

The rooms the Indians occupied were quite attractive. The sitting room was ample in size with a sofa and four comfortable lounge chairs. There was a roll-up desk in the corner with a high-back chair. It was this room that Sal, Carlo and Lisa were ushered into by Sita to await Anand who was still downstairs in the breakfast lounge.

Paolo had followed his marks dressed as an old woman. When he wanted to, he could transform himself into someone so totally different. It was the secret of his many successes in his field. He was aware of the room his targets were visiting but because of the layout of the hotel, he had no idea of what they were doing or with whom. This changed somewhat when he watched a fine looking Indian young man come up the stairs and enter the very apartment his charges were in.

Anand opened the door to the sitting room of his hotel apartment to see the three young people he had met the other day. With them he immediately spied the two vases they had with them. These were unwrapped and sitting on the table situated between the lounge chairs and sofa. He quickly studied the Sanskrit that adorned the vases and became quite excited noting how old the vases looked.

Looking up at those in front of him he asked, "Where did you get these beautiful pieces of art? They look like they should be in a museum in my country."

Carlo looked at Lisa and she in turn began to relay the story of how her family owned them and the box that seemed to be attached to them. She explained that her uncle had died with a secret about that box and seemed to give a hint that these vases could help unlock that secret and help them relocate the stolen box. As they said before, they only need someone who can translate Sanskrit.

"It is a strange coincidence that you should find me the other day, because I am probably the only person in the whole of Europe at this time who can do such a thing. It appears that their fates are linked together somehow. So, let's see what these beauties say."

"First of all, this is not Sanskrit on the vases but Pali. Pali is a language used by many Hindu texts and virtually all Buddhist texts. It is thought to be derived from Sanskrit, but that is somewhat in dispute. A mystic quality is often attributed to this language as it was often used in charms and such. It was the language of the Buddha and is very often associated with him and his times."

"Luckily I am also proficient in Pali, as well as Sanskrit."

"So, Anand, what does the writing say?" Sal broke in with anticipation.

"Let's see, this vase that I am holding seems to be both an invitation and a warning of some kind. It also seems to be Buddhist in nature because it speaks of dharma. Literal translation is: 'The dharma of he who reads these words, if pure of heart, will be changed into finding the miraculous. Those of evil and selfish intent will be thrown violently to the four winds, beware.'"

"Boy," said Carlo, "That sounds melodramatically ominous."

Anand picked up the second vase. "The other vase reads: 'That which lies within the container will open the world of man to that which is beyond the stars, seek the talisman held by the "Man Who Does Not Know" to find the further key.'"

"This is crazy," Sal quietly says. "What could that possibly mean?"

"I do not know what it means, but the term 'Man Who Does Not Know' is written as if it were a title of some kind — every first letter is capitalized," answered Anand.

"Is there anything more said, my husband?" Sita asked.

Anand responded with blandness. "Nothing more. Does it have meaning to any of you?"

No one answered, and after a short period of time Sal, Lisa and Carlo got up and left the apartment not knowing what to do next.

15

"What do you do when you are confronted with an impossible task?" I asked Amrit.

We were sitting in Vrindavan, the ashram's cafeteria, each nursing a cup of chai.

"I have no idea what you do," was Amrit's response. "What impossible task are you talking about anyway?"

I was contemplating telling him that my obsessive-compulsive mind had plagued me since puberty with commands to do things that I had no wish to do, such as become a monk. Why it did this, both mystified me and bothered me to no end. There were other obsessive ideas that followed the same pattern, both in their innocence and their 'must do' and 'don't want to do' character.

Now, however, I had a real-life situation thrown at me that mimicked my crazy mind's obsessions to the max.

"I was minding my own business last week when I noticed a woman-friend named Sona hanging around me and my companions. I was very caught up in meditation and seeking enlightenment. At first, I did not notice her around me that often. However, it did grab the attention of Govind, because he told me that Sona seemed to be after one of us as relationship material. Everywhere we went Sona seemed to be there. I blew off his observation thinking it must be him that she was after."

"Sure enough, last night while waiting to go into darshan (a meeting with the master) with around ten others I found myself sitting next to Sona who just happened to book a darshan the same night as I had - such a coincidence. While sitting there she told me a story about how a week ago from that very day she had gone to another darshan where Bhagwan told her to go find a man to walk through life with and commanded her to bring him back to see him when she had found him. She was to do this in a week's time and that time was up that very night."

"Wow!", I said to her. "What a story." Of course, I was curious and asked her if she had found her lover and if so, who was he? She sheepishly reached out her hand and touched my arm and exclaimed that it was me.

"Are you kidding me, Sona!" I nearly shouted in the darshan's silent waiting zone. I just about fell off my chair and told her 'I like you as a friend, but that's as far as it goes.' She simply smiled, and then we were called into darshan as if the timing was choreographed."

"The protocol during the darshan was for the group of us to sit in a semicircle facing Bhagwan. We each had a turn to be directly in front of him and ask questions, or make conversation with him for a brief time. I was the first to go since I sat furthest left, and he called us up left to right."

"My reason for being there was simply to sit with the master, so I did not go to sit in front of him, but told him that I had no particular reason or issue to bring to him at the time. He quickly moved on to the person who sat to my right and after a few other interviews came to Sona, who was seated five people down from my position."

As she sat in front of Bhagwan. He asked her, "So, Sona, did you find someone?"

"She responded by telling him that she had, but that he was a little reluctant at which point everyone sitting there laughed, including myself. Bhagwan then told her not to worry, and that if she was to keep pursuing her desired man he would eventually give in."

"Since that moment, Amrit, Sona has been all over me and my obsessive-compulsive mind is driving me crazy. I feel I must give into her advances, especially since she has the full permission of our master to do so. After all, a good disciple would surrender to the master, but for the life of me I have no interest in being with her."

Amrit proceeded to laugh and laugh. He had no idea what I was going through. "Just do what you want!" he finally advised, but he did not have my particular brand of craziness. I was stuck in being compelled to do something I did not want to do. It would take me many years to be rid of this internal obsessiveness. At that time, I was consumed by it.

It did amaze me how the master and the commune surrounding him could in a very short time confront me with the obsessive mind I had been dealing with for years and years. Although it may seem silly for most, this was torture for me. I could not easily resolve my dilemma in a straightforward manner.

After trying to make attempts to placate Sona I eventually ran off with another woman which got Sona to close the door to this episode. This was the beginning of the end of this mental issue, although it took many years to finally resolve it.

As time passed, I found out that all who entered Bhagwan's commune found themselves confronted with their own brand of monkey mind.

"Monkey mind" is a term to denote the human fixation of focusing on the mental chatter of ideas, concepts, judgments, definitions and our emotional response to the mental chatter that we are all brought up to fixate on.

I was to discover that what lies behind the monkey mind is what all life strives to remember. I call it 'intimate-isness'.

16

As I sat on my favorite stoop, Maria and I were talking about Italy and being of Italian descent. Although both of us had been to Italy before, we each wanted to explore it more fully. We had been hanging out together off and on for the past six months, and I was finding myself in the opposite situation that I had with Shanti. I increasingly found Maria attractive and wanted more intimacy with her, but hadn't quite broached the subject for fear that it would somehow ruin our relaxed friendship.

For her part Maria seemed to be quite content with the way we were together, and this also made me reluctant to push things. I found myself fantasizing about traveling to Italy with Maria, and thinking how wonderful that would be.

"Maybe we should go to Italy together," I said haltingly. "I've always wanted to go, and I know you have, too. We could share the expense and I think it would be fun. I mean, I believe, we would make great traveling companions."

Maria looked up directly into my eyes and she held her stare for quite some time. "That would really be an interesting trip if we were to do so, but I am not so sure about traveling with you. Besides, what would I do with Joey?"

"He could come with us, or Isabella could care for him while you're away. What do you think?" I asked her with some hesitancy.

"I don't know, Prem - maybe, sometime in the future. One thing I know though is if I was to go to Italy I would want to start off in Rome and work my way up to Milan where I still have relatives. It would be great to see some of my cousins again. I can't go now, so if we were to do such a thing it would be sometime in the future. Nice thought, though."

Funny how I was so unsure about my relationship with Maria, especially since I had spent time with many other women over the course of life. *Interesting*, to say the least. I remember thinking right after this conversation - *Do I push it or just go with the status quo?*

I also remember pondering how it would be great to go to Milan as it is the starting point of my narrative adventure.

Our conversation finished and Maria left to give me space to continue the story unfolding before me.

Paolo watched from a boutique across the street of the hotel as our trio departed. He was to keep an eye on them and relay back their activities to his telephone contact.

He noticed that all three of his targeted subjects were not talking to each other as they walked away and two of them, one of the boys and the girl looked rather dejected for some reason. Unfortunately, he was not able to overhear what took place in the hotel room and didn't have any idea what they went there for. They were still carrying the vases they had brought to the hotel room. In a short time, he realized that they were simply heading back to their own apartment.

At this point he broke off from following them and returned swiftly to his own occupancy across the street from their rooms. He called his handler and relayed their trip, including his impressions of their mood after leaving their meeting. He also asked if there was anything that he could tell him about the situation. The answer was "No." The voice on the other line thanked him for his diligence and told him that he still needed to watch them to see where they would go next.

After hanging up he wondered why this relatively ordinary, rather unaware trio was of interest to his employers whom he knew were a very powerful and influential group. "Seems odd," he thought. "But, a job is a job. Besides, they pay well even if the work is boring."

17

"*This is an impossible task," Sal moaned to no one in particular. Lisa and Carlo were looking at each other, not quite sure what to say as they too could see no way forward. "Maybe we should just give up," Sal continued. "After all, how can we possibly find this guy, 'The Man Who Does Not Know?' Anyway, how do we know if this guy is a real person in the first place?"*

"Maybe this guy is me," Carlo piped up. "It certainly could be me because I am the guy who does not know, or perhaps it's a girl. It could be Lisa, because I can see in her eyes that she does not know either. By golly it could even be you, Sal."

"What the hell!" exclaimed Sal looking at Lisa as if to say he's gone completely crazy.

"You two just stop it!" Lisa commanded. "We are going to find out the meaning of this next clue somehow, I am sure. The vases would not give us a message that couldn't be answered, and I am going to find out how to answer it, and you two are going to help me, understand?"

"Who lit a fire under her?" Carlo whispered to Sal. He was smiling and thoroughly enjoying Lisa in her fiery persona, although he didn't want her to know that.

"We need to go back to the libraries," Lisa continued without comment to Carlo's sarcastic remark. "We need to find out everything we can about this 'Man Who Does Not Know'. Let's

start off by suspecting that it is a person we are looking for who has some sort of a talisman, whatever that is. By the way, let's just call this guy "TMW" from now on short for 'The Man Who.'"

Obsession at times can be a good thing if it can galvanize one to follow through with an impossible task. Lisa became obsessed with her mission, and she dragged her two cohorts along to library after library looking for anything on this enigma of a person. They, of course, found nothing.

They had not forgotten that they were being followed and once or twice glimpsed Paolo from afar. They all knew that they should try to find out more about the spy, but were now hell bent on spending all of their energy looking to solve the clues of the two vases.

Then it happened and it happened, suddenly. It all came together as if existence itself orchestrated the whole thing. Sal was shocked when he bumped into their nemesis in one of the rows of the twelfth library they were canvassing.

A stunned Sal exclaimed a little loudly, "What the hell!" after he realized just who he bumped into.

"Sorry," exclaimed Paolo. "Didn't see you when I turned the corner."

"Never mind that," Sal said. "Who are you and why have you been following us?" Sal then called out to his friends who were in the next aisle to come and see who he caught.

All three of the Milano residents stared intently at Paolo waiting to hear what he had to say. He looked at them and shrugged his shoulders.

"I guess I didn't do that great a job of keeping my activity a secret," he started. He then reached into his inside pocket and took out a badge indicating his status as a member of the Roman police force, detective division. "My name is detective Giuseppe DiMarco, and I am with Rome's finest. I was watching you because I noticed that you seemed to be catching the interest of some pretty nasty people. These people belong to an organization

called the 'Brotherhood of the Not Knowing.' I wanted to know why they were interested in you, and thought that if I followed you, I might be able to find out."

"We don't know of any 'Brotherhood of the Not Knowing'," Lisa informed. *"What could they possibly want with us?"*

"That is exactly what I want to know," said Paolo. "Now that I have blown my cover, I need to ask what you're doing here to attract their attention?"

By this time Paolo's badge was back in his pocket and his air of authority was all he presented to the three in order to find out more of what was going on. He had been following them for over a month now and decided that he needed to find out why. He did this without the permission of his handler, but had decided that he could pull off this deception and cover them from the inside rather than following them around. Indeed, it was working.

"Not so fast," Carlo interspersed himself between Lisa and Giuseppe. "What you are saying doesn't sound right. You're the only one that we saw following us - we don't have to tell you anything about ourselves. By the way, 'The Brotherhood of Not Knowing' sounds a little ridiculous."

"First of all," Paolo countered, "you saw my badge and second, follow me to find out for yourselves."

Paolo proceeded to take them down several aisles over from where they had been standing. He then reached up to the highest level of the bookshelf before him and brought out a book. Its title was: "The Secret Societies of Europe." He began thumbing through the book until he was some two thirds of the way through it when he stopped and handed it to Lisa. On the open page was written "The Brotherhood of the Not Knowing."

Taking up the book, Lisa proceeded to read a two-page description of the 'Brotherhood' to her three companions. In summary, the two pages explained that this secret brotherhood was believed to have been started in Athens and was connected to Socrates. The great oracle of Delphi had declared Socrates the wisest man in the world, because he knew that he did not know – his not knowing was not only innocence, but wisdom itself.

The society started in Greece and as it grew spread into Europe, Asia and parts of Africa. It was thought that this society was the keeper of secrets that would literally change the world as we know it. Contrary to the name this society seemed to have plenty of esoteric knowledge. This knowledge had been kept so secret that not much has been leaked of it over its many years of existence. After turning to the second page, she came across a sentence that simply stunned her. Following a pause, she read out loud, "The Brotherhood is headed by an individual who is known as the 'The Man Who Does Not Know.'"

18

Midday at the Bhagwan's commune the Nadabrahma meditation was run for all who cared to partake. It was another of the master's active meditations that is done in four parts. However, this mediation is much less active than either of the Dynamic or Kundalini meditations.

Sitting in a relaxed position I begin the meditation listening to bells of various pitches and at the same time I start to hum along with all the others in Buddha Hall. We created a chorus of humming. This builds up the energy in the whole of the hall as well as in my inner being and within the beings of my fellow meditators. After humming for a half hour, the energy within is built up to a feverish extent, and at that time music is introduced that informs the meditator to stop humming and begin to bend his elbows so that his hands and elbows are parallel to the floor.

In this position the meditators commence to rotate their arms outward bringing their hands together and moving away from the body in a circular motion pushing the energy just built up outward into the world at large. This is done in as slow a motion as is possible and lasts for seven and a half minutes, or until the music pauses for a short moment and restarts again.

After the pause, the meditators reverse the rotation of the arms and create the movement to bring the energy back into themselves. Arms that had circulated outward are brought together and drawn inward to the center of the body taking back that which was so freely given. After another seven and a half minutes the music stops and the meditator sinks into the pregnant silence. Deep into the witness of all that is going on inside, yet in some mysterious way far away from all that is happening inside as well. All perceptions, sensations, thoughts, and emotions are there, yet somehow not there.

In this way all meditations are an attempt to aid the meditators to see that all the various expressions of energy can be experienced as only energy devoid of content. The content comes from the attachment to, and focus on the particular expression rather than the a-priori energy alone. When this insight happens, one sees beyond the veil of *little self* into the view of the *bigger Self* that has always been there.

Several times while doing Nadabrahma meditation, I had the experience of being in the center of a cyclone. During the humming part I started to feel as if the whole world was spinning and spinning in a whirlwind so intense that it spun both clockwise and counterclockwise at the same time. The first time this happened I got so scared that I opened my eyes and stopped humming to stop the sick feeling the spinning created.

When the humming elicited the same spinning effect in a subsequent meditation I sat through the sickness and kept humming only to find myself in stillness as if I was in the center of a whirlpool. All was spinning yet all was so still and peaceful. No longer identified with the energy I became stillness itself while the energy had not gone anywhere.

It was experiences such as these that made me start to feel the magic of the spiritual field that I found myself in. Later, I discovered that this place was a highly charged energy vortex that promoted these kinds of insights and discovery, and later still I realized that the world, no, the universe itself, held all the magic one could uncover anywhere within it.

During the fifth week we were at the commune Govind asked me if I would not like to see other parts of India. He had heard that Goa was a sheer paradise and wanted to go see for himself. Although I was comfortable with just staying in this magical ashram I said that I was open to accompanying him to Goa just for the adventure.

A week later we took a train from Poona to Bombay with the idea that we would catch another train or bus that would take us down to Goa.

Going third class on an Indian train was an adventure in and of itself. Barefoot Indians with dirty clothes and nothing more would crowd into what could only be described as cattle cars. People could be hanging out the open doorways at times holding on for dear life. Everyone's climbing, touching, intimately crowding in on everyone else. Others would be scrunched up in a corner sleeping on the floor of the train car next to others sleeping on top of them.

For two guys from the USA this was beyond tolerable. We had purchased the ticket, however and were forced to tolerate it. Could I see this over crowdedness as just energy without getting caught up in the various judgments and emotional reactions brought up within me? Not at this time, I couldn't.

Upon exiting that first Indian train ride, both Govind and I were beyond relief and swore never to purchase another third-class ticket again. India was not so expensive for us Americans and we vowed to ride first class from then on. With that in mind, we went seeking first class train tickets for Goa that same day, but were told that all tickets were sold out for the next four days.

Then we went to the bus station only to be told that buses heading for Goa were also sold out for the entire week ahead. Disappointed, we headed for the Amir Hotel where we originally stayed to book a room and regroup.

That evening we wandered over to the Taj-Mahal Hotel to get a bite to eat. Stopping by the concierge we discovered that a boat goes down to Goa every day, and it was leaving for Goa the next morning at 7:30 from a pier nearby.

Getting up early the next morning we decided to forego breakfast and headed directly to the pier to purchase tickets for the boat ride to Goa. The ferry took about twenty hours to traverse the distance to Goa along the West Indian coastline, and we succeeded in securing two tickets.

We went happily off to Goa. The ferry meandered along the coast that was filled with lush tropical vegetation. For many years at that time in my life I was enamored toward palm trees. Palm trees represented warmth and comfort.

For most of that ride Govind and I stayed outside on a broad flat deck where people crowded every corner. Traveling around India made one very aware that it was the second most populated country on the planet. People were everywhere on any mode of transportation.

Our pleasant ride and our expectations were both blown apart when Govind noticed that after about nineteen-hours of motoring down the coast the ferry began to turn around. My eyes were closed while enjoying the sun when this happened. Opening my eyes, I was shocked to see that he wasn't kidding.

Had we come to our port of call? Oddly, the boat began motoring up the coastline. "What's going on?" We did not have to wait long for our answer. The captain sent word down that we were going back directly to Bombay. But we couldn't have been more than three quarters of an hour from our destination.

A cyclone was forecast as a possibility to hit India's west coast and the crew was not going to take any chances. They refused to stop and let us off as most of us requested. We could have probably walked to Goa from where we were. Only in India!

Thus, we took a forty-hour boat ride from Bombay to Bombay arriving at the pier of debarkation around 2:00 in the morning following the day of our departure.

A bit shell shocked and tired, we decided that we were going to go somewhere so we took a taxi to the train station and proceeded to try to buy a first-class ticket to a variety of northern India destinations. Each time we were unable to for one reason or another.

Looking at Govind and seeing in his face the frustration I was experiencing, I told him that if we could get an immediate train back to Poona, I was going to take that as a sign that we were not meant to be gallivanting around India. Sure enough, two tickets to Poona were readily available when everything else was blocked.

Immediately, the old Sadhu we had met on the Isle of Elephanta came into my vision. He had told us not to go anywhere else in India because what we were seeking was nowhere else to be found except in Poona. I for one was not only resigned to my fate, but relished it.

19

*P*aolo had left the three young people several hours ago. He had talked to them over a lunch they shared, and although he had not totally convinced all of them of his good intentions, he was sure that he was well on his way to doing so.

This strategy of his was risky business, and something he had never ever considered in the twelve years he had been doing this kind of work. He attempted to convince himself that it was fine to follow this path, because it gave him an insider's position in case something had to be done with any of his subjects.

It was a concern that he was not authorized to befriend his targets by the powers that be, but he was sure that he could get them to come on board with his plan.

He was aware that the reason he proceeded with such an audacious action was because he could not contain his need to know just what was going on with these three very innocent and naïve young Italians. What could the group possibly want with them or how could they be any threat to such a powerful organization? There might be something that he could take advantage of in this situation.

Truth be known, Paolo was tired of being just a low-level peon and began to have dreams of becoming his own man. This just might be the perfect opportunity, and anyway he knew that with his false portrayal of being a police officer he could gain his target's trust. In doing so he would be in an easy position to carry out the group's directives concerning them. On the other hand, these three just might have something going that if he got his hand on it could set him up as a force to be reckoned with.

He just needed to get more information about what was going on here, and for that he would attempt to stay close to his subjects and get them to tell him what they were doing. He'd get the information he needed with guile or possibly force if necessary.

Right now, they were more than half convinced he was a cop, and that persona would work to get them to trust him, although he had some doubts about the one called Carlo. The girl and her brother were a sure bet.

With all this in mind he set up another meeting with them for the day after tomorrow. They bought the secret society bullshit, and he told them that he would try to uncover the leader of it, as their main interest seemed to lie there. Strange he thought, why are they so concerned with 'The Man Who Does Not Know.' They hadn't told him, and only asked if he knew who he was. He had used 'The Brotherhood of Not Knowing' as a ploy only because a friend of his had mentioned them as a secret society that he might possibly work for one day. He had no idea about them. Somehow, he had accidently picked the right group to use as a cover.

"Till Thursday," he set up a date with them.

While Paolo was thinking over his strategy Lisa, Carlo and Sal were in their apartment frantically talking about all that just happened.

"I do not trust or believe this so-called policeman Giuseppe DiMarco. He's lying to us – I just feel it," Carlo insisted.

"Come on Carlo," Sal countered. "He showed us his badge which was all too real, and he brought down that book. Could you believe how crazily synchronistic that was? Giuseppe comes to us at the right time and unknowingly points to the answer to

the very question we have been searching for. He is authentic, he must be."

"It is creepy that this secret society has been spying on us. They must know what was said on those vases, but if they did, why would they leave the vases with us when they stole the box?" Lisa was concerned.

"That is troubling I will admit. The fact that he pointed out the society we were told to find gives his story some credibility, but then again, he could have stolen that badge, and synchronicity could just be coincidence. There is something about Mr. DiMarco I just don't trust.

Looking at my last sentence I became engrossed in the idea of synchronicity in everyday life.

I was particularly thinking about the many synchronistic events that seem to be happening between Maria and I, especially concerning my writing.

I had picked Milan, Italy as the place to begin my novel completely on a whim, and then met a woman living in the apartment of the stairs where I began writing this novel. She just happens to be practically the only Italian in East Boston whose origins were from Milan. Over the course of our friendship, I had further discovered that her family had a secret that was handed down from father to son for as long as Maria could remember. This information had come to her from her mother, who wasn't sure how far back they could trace her uncle's secret. Maria had no idea just what they were hiding, but was confident that her mother was not just shining her on. Her mother had told her that the secrecy had gone on for a long, long time.

This morning Maria told me that her family had some connection with Athens, Greece, but was not sure what it was. This happened after I had written the chapter about the 'Brotherhood of Not Knowing' and its Athenian connection.

That was enough coincidences to give me shivers, and although I had no idea what it all meant I was beginning to suspect that my connection with Maria was more than my innocence would have me believe.

Everything about all this was strange to say the least.

20

As a child I remember asking myself what love was. I had heard it mentioned repeatedly by the priests and nuns at school, but never got a satisfactory answer from them. They only gave me repetitious threats about hell and enticements of an unclear heaven. These gave me no solace, as to my yearning. God I was told was loving, but the sad image of his son Jesus hanging from his cross did not seem to be very loving. It didn't take much insight to see the heavy sadness surrounding the religion I was brought into.

I had heard love talked about on TV and in books, but for the life of me I just didn't feel this supposed wonderful feeling called love in my life. Surely some of the characters on the shows seemed to be thoughtful and concerned, but often they were wooden and too predictable, and for sure nowhere near the image of the people I had to deal with day to day.

Both my parents seemed to be at each other's throats, arguing and shouting all the time. My father was distant and cold. Most of my interaction with him had to do with being told I was stupid or worse. My mother was caring, but she was also somewhat stoic, and thought I was too attached to her. In truth I felt abandoned by her although I know her actions were done to develop a sense of independence in me. Independence was her own desire, and, of course, what was good for her was good for me. Neither of my parents were people you could have a deep conversation with concerning life's difficulties and challenges. As for my sisters they were often there for me, but caught up in their own worlds, and dealing with my parents themselves.

My grandmother, aunts, uncles, and cousins were quite close to me, but I still missed a sense of love. All these people were not very demonstrative of what I had thought love was supposed to be. They were never very physically affectionate, nor did anyone ever say *I love you.* Neither were they well-springs of positive feedback, nor was I able to be vulnerable with them with the expectation that they could listen and truly respond in kind. I experienced more fear in my childhood than love. Hence, I ended up pondering, *what love really is.*

By the time I found Bhagwan I'd had a girlfriend and explored passion and intimacy, but I was never sure I was in love or was truly loved. So much about relationships seemed to be about compromise and just getting along. I sensed much was missing. Don't get me wrong, I thoroughly enjoyed the physical connection of sex, but was that love?

Love was elusive, until I met Bhagwan. Just listening to him I felt for the first time that someone really knew me. He connected with my fears and my desires, my thoughts and feelings. Listening to his taped discourses while in Boston I began to have an inkling of what love was.

Sitting in Buddha Hall with Bhagwan with two thousand of his lovers heightened the love I glimpsed while in Boston. In the profound silence deepened by so many other souls, Master spoke about how society in general including parents, relatives, teachers, friends, priests, on and on gave us our beliefs out of their beliefs. With those beliefs came guilt and shame, anger and sadness, and with these feelings came protectiveness and the enhancement of a sense of us against them. It reminded me of how proud I felt for being an Italian as if that was a badge of honor, no, a protection against the outside world.

He spoke on how the rules of society so often condemn what is so natural in the world: sexual taboos, taboos around death and dying, the holding back of women, the discrimination of large groups of people by other large groups of people; including the layering of people into classes and more were expounded on by Bhagwan. These things we have been taught in a thousand ways he told us. We believed them even at times despite ourselves. Love and society as such did not appear to walk hand and hand together, but rather it appeared that society walked a path opposite to love. We had to find out who we were before society took root in us. So heartfelt was the master's understanding of these things, and so eloquent were his words that conveyed this understanding that the thousands listening could only absorb the truth of it.

Bhagwan, although sitting so far away from me on the podium in Buddha Hall instilled an intimacy so profound as to elicit powerful feelings of love that I had only guessed at before. In a moment I realized that love was experienced whenever one felt really heard, totally seen, and completely accepted by another. Later, I was to learn that love does not even need another to be experienced, but at that time his miraculous understanding of the human condition and his ability to share those feelings arising out of it and his complete acceptance of them was love.

My deepest question was answered and by someone I didn't really know in the conventional way. We never had a one-on-one conversation, nor shared a meal, nor even casually conversed at a party. I loved this man more dearly than I had ever loved another, yet we had no relationship as such. True intimacy does not necessarily even need a relationship. I had come to India to seek out a spiritual master, but what I found was so much more – a true human being. True intimacy is sharing a profound sense of humanness with another human being.

I was so overjoyed that Govind and I could not get out of Bombay to wander India, because what I really needed was the time to sit in Buddha Hall with the master to take in the true meaning of what I came to India for in the first place. The inner journey's start had presented itself as a rich adventure that had no parallel.

Govind for his part was also glad that we had to return to Poona. He had connected with a woman named Sudha and became a guard for Bhagwan sitting in the lovely garden at Lao Tzu villa just outside the master's bedroom window. It was not all peaches and cream for Govind, however, as his feeling of being overly vulnerable in India would not leave him, and a meeting he had with Bhagwan disturbed him greatly.

It was the very first darshan we had together with the master. Darshan as I had said consisted of about ten people sitting in front of Bhagwan in a semicircle. One person at a time would move closer to him and sit directly in front of him. Usually, a short conversation would ensue. Many people would ask Bhagwan a question about something going on in their lives. They expected, and usually got wise advice.

The very first time Govind sat in front of Bhagwan he did something I had never seen him do before or since. Normally a very loquacious and spontaneous individual, Govind became completely tongue-tied. He was unable to speak and was locked in eye-to-eye contact with the Master; so much so that Bhagwan had to tell him to go back to his seat in the semi-circle. He told him to meditate for a week before coming back to complete his darshan.

When we came out of the gathering, I asked him what happened, but he would not tell me. He just went silent. I accepted his need for privacy, but knew something exceptional happened in Lao Tzu Hall that night for him. Years later he finally confided in me what took place, and then I understood why he began to want to leave India sooner than we had planned.

He fell into a bottomless abyss looking into the master's eyes – no one was there. It scared the shit out of him.

21

"We must go to Athens," Carlo said, looking intently at his comrades. Of course, they were both in agreement, although it meant a journey that had not been planned for, and a cost they needed to deal with.

Thinking out loud, Sal blurted, "What about Anand and Sita? They said they were interested in discovering more of what the message meant. I wonder if they would help us with funding. Who knows, they may even be interested in coming with us on this journey."

Lisa was not so sure that the latter part of her brother's thought was such a good idea. "Sal, you really think we need more people tagging along with us uncovering our family's secret?"

"Why not, Lisa, we need the money to go on further, and who knows how much further we will have to go after Athens. Besides, we might need more help with these Asian languages, and they seemed very sympathetic to our cause. We should at least explore the possibility and see if they're interested. What do you say, Carlo?"

"I still have some money," Carlo responded. "Lisa told me that you both have a bit left, but I have no idea how expensive this venture is going to be. Our two Indian friends seem to be quite well off, and they are explorers of a kind so their help may be very valuable, especially if this search gets more difficult."

"We wouldn't want them to get into any danger because of us," Lisa worried. "I'm just not sure."

"Let's leave it for now," Sal decided. "We have a meeting with DiMarco tomorrow, and that may give us more of an idea as to what to do."

"I'm not sure, why are we meeting with this guy?" Carlo bellowed.

"Carlo, hold down your paranoia, he told us that he would look into where we might find this guy who doesn't know, and after all he is a policeman with contacts. We need to follow through with him, and anyway, it would give us more time to figure out if you might be right to distrust him. Believe me, I have some doubts, myself; although I found his explanation of why he was following us to be plausible. Still, it's better to be safe than sorry and what better way to be safe than to meet him again and check out his story further," Sal shared.

Paolo had contacted his handler and had the devil of a time convincing him of the action he took contacting his young charges. "Are you crazy?" his handler shouted when he heard what Paolo had done. "You were never told to contact them. Are you an idiot!" He went on at some length with both threats and insults.

"I knew he wouldn't be happy, but I didn't believe that he would be this bad," thought Paolo.

"Look, I know you're upset," Paolo pleaded, "but these guys knew I was following them. This way I can follow them without them thinking I am doing so. They are very naïve and don't suspect anything but what I told them." He knew that he was stretching the truth here, but he was very confident in his abilities. Besides, he already took this turn, so he thought it better to follow through with it. He was aware that his reputation and maybe even his life might be on the line.

"Tell me exactly what they told you about what they're doing," the voice on the phone commanded Paolo.

At that moment, Paolo knew he had to lie, or he may never get the information on what exactly his charges were up to, or why the organization wanted him to follow them so badly.

"They didn't tell me much yet, only that they came to Rome to have some vases appraised." So far that is all I got out of them, but I am meeting with them tomorrow so I may know more for you then."

"Paolo don't fuck with us," the caller threatened. "You better have more information tomorrow and it better be good."

"Well, that went well," Paolo nervously chuckled to himself. What was he doing here? Did he really think he could fuck with the organization and get away with it, and for what? Why was he so curious about these marks anyway? He was following an inner voice he had in doing this. He remembered having hunches like this before, although very rarely, and they always seemed to lead to something good.

The meeting between DiMarco and the trio was set for one o'clock in the afternoon. It was to commence in front of the famous Trevi Fountain. The three Italians were there first, and each of them threw a coin in the fountain. The three wishes each coin represented were similar in nature. Each wanted to uncover the secret they were pursuing. In addition, Lisa wanted safety for herself and her companions. Sal wanted a conclusion to this journey with the outcome of more wealth for his family, while Carlo wanted a deeper relationship with Lisa.

Before going to the fountain Paolo considered what his next strategy would be and what he expected to get out of this risk he was taking. If this group had some information his employers wanted or was trying to protect, it could be worth a lot of money if he could get his hands on it. Perhaps, he would be able to be independent from the organization and create his own agency. However, going against these powerful people was very dangerous. If he guessed wrong and the information was not as valuable as he assumed he needed an exit plan which unfortunately meant *killing someone. This he did not want to do. Extortion, thievery, spying, and just about everything short of murder were his gigs, but he had avoided adding killing to his repertoire until now. It would be amazing if he did not end up having to destroy a life in this venture. It was time to take the risk, or otherwise languish in being a lackey the rest of his life.*

These were his thoughts as he approached the Trevi Fountain, and so when he reached the rendezvous point and threw his own coin in the water, he wished that he would succeed in gaining independence and power.

"Hi guys", Paolo said.

"Hi, Officer DiMarco," Sal said, greeting him.

"Please don't call me Officer DiMarco. Just call me Giuseppe," Paolo said with an unusual grin.

"So, Giuseppe, do you have any more information for us?" Carlo asked watching officer DiMarco with nothing but suspicion on his mind.

"Still don't trust me Carlo, do you? Well, I don't blame you after I followed you for two weeks, I wouldn't trust me either. What about you two?" turning his attention toward Lisa and Sal. "You know it doesn't really matter. I got a job to do, and it seems you are helping me not only do it, but helping me discover just what must be done."

"I looked into your little friend 'The Man Who Does Not Know,' and discovered that he is a mysterious figure who's wanted by quite a few European police forces including the Italian State Police. By the way, did you know that the Italian State Police was formed in 1848, and that this so-called unknowing man has been wanted since 1886. Seems that the original guy wanted, who was probably a predecessor of whoever currently has the position. Heck, who knows how many 'Men Who Do Not Know' there have been. Funny, though, that the police still list this man as wanted presently - crazy."

"What led you to become interested in such a character, any-way?" Giuseppe continued. "He may be still wanted by police, but really has been off the radar for many decades, and now you show up interested in him. You know I am very aware of the Not Knowing Society but was clueless as to what its leader was called until now. I need to know what's going on here."

Carlo took over before either of his companions could say anything. "It really isn't anything about police business, and we would rather not say why he interests us. Let's just say that we have heard of him through some books we have read."

"This leads us into a bit of an impasse. How can I possibly help you any further if you don't trust me at all? I want to catch this guy – it would be a feather in my cap. I need a little coop-eration on your part however to convince my superiors to pursue him. I know you are very interested in finding him yourselves. It would be easier if we could work together. I'm going to the men's room now so why don't you guys talk it over as to whether we do this together or say goodbye and you do this on your own, or maybe, not at all." Paolo in the guise of Giuseppe got up and left.

The trio wasted no time in discussing the pros and cons of trusting DiMarco with some information in order to get his further cooperation. They all agreed not to tell him the entire story yet. If they were to give him any information, they would tell him that the family had a secret, and they heard mention of the Brotherhood from their family in connection to it. They would not explain the clue leading to TMW. No mention of the box was to be made or the danger suggested. By the time DiMarco was seen returning they still hadn't agreed to tell him even this much. Hastily, they put it to a vote just before he came to the table - Lisa and her brother, for, and Carlo against. They would tell him.

Lisa began telling Paolo the story. He sat quietly and lis-tened, although as time went by, he wondered just how crazy his idea was since their story did not seem to hold great promise to *finding something worth a fortune. He was helping them look for a family secret – what would that get him? Yet, the organization was somehow mixed up in all of this so he shouldn't give up on it just yet.*

When Lisa finished Paolo wasn't sure what to make of it all. He was driving on a particular course, however, so he decided to continue to gather more information. He knew that she had not told him everything, and he had expected she wouldn't. Whether the story that was missing was enough to give him what he wanted was completely unknown to him. He decided to help the trio seek out the mysterious TMW. Perhaps things would become clearer if they found him.

In his guise as DiMarco, Paulo sat for an hour with his three companions, explaining more of what he did on the police force and getting more information about their Milano lives. Building trust was his mission, and after this bonding period he felt that even Carlo was more willing to see him as, at least, not an enemy. Being on the other side of the law gave him ample information to describe what cops did in their work capacity, and he was beginning to like playing this role.

He told Lisa and the boys that he had to go to his lieutenant to ask him if he could pursue this case further, and that it might mean he would take a technical leave of absence from the force, because they would need to go outside Italy to Athens to find this guy. He'd need to find out everything the force had on the head of the esoteric organization. He had to contact his handler and convince him that he should keep up this charade and see if they knew anything about TMW.

Meanwhile, none of the trio mentioned anything about needing to go to their newfound Indian friends to procure funds to be able to go on the next leg of the search. After they left DiMarco they straightaway called Anand and Sita using the telephone at the railway station. They had to leave a message for them at the hotel desk asking if they could see them later that day, and they planned to go by the hotel in the evening hoping that they would be available for a meeting.

The three friends became excited, but also shared with each other that they were more fearful than ever with this turn in their quest and with getting involved with more people, especially Giuseppe DiMarco. Oddly, they were not inclined to go to the police to check out Paolo's 'Giuseppe' story. If they had, Paolo had it covered, because Giuseppe DiMarco was really a cop on the police force. It didn't occur to them to pursue this kind of inquiry, so they were left up in the air whether to trust him or not.

22

"*They wanted to go find the 'The Man Who Does Not Know' and I told them that he was wanted by the police and that I would help them find him.*" Paolo was talking to the voice on the phone again.

"*You're getting thick into this Paulo, aren't you? I ran all this by the committee, and we are cautiously okay with you continuing for now. However, we do not want them to have contact with this man, but we would like to find him ourselves. I doubt very much even with your help that they could make contact. We have been trying to find out who he is for years with no luck at all; I don't think it will be much of a problem if you try helping them. If you fail you can use your influence to discourage them from looking any further into the matter, and we can finish this whole affair without much messiness.*"

"*If you do somehow find the 'Man Who Does Not Know,' you are to contact me immediately and prevent our trio from contacting him by whatever means necessary. Do you understand me Paolo? We will take care of him in another way that suits our purpose.*"

"*I understand,*" was all that Paolo responded. He understood that he would have to make a life changing decision if he and his cohorts somehow stumbled onto the mystery man.

He would get no help from the group on finding this guy. Heck, he wasn't even sure he wanted to find him. Just getting these Italians away from whoever they were looking for might put him in enough stead with the organization to help him climb a little higher in status. Then again, he would still be a lackey, and he wanted more.

Paolo then went out on a limb. He stole a cop car to pick up his marks just to quickly tell them that he was going to travel with them and to set up a meeting for later that same day to plan their next step. The car would seal the trust he was falsely pursuing and assuredly went a long way to doing so. Although, Carlo seemed to still have some reservations.

While Paolo was busy contacting the group and doing the rest of his shenanigans, Carlo and his friends spent time with their Hindu acquaintances. They told Anand and Sita all that transpired since they had left their hotel room five days ago. Lisa recounted their library searches and bumping into DiMarco, finding the book and their need to go to Athens to continue the search. They were sure that if they could find the head of the ancient society described in the book, they would be well on their way to finding the box and its unknown contents.

Anand wondered what could possibly be in this box Lisa had told him about to warrant such intrigue and difficulty. This may be a discovery of a lifetime or just a useless venture. When they told him that they needed more funds going forward he perked up. When they asked him if he would provide the funds, he became extremely unsure as to the merit of honoring their request. Even after they asked him and Sita to accompany them on their search, he was hesitant to commit. The money was really no object for him as his family was indeed very wealthy. He just did not want to go on a fruitless and possibly unrewarding search for God knows what and then to drag Sita along? He would have to talk it over with her, and was himself, inclined to say no to his young new friends.

"Let me talk it over with Sita," was all he left them with, and that is all they knew when they met DiMarco in his police car.

"I told you he was the real thing," Sal directed his certainty to Carlo after getting out of the car.

"I'll admit that I was probably wrong about him, but I still don't trust him. I don't know why. There is just something about him."

"You just can't admit when you're wrong, Carlo. Anyway, we need to find a way to get more money. We can't tell Giuseppe that we can't go along with him. Any ideas Lisa?" Sal was concerned.

"I have not given up on Anand and Sita, yet." This was all that Lisa could contribute looking at Carlo for some other feedback…none came.

Money is such an issue in life, isn't it? It does make for some interesting twists and turns on one's journey, but it is the vehicle of much enslavement for most of us.

Luckily, I had done well with money for myself over the years. Being involved with accounting I was able to command a very good income and I still do for that matter. Maria on the other hand was not so fortunate. As a bartender her salary was limited and having a son and mother to take care of was positively no help financially. Even with her mother's social security the family lived from paycheck to paycheck.

Money was one of the reasons why Maria was reluctant to go to Italy with me, although it was only one reason among several. The others were her reluctance to get more involved with me and leaving her son and mother at home.

Over the many months of our friendship, I had told Maria of my exploits traveling the world and being involved with more than several lovers and friends through my sannyasin network. As a sannyasin, Bhagwan taught us to identify and go beyond repressive ideas and idioms instilled in us by society. As I said before, much of this repression centered around sexual taboos and norms, emotional restrictions, and social niceties.

Some of my stories that explored *letting go* both excited and scared Maria so much that she was still hesitant to accept some of my more affectionate gestures I was directing toward her of late.

One example was a story I told her about a past lover I had in Cambridge, MA. Tammy and I had lived together for almost a year. We were both sannyasins and had listened to Bhagwan declaring the need to let go of attachments in order to achieve spiritual freedom. One day I came home from work to have a quick lunch and walked into our shared bedroom to get a new pair of socks. As I entered the bedroom I was met with the image of my girlfriend in bed with another man.

I became so distraught and jealous, and reacted by freezing inside. Not even looking at them I got my socks and left the room without saying a word. "It's over," I thought as I walked away from the bedroom door. Then, I stopped in my tracks, and thought, "What would a Buddhist monk do in this situation?" The answer came immediately, go back into the room and witness the situation as if meditating. This is what I ended up doing.

Walking into the bedroom I sat on the bed and simply watched these two people in bed together. Of course, they sat up and started talking to me. I told them that I was just there to witness them and not to engage with them. I was there to witness my reaction to the scene without doing anything. After sitting with them in silence for several minutes I felt a calm descend on me and I got up and left Tammy in bed with some guy. From that day onward, I had no issue with jealousy.

My relationship with Tammy at the time continued for another year after this event, and at the time I was seeing Maria, Tammy and I were still very good friends.

Most people with whom I came into contact did not understand this story or my reaction to it, yet I was of the mind to be as open as possible to anyone I felt close to. This and other stories had Maria reluctant to become romantically involved with me as they were not in any way conventional.

With all this pushing the envelope against Maria's conventionality I was still hopeful that the connection we truly had would deepen and our relationship would become more intimate.

It seemed to be heading that way as Maria and I were spending more and more time together going out to dinner, plays, and just hanging out. On another note, by the time Maria and I started seeing each other I had already thoroughly explored the idea of non-attachment.

Non-attachment is the visceral understanding that there is nothing outside of you that will save you or fulfill you. All that is 'other than you' is transitory and ultimately non-substantial. Thus, attachment to it is equivalent to pain and suffering either now or in the future. The suffering is derived from the attachment to that which is not you. There is indeed sadness and pain in losing a relationship, job, or other affection, but these are transitory. All feelings when deeply felt transformed themselves into something beautiful. Long suffering comes from holding onto the idea of that which has left or changed.

Love fosters deep intimacy and a feeling of oneness with that which is loved. Love can also lead an unaware mind and heart into illusion. This illusion is the idea that that which you love is yours because it completes you or fulfills you. This attached love is not really love at all, but is something that you are using to falsely fulfill yourself.

Saying all this to Maria was not so helpful, because even if she understood all of it mentally, and I doubt that she did, it did no good. Unless one has experienced the truth of it, it remains only hearsay.

The pain of loss is very real pain. The fact that you attribute that pain to losing the person or object outside of you is not only not correct, but misleading, and only perpetuates the agony. Seeing the pain as generated by holding onto an illusion of permanence is ultimately very freeing.

The nature of things is the nature of things, and there is nothing to be done about it, except for being in awe and acceptance. Can you fight a cloud or scream at the moon for simply being?

This was my understanding while connecting with Maria, and there was no need to act out non-attachment because it became for me part of the nature of what is; just as intimacy is fulfilling unto itself.

I understood that my expressing all this to her was not very comforting, but I was being true to myself; yet assuring her of my affection still did not instill much confidence.

Still, I invited Maria to travel with me to Italy in September of the following year and I told her I would pay for the entire trip.

"Sita, they want me to fund their family search and they suggested that we go on the quest with them. I told them that I would ask you, but I think it is a crazy idea. I admit those vases are ancient for sure and the fact that they had a weird message written on them in Pali has stoked my interest, but it really doesn't seem promising, and I am inclined to say no to them. What do you think?"

Having just got up from her evening mantra meditation, Sita was alert, yet serene. Coming from a place of centeredness, she said, "I sense that there is a part of you that would like to throw caution to the wind Anand, but I tend to agree with your assessment here. You know we came to Rome to see if we could find a lead on the Veda's referencing Vimanas. We were led to the Vatican Library, and we need to focus on that job, although it seems that we may not find what we are looking for. We still have a few more places to look. We just don't need to get caught up in another, how do they say, goose chase."

It seemed to be settled – they would not be the vehicle for these young Italians to continue their odyssey.

"I will send Carlo a message in that regard and convey our full condolences for not being able to help them," Anand acknowledged Sita.

It was the following day that Sal opened the door to find a messenger handing him an envelope. "I was told to deliver this to Carlo," the young man said. Sal took it and conveyed to his sister and friend the disappointing news. The small group began to grasp the difficulty with being able to further their pursuit.

The previous night they had calculated that even with the money they had left they could not possibly put enough together for even two of them to make the trip to Greece.

23

As I sat on the stoop listening to the ringing in my ears, Maria came out to join me. She looked lovely in a stylish light green pantsuit. Her silky hair was long and dark in contrast to her blue eyes. She was getting ready to go to work and came out to share some photos of her son playing baseball. He had joined a little league team and her pride for him was shown through the twinkle in her eyes.

"Doesn't he look great in the uniform!" she exclaimed. "He did so great the other day and seems to be one of the best hitters on the team. Perhaps you can come with me to see his next game, and give him some manly support?"

"But of course." I told her. I was not a great fan of baseball. I found it boring and was much more inclined toward basketball and football. I had to support Joey, however, and I was so caught up with Maria that baseball was my new interest.

Even though Maria and I weren't an item, yet I could feel her sliding me into the role of stepfather to Joey. Having seen myself as too much of a child to be a father to anyone I was quite a bit uncomfortable with the role, but decided to meditate on it as I did with most things in my life. I needed to let this process unfold and take it wherever it would lead.

Anyway, Maria left for work, and I was left with the continuation of my story. Exactly where do I go from here? I was starting to realize that writing longer pieces was tedious and needed more of my focus. It seemed that I was being asked to get more involved with additional responsibilities.

After receiving the message from Anand & Sita, the Milano's became most depressed and uncertain. They would have to go back home and work to get the money together, which meant that time would pass and the possibility of them recovering the box would dwindle.

The worst part about the situation was that they would have to tell DiMarco they could not join him and were afraid he might discover the mystery man on his own thus ruining any chance they might have of finding the next clue.

Sal at one point began arguing with his sister. He had concluded that one of them should continue with the search and that he was the logical choice. If they could pool all their money together it would suffice for him to go to Athens alone with DiMarco and find the answers they needed.

Lisa strongly disagreed and the siblings bickered the whole afternoon.

Without much to say, Carlo watched his friends arguing. He could see no way for them to proceed together. He wasn't a fan of having Sal travel the trail alone, but realized that it might be their only chance to do so.

In the end Lisa won. There was just no way she would let any one of them go forward alone. Although they had no major trouble going down this path yet, her late brother's warning rang loudly in her ears. They would just have to delay the whole search and tell detective DiMarco. Anyway, he might not be able to go to Athens by himself.

Wasting no time, they contacted DiMarco and told them of their dilemma, and the need to postpone their journey going forward.

Paolo was torn when he heard the news. For whatever reason he had become excited about going in search of TMW and the possibility of where this might lead for him. Yet here he was presented with the successful conclusion of his task without any further complications. He could take his money and go on a vacation. It was true that this opportunity of making a name for himself would be gone, but there would always be other possibilities in the future.

Initially, Paolo as DiMarco expressed disappointment when he heard the news. When asked if he would pursue the trail by himself, DiMarco said that he didn't think so. He didn't think going it alone would work and told Sal to keep him informed if they ever got it together to go. His job was done with no harm, no foul. He wouldn't have to kill anyone after all.

Earlier, he had responded so, but later after the evening passed Paolo became anxious and unusually despondent. He kept thinking what could be wrong with him. He never felt this kind of inner-agitation. He had this compelling feeling that he shouldn't just walk away, but wasn't sure why he felt that way. Something was happening here that was unusual for him. He kept getting the sense that he needed to continue with this quest and furthermore he needed to bring the trio with him.

"What the fuck", arguing with his internal urge, "is going on?" This was very unprofessional, and he wasn't clear that he felt this way solely because he wanted to make a name for himself. Whatever it was he couldn't shake the feeling and was in misery because of it.

The decision was made. Lisa, Sal, and Carlo would depart for Milan in three days. There was nothing more for them to do except say goodbye to their new Indian friends and to Roma itself. All three were experiencing their own despondency, although Carlo and Lisa seemed to be doing better than Sal. Carlo and Lisa mainly spent time consoling each other during this period, inhaling Rome's romantic aroma during their long walks through softly lit ancient streets.

The night before they were to leave, they stood by the river holding each other in an intimate embrace. This grew into a long and passionate kiss. "We better not go home right now Carlo," Lisa said after they came up for air. "I don't know if I can trust myself alone with you in the apartment. We need to take this slowly, I think."

Looking at her with a soft, but longing stare Carlo could only respond by telling her, "Whatever you want, Lisa. Right now, I don't want to stop kissing you."

The next half hour was full of stars for both of them, and it left them with the certainty that they would be spending more and more time together wherever they landed next.

Sal, on the other hand, found himself spending much of those three days sipping coffee alone at various cafes trying to figure out how he could continue the journey, but came up with no answers. To say that he was extremely disappointed was an understatement.

That night after the lovebirds finally felt in control enough, they returned to the apartment that was vacant since Sal was still out. They were shocked to find their apartment in shambles. Some of the furniture was overturned. All three bedrooms were a mess with the bedding undone and the mattresses halfway on the floor. Drawers were opened and clothes were thrown all over the place.

"Oh, my god!" Carlo exclaimed.

He hadn't immediately noticed but Lisa had. "The vases are gone!" she shouted. "The vases are stolen Carlo. God! What are we going to do?"

A short time after that disastrous moment Sal came in and the three of them huddled together shaken and in disbelief. What were they going to do? Of course, they called the police and during their conversation they asked for Giuseppe DiMarco. They were told that he was unavailable, but that they would send over two other agents to take their statements.

Since they had Giuseppe's telephone number, they decided to call him directly, and told him the whole story including that they called the police and asked for him.

Paolo had to think fast on his feet when he heard what went down and the fact that they asked for the real Giuseppe DiMarco to come check out the crime scene. Luckily, the real Giuseppe was not there, or he would have been screwed. He had to stop them from connecting with the real DiMarco immediately, but how?

"Just give the officers who come to you everything you know about the robbery and let them do their job. No need to ask for me, because after I finish what I am doing now I will come to the apartment immediately. I was going to call you anyway, because I have some good news to share with you." Paolo spoke swiftly.

He thought to himself that this sealed the deal. He had to get the trio out of Rome fast or else his story would be blown to smithereens. He also thought that it was weird that his compulsion to continue with the search was being pushed along by this surprising event.

He paced back and forth while he waited for the two police officers to finish their inquiry. As he watched the whole gathering of evidence from his apartment he planned to rush there immediately after the police left the premises. If his fraud was discovered by his charges talking to the police, there was nothing he could do about it, but if they had not discovered his deception he needed all of them to move without haste.

The whole police scene took about an hour and half, and Paulo raced across the street just at its completion.

"I got over here as fast as I could," DiMarco said a little out of breath. "How did it go?"

"They took all our information," Lisa shared. "Someone is obviously still watching us, and the fact that they took the vases suggests that they know what we were doing."

Paolo relaxed just a little believing that his story was not blown yet.

"What did you want to contact us for?" Sal asked

"I've got some news that you might like, especially after this disaster. I've decided to continue with the search for TMW and I got enough funds to cover all four of us to do so."

"What!" the trio shouted in unison.

"The only thing is we must leave tonight. I have a time restraint with my captain, and we need to leave now. Can you pack up and go in an hour?" Paulo was in a hurry.

24

*T*hey all met an hour later outside their apartment. DiMarco led them on a walk to the train station that was only six blocks away. They took the train to Bari, Italy which was a small village on the east coast. From there they would take a boat to Patra on Greece's western shore and from there, a train to Athens. It would be a 35-hour trip all together, and who knows how long it would take them to find their quarry.

Before Paolo had met his marks, he contacted his handler. Over the telephone he took great care in asking his contact why the organization had stolen the vases.

The voice on the telephone told him that he was to mind his own business, and that they had their reasons. He was told just to continue with his plan, although the organization thought he had a slim to none chance of finding the man they were looking for. Paolo was told that although they would appreciate very much if he did indeed find the 'The Man Who Does Not Know' they would also be quite okay with failure here. "Either way it is a win for us," the voice informed him.

One positive communication that Paolo did not expect was when his contact said that he should start his search at the Algiers Café in the old town of Athens. The group knew this to be a contact point for the society he was seeking.

During the long trip he learned of Lisa and Sal's family history – the loss of their father and brothers during the war, and their subsequent survival in Milano.

He in turn told them something of his own history in Spain. He stuck close to the truth about his past, although he left out some key identifiers, and he told them a fabrication of his story after leaving Barcelona.

As for Carlo he didn't share much of himself. He simply listened to all the stories, some of which he was aware of and some not so much. He and Lisa spent quite a bit of time strolling the deck while they were on the ferry.

"You still don't trust our friend, do you?" Lisa asked on one of their deck walks.

"No, I don't," was all the response she would get.

After some time while they strolled arm in arm he added, "I know that he is the reason why we can continue this journey, but I think we should be very cautious around him. Please don't tell him about the box, at least, not yet. Promise me and tell Sal not to either."

She turned and kissed him deeply under the brilliantly shining Milky Way. "I promise for now, Carlo."

The trip took a little longer than they had expected, but after nearly two days they found themselves in Athens, and because none of them had been to Athens before they were a little lost as to where to plant themselves.

The first order of business was to find a three-room apartment. Lisa needed her own room as usual, while Carlo and Sal would share a bedroom. DiMarco would have his own room as well. Over the course of their trip, they had discussed what it would take to find TMW, and they concluded that they might have needed an extended stay in Athens. DiMarco told them that he had funds enough to cover two months, and that if it took longer than that they were out of luck.

*After they got settled in a flat on Syngrou Avenue, DiMarco
informed the group that his captain had a lead as to where to
start the search. It was off to the Algiers Café; they found themselves going the following morning. There was no time to waste.*

Shanti and I were sitting having lunch at a small, but
famous Italian restaurant called Riso's on Trenton Street in
East Boston. Eastie had quite a few good Italian restaurants,
but this one was a cut above the rest with its homemade
pasta and sauces.

We were talking about some of our experiences at the
commune in India, and about the synchronistic events that
seemed to be a daily occurrence there. She was telling me a
story about how during her second time visiting the ashram
she was trying to decide whether to stay there and make it her
home or leave and go back to the States. She was conflicted
around this one question. She loved the depth of silence and
peace she felt, especially during Bhagwan's lectures. Valuing
the intimate connections she was making with many of the
people she met, she was also butting heads with the woman
who ran the place and her overall power over the workers and
disciples that became part of the scene.

With this question whether to stay or go running ram-
pant through her mind, she entered the ashram bookstore
and randomly picked up a book and opened it to a page that
coincidentally had a question directed toward Bhagwan by a
man asking him whether he should stay in the commune or
leave it. Just as coincidently his issue centered around loving the commune itself but having difficulty with its power
structure. The answer came in an apology from Bhagwan. To
paraphrase, he was sorry about the power structure that was
growing around him, but in so many ways it was a necessity
in order to create a safe place in which his disciples could
experiment with meditation and spiritual growth. "That was

just what I needed to hear, so I stayed," Shanti shared. "How about those amazing coincidences!"

I told her that that kind of thing would happen all the time to me and to just about everyone I knew. There might be a friend you were thinking of and missing because they were somewhere else on the planet and then you would look up and bingo, they are in front of you. You would have an emotional difficulty you were working through and someone dealing with the same issue would ask Bhagwan a question about it that same day during lecture. It was such a common everyday experience that my friends and I started thinking that we were living in a magical field.

Bhagwan shared with us that what was being created around him was what he called a Buddhafield. Shanti and I laughed just thinking about it. I told her that synchronicity is everywhere if you are open to it, but it was the daily routine at the ashram.

Shanti and I first met the very first time I went to Poona. I was walking down the main lane in the commune when I saw my friend Nirmal. As would often happen within the commune we stopped and gave each other an intimate hug. After we released each other from our embrace she turned to the woman she had been walking with to introduce her to me, and we, of course, hugged each other. This hug had quite a charge to it, and we remained in each other's arms for what felt like ten minutes. It was not, but it sure felt like it. We then looked into each other's eyes, both of us knowing that the embrace would lead to something even more meaningful.

There was much ‘*connecting*’ going on in Bhagwan's ashram as we were allowed the freedom to explore sex and love to an extent and with an acceptance not common even for the 60's generation.

We looked into each other's eyes acknowledging the depth of feeling we still had for each other even though the sexual element was no longer there.

"Boy I wish my relationship with Maria could be as easy and free flowing as yours and mine was," I whined to Shanti. "We acknowledged our attraction to each other quickly and there was no hesitation on either of our parts. My connection with Maria is so much more complicated than it should be, and I seem to be more complicated in it than I need to be. It is another world out here away from the ashram."

"Yeah," said Shanti. "Everything is so much more serious out here, but to tell you the truth I think that's not such a bad thing. Maybe if we weren't so casual in our sexual relationship it might have gone deeper and longer than it did. Sometimes I regret all the quote unquote 'spontaneous sex' that happened in the ashram. It might have been satisfying for all you guys, but many of my female friends there have voiced some regret for being so open so fast."

"Shanti, are you kidding me? I didn't feel any resistance from the various women I went to bed with while in our ashram during the years I was there. Now, are you telling me they are second-guessing themselves? I just don't believe it."

"Swami with all your great knowledge you still don't understand women, after all how could you – you're just a man. Anyway, you and Maria have been having foreplay for quite some time now. What gives?"

"I don't know. It was partially my fault in the beginning. I just wanted to remain platonic friends and not have sex fuck up our connection, but now she has held back probably because she knows something of my sannyasin past."

Just as I was saying this, who do you suppose walked into Riso's? Maria, Isabella, and Joey sat down two tables away from us, and the theme of our conversation abruptly ended. All three of them got up when they noticed Shanti and I and said hello.

Synchronicity is everywhere if you are open to it.

Paolo realized that they were being followed the moment they walked out of their flat on route to the Algiers Cafe. He thought, "They don't trust me."

He knew that making a name for himself by taking advantage of a situation dealing with the organization was never going to be easy and he still thought that they don't know anything yet, and if it doesn't work out, he could still come out of this cleanly with them. He just needed to be very careful.

25

*T*he Algiers Café was quite a 'happening' place. Filled with locals it was situated in a dense part of the old city. Small alleys crisscrossed small streets to make a maze of tunnels running through three and four-story residential buildings. Some of the buildings looked like they were built in the time of Socrates.

On one corner in the middle of the maze was the Algiers Cafe. It was big as cafes go, especially in that part of town. The place sat dozens of people mostly in a piazza just outside the building itself. The aroma of Greek coffee and regular coffee dominated the place although anyone with good olfactory senses could pick up a multitude of spices from cardamom and ginger, to nutmeg and turmeric.

People could be found in pairs or in groups occupying every table and all the counter space. When the Italians and DiMarco arrived, there was nowhere to sit so they ended up getting coffee and pastries and stood up by the picture window overlooking the piazza.

Sal gave DiMarco a clear look that said how do we do this? It was Carlo who came up with the way to proceed, however, when he asked the waitress walking by him if she knew anything about 'The Brotherhood of Not Knowing.' She stood still as if shocked by the question, but then shook her head vigorously, NO!

Carlo's companions all gave him the stink eye as if he just did the worst possible thing that could be done. Lisa said "Carlo what are you doing, that's no way to find out what we need to know, and you are going to make trouble for us. Stop it."

"What do you mean 'stop it?'" he responded. "The best route is usually the most direct. What else can we do, and do you have a better idea?"

DiMarco played the mediator here by telling them to calm down. "Perhaps we should not go so boldly forward just yet, Carlo. How about we just get a feel for the place before we start asking such direct questions toward just anyone. I would say that it might be better that we split up here and wander listening to whoever we are near. Perhaps we might pick up something without giving ourselves away, just yet."

"That sounds like a great idea," Lisa responded while giving Carlo a look that told him so. "We need to be more careful, don't you think?" again directing her comment to Carlo who sheepishly got the message.

For a good twenty-five or thirty minutes they mingled with the patrons wandering and standing in one place here and there. After that Sal found them a table in a great location just outside the Café surrounded by a multitude of tables all of which were occupied.

After three hours and several various coffee drinks they were no nearer to their goal as not one of them had heard anything of significance. Not once did any of them hear even anything about knowing or not knowing. they were spent and got up to go. Carlo couldn't help but face his three companions and smirk. "Well that went perfectly, didn't it?"

No one answered him and no one said a word. They began to return to their newly found flat; however, just as they turned into their street a car came bolting around stopping in front of them. Two rather large guys got out both holstering guns easily seen in their open jackets. There was a small alley the two directed them to go down. While all four of our friends moved toward the alley another tall, but not burly individual alighted from the vehicle and walked toward them.

"Who exactly are you people and what do you want with STINK?" the tall man demanded.

Carlo, who had sweat pouring out of his armpits managed to say, "We were looking for 'The Society That Does Not Know', we know nothing about STINK."

"Are you a buffoon or do you just look like one? The two are the same in essence. Now answer me! Why are you looking for the Brotherhood? This better be good for your sake."

Lisa went into an answer that tried to explain the vases and the writing on them telling them to find TMW. In her nervousness the way she blurted out her explanation made very little sense to the men listening to her.

The tall man stopped her mid-sentence and told them that if they valued their lives, it would be better if they left Athens and their quest. He said that he would know if they hadn't, and that he had very little patience to play around with them. Then, he and the two thugs got back into the car where a fourth man was waiting behind the wheel to drive them away.

After the men drove away, our seekers rushed back into the apartment. Carlo made an off-handed comment about how well his direct approach worked regardless of all their admonishments. No one was very open to listening to him, and as a matter-of-fact Sal became quite angry telling Carlo that his approach nearly got them killed. He was so angry that he called Carlo an idiot during his little speech.

"Stop it Sal," Lisa yelled. It wasn't Carlo's fault. After all, we came to find TMW and we had to ask someone sometime."

All this time DiMarco was eyeing Lisa with some intensity. Lisa speculated that among all of them, he didn't seem all that freaked out probably because he was a policeman. Anyway,

Lisa noticed DiMarco's intense stare and asked him why he was staring so much.

"You never told me that the vases had writing on them," he said. "You said that you were having them appraised. Exactly what is going on here? What exactly did those vases reveal to you?"

Lisa looked red-faced at DiMarco and was speechless.

"Don't be hard on us," Sal answered for the threesome. "We didn't think you needed to know about the vases. Anyway, we told you that we got the information about TMW from writing we came across. What difference does it make if the writing was on the vases or not?"

"What difference does it make?" DiMarco was yelling now. "What difference does it make? How about the difference between getting us killed or not. You told me that TMW was someone who you read about who could help you find your family's secret, but did you ever think that he could be the guy who wants to keep the secret as a secret. If I had known this little fact, I probably wouldn't have gone on this wild goose chase. After all, did you not wonder who stole the vases? I thought the vases were stolen because they were worth a lot of money, but now it would seem that they may have been stolen by the Brotherhood itself.

Paolo was overjoyed that this fact had come out, and now he had to take advantage of its revelation to instill fear and urgency for them to reveal to him more of what was going on.

DiMarco continued, "You need to tell me exactly what was written on those vases right now before we even think of continuing."

And, without much hesitation Sal went into his backpack and pulled out a piece of paper with the exact translation they had received from Anand.

DiMarco began reading out loud:

"The dharma of he who reads these words will be changed to finding the miraculous if he who reads is pure of heart. Those of evil and selfish intent will be thrown violently to the four winds,

beware. That which lies within the container will open the world of man to that which is beyond the stars, seek the talisman held by the 'The Man Who Does Not Know' to find the further key."

Carlo looked at Lisa with consternation written all over his face, but said nothing as DiMarco finished reading.

DiMarco looked up at Sal with a look of bewilderment, and Sal began to speak.

I sat on the stairs speechless. How to go on here and where was I going with this? Maybe I should go back to Riso's and have some pasta, because my mind was blank.

26

"*Do you see now why we need to find TMW? We need to get him to show us his talisman. I don't believe it was him or the Brotherhood that stole the vases. What sense does it make? TMW must have known about the vases already and the message that was left on them. He must know that he is the key that leads us to the secret we are seeking, otherwise the existence of the vases makes no sense." Sal was on a roll.*

"You make no sense Sal," DiMarco responded. "Whoever wrote on those vases could have known about TMW without TMW knowing. He may have no part in helping to reveal whatever secret you are talking about. Are you kidding!"

Paolo pressed his advantage. "What secret are we talking about here? I need to know. What kind of secret can 'open the world of man to that which is beyond the stars'. I'm of a mind to just leave you here on your own and be finished with this farce unless you come clean with me. What more are you not sharing?"

The three Italians looked at each other, and then turned their heads towards Carlo.

"We need to tell him Carlo," Lisa pleaded.

"Yes, Carlo, we need to tell him." Sal continued.

"I disagree," Carlo said slowly. "But do what you want, after all it is your family's secret not mine."

All this was said in front of Paolo, while he waited internally knowing that they had no option but to tell him everything. While they were going through this needless ritual, he was thinking that now he would have enough information to continue his dubious ploy or melt into the ethers and leave these innocent idiots to their fate.

"We need to do this Lisa," her brother was saying. "Tell him."

And so, Lisa told Paolo the whole tale without leaving anything out. For his part Paolo listened carefully. When he heard about the box he perked up. This is what they were looking for and this is what could supposedly hold the key to the prophetic possibility the vases allured to. When Lisa got to her father dying in some strange explosion in the Milan Library he immediately and intuitively knew that the organization must have killed him. Just as he was sure his story about the Brotherhood was only that, a story.

Realizing that he was chasing after a box Lisa and Sal's family had in their possession for centuries excited him. Should he go on with his crazy plan or not? Strangely he felt compelled to go through with it and find this secret whatever it was for himself, although he was a little apprehensive about the warning that was written about those with evil and selfish intent. Wasn't it true, he thought, that all these ancient treasures had warnings to frighten people from trying to find anything about their secrets? He wouldn't be so gullible.

Sal for his part began trusting DiMarco more so his question regarding where they go from here was mostly directed toward the man he knew as a detective.

"We can't be so easily scared off," DiMarco insisted. He needed to backtrack from his story blaming the Brotherhood. "Hopefully Sal is right about TMW and his society not being the ones who are trying to keep the box away from you, otherwise what I am proposing could be very dangerous to our health. We need to go back to the Algiers Café and get them to pick us up at which

time we must find a way to convince them to send word to their leader. If these guys really are your thieves, maybe we get our heads broken. I don't see any other way that this goes down."

So, the four of them went back to the Algiers Café the next day, but nothing seemed to happen. They went back the day after that and asked the people behind the counter for the Brotherhood, but again nothing happened. They went back day after day after day without any success.

One week went by, then two weeks and then a month, but no further contact was made with the Brotherhood.

They waited on pins and needles expecting any day to be the one that could be the breakthrough. Nothing happened except for Lisa receiving a letter from Anand and Sita that informed her that they were leaving Roma. Their research was now going to continue in Athens. The letter was dated two weeks after Lisa and her companions had left Rome. It further suggested that Lisa, her brother and Carlo meet them at the Hotel Amir in the old quarter soon after their arrival in Athens.

The day the Indians arrived, the trio and Paolo went off to the Hotel Amir. It was that same day that Paolo came to a final decision. Although the Italians were downtrodden with their lack of progress it was Paolo who was really getting exasperated. The day before he had reminded his marks of the time that had elapsed, some thirty-five days, without any progress whatsoever.

During that time Paulo even went to the Athenian police under cover of his false identity to try to uncover anything he could on the Brotherhood. They simply laughed at him. His companions searched out information at the libraries to no avail. Nothing was happening and he was ready to call it quits. He would take his paycheck, his reputation and drop his ambition for now, despite the nagging feeling that urged him to continue. He'd give it four or five more days and "finito", as they say.

He'd give his new-found friends a ticket back to Milan on the group's dime, of course. No need for them to go back to Rome and possibly discover his deception.

The Hotel Amir was located Near Syntagaru Square right next to Adrianou Street on a small tree lined lane. It was a relatively new establishment, and like much of the surrounding area was part of the rebuilding that occurred after the Greek War of Independence. The Indian name of the hotel was a result of the owner being of Indian/Greek descent.

Carlo asked the hotel attendant for the room of Anand and Sita and was told that they had informed the desk that they were awaiting guests. When the attendant rang the room Sita answered and excitedly said she and her husband would meet the foursome in the lobby in a few minutes.

A grand reunion took place with lots of hugging and laughing. Sal introduced DiMarco to his Indian friends who knew of him, and for the first time met him in person.

After all the pleasantries and catch-up, Sal told the two researchers of the lack of progress in finding TMW. He told them how they were accosted the first day they were in Athens, right after they had asked for the Brotherhood at the Algiers Café. Since that day he said they decided to brave the threat they received and visit the Algiers Café again and again only to receive silence.

Carlo was being his quiet self, but obviously was having good feelings being around the two Indians. He suggested they prolong their visit, and go to the Algiers Cafe for lunch.

At the Algiers Café they miraculously found a table big enough for all of them. As they were placing their order, a spontaneous idea arose in DiMarco. When it came to his time to order his food he purposely blurted out that it was urgent to contact the Brotherhood now that they had their two lead researchers present.

Everyone looked at DiMarco in disbelief, and everyone said nothing except for the waitress who let out an exasperated sigh and said "I told you ten times already that I know nothing about this Brotherhood already. Just give me your food order please."

Nothing happened although DiMarco was put to task as to how inappropriate he had been using Sita and Anand as a lure to get something to happen. It was Lisa who told off DiMarco in no uncertain terms what an ass he was for doing so. She was extremely embarrassed with what he had done and worried that he might have gotten her friends in trouble. A trouble, she emphatically told him that should have had nothing to do with them.

Anand and Sita remained quiet even as DiMarco defended himself explaining that his was a last-ditch effort to get the Brotherhood to come out of the closet one way or another.

Nothing happened when they walked the Indians home, nor when they proceeded to their own apartment. Nothing happened at all.

Later that afternoon while the three guys were lethargically hanging out in the apartment Lisa went out to a food market near their flat to get something for dinner. While testing the ripeness of a tomato she was accidentally bumped by a kindly looking older gentleman. He pardoned himself in Greek and Lisa responded, "It's okay," in Italian.

He started asking her how she knew Italian and soon realized that her Greek was limited, at which point he said in fluent Italian with a Roman accent, "You are an Italian tourist? We don't get many Italian tourists in this part of town, and especially at this market."

Lisa told him that she was visiting for a couple of months with friends, and that they had decided to get a flat because it was so much cheaper than staying in a hotel.

"What are you here for, may I ask?" his eyes sparkled in the afternoon light. Her answer was that it was a long story with a great element of frustration to it. At this point he smiled and said he would love to hear more about it, and it would afford

him a chance to practice his Italian. "Would you join me for tea at that stall at the end of this row and tell me more?"

Lisa realized that she relished the idea of telling someone other than her companions of the past month's disappointment and longing around their search. It was about to come to an end she sensed anyway, and they already had put themselves in harm's way so there was nothing more she needed to share. And so, she began her saga.

"We came here looking for the 'Brotherhood of The Not Knowing' and specifically for its leader 'The Man Who Does Not Know.' From there she went on for an hour and a half retelling the whole story from her mother's childhood longing to the present dilemma.

The old man listened and asked questions here and there, in his fluent Italian. He seemed to be most interested in finding out about DiMarco and the Indians. "What's DiMarco's background and what are Anand and Sita researching?" he asked. She told him what she knew.

When Lisa finished her story, she felt a sense of relief from much of the anxiety that had been building. The old man thanked her for sharing her story, and said he understood why she might have sleepless nights. He wished her luck in her quest and gave her his address in case he could be of any service, although quite frankly, he said he had no idea how he could help. "Perhaps, if you just want to talk again," he said to her just before leaving.

What a friendly soul Lisa thought as she left the market. She would have to tell Carlo about him when she got into the apartment. On the way back to her flat she thought about her inclination to tell Carlo and realized she was getting involved more deeply and realized further that she relished it.

Sal and Carlo were back at the flat each in separate rooms. Carlo was in their shared bedroom whereas Sal was writing at the small desk in the parlor.

Lisa greeted her brother and then made herself a cup of tea. She then went into the bedroom where Carlo was lying down. She wanted to give him a passionate kiss, but instead she sat on the bed. "Carlo are you awake?" He responded in the affirmative.

"I met this very sweet old Greek man at the market and shared with him our story. It felt good to talk with someone else for a change. He was kind enough to listen and just by talking I began to understand just how impossible our task is. I realized that if we never found the box or its secret it would not be the end of the world, and Carlo I realized just how much I care for you." Certainly, they would have kissed then, however Sal walked into the room.

"I wonder where DiMarco is. He left to take a walk shortly after you went to the market and that was three hours ago. What do you think?" Sal was concerned.

Lisa and Carlo turned from Sal and glanced at each other laughing nervously.

Sal looked annoyed, "What are you two laughing about? Oh, did I interrupt something?"

Carlo smiled and simply proposed that they all go out to dinner. "By the time we're back DiMarco will be here, I'm sure." They proceeded to walk to their favorite Greek café not far away.

They returned two hours later, but DiMarco was still not back. Nor would he return the following morning.

"We need to find him somehow." Sal directed his statement to Lisa & Carlo.

"Yah!" Lisa said. "But how?"

27

The tall thin man was directing his questions at Paolo who was tied to a chair in the middle of a large warehouse room. Water could be heard lapping up against a pier or siding of some kind. Paulo figured that he must be somewhere by the river. He was mentally beating himself up for getting surprised the way he did. He knew he was being followed as he had known for a while now, but he neglected to see the three guys hidden ahead of him in the doorways on either side of the street. Four guys against one he didn't stand a chance. Well, he knew that this would probably be the likely outcome if he kept pushing the Brotherhood to show themselves.

His interrogators asked, "Who do you work for, and why are you with these Italian youths?" Paulo said nothing upon which one of the heavies punched him in the jaw. Again, the question, and again no answer and again his head snapped back when the blow came.

"So, you're with the Rome Police Department?" the tall man said as he changed his tactic. Funny we have connections with the police in Rome and Giuseppe DiMarco who is on the force there is a short balding guy. "Who are you really? We can go at this all night. It's up to you."

I should have known that they would know I wasn't my alias, Paolo thought. "How the hell am I going to get out of this?" he

140

thought to himself. Another punch came and this time he felt it loosen a tooth.

"Who do you work for and what is your name?" repeated the tall thin man.

Lisa, Carlo and Sal decided to go to the police, although they weren't sure just how welcome they would be. The short of it was that Carlo ended up being their spokesman with the police and they relayed the fact that DiMarco, who was a member of the Rome police department was missing and that they thought it was the 'Brotherhood of the Not Knowing' who took him.

Whereas before when they inquired about the Brotherhood, they got laughed out of the station. This time they spoke to an officer named Zorba who took down all the information quietly and efficiently without any hint of unprofessionalism. When the trio left the station, they felt confident that at least the Greek police would seriously investigate the disappearance.

"My name is Paolo Garcia, and I'm originally from Barcelona. I thought to con my Italian friends out of some money, and I needed to get their confidence, so I did it by posing as an Italian police officer. I found out that they had no money to speak of, but they were on a quest to find this missing box that they said was very valuable. I thought I could help them find it and then steal it from them later." He had to tell them something.

"Who do you work for, Paulo?"

"I don't work for anyone, just myself. I swear it."

"We'll see," said the tall man. He turned to one of the heavies and told him to make sure Paolo was tied tightly enough. "Just know that if you're lying to me you will wish you hadn't." At this point the inquisitor, the heavy and the guard all got up, walked out of the room and bolted the door.

They all moved to an adjacent room in the warehouse where Sita was tied to a chair in the same manner as Paolo.

The tall man's hand gently caressed Sita's face and hair. "You are lovely my dear. Such fine hair and high cheekbones, and those eyes are royal. Now tell me what you are really doing in Athens. Why are you interested in the Brotherhood and who sent you?"

Sita was petrified. Although the young Italians mentioned that there could be some danger with their search, she never thought that looking for a family heirloom, as she conceived it, could put her into the situation that she found herself now.

With a shaky voice Sita explained that she was not really interested in the Brotherhood other than to help her Italian friends follow up on something her husband Anand had translated on the vases he was shown. She told her captives the translation of the Pali writing, and how it indicated that the leader of the Brotherhood had a talisman important to their search.

"So, you mean to tell me that you and your husband are not the leaders of this group of yours, and that you're not truly involved. Are you bullshitting me?"

Adonis was a fine reader of people. He had been a therapist for many years before coming to the Brotherhood, and still was for that matter. He, himself, had been overwhelmingly distraught and traumatized by the accidental death of his wife, and it was the Brotherhood and its leader who befriended him and helped him get back on his feet. Eternally grateful to the organization and the people in it for bringing him back from the brink of suicide he had decided to work for them.

He could tell that the woman in front of him was basically telling the truth, although there was something she was not sharing. He also knew that she was not equipped to hold her secret for long.

"There is something you are not telling me. What is it?"

"I have told you everything," she answered. "There is nothing else I know."

"You said that Anand, is it, and you stayed in Rome after the young trio and detective DiMarco came to Athens. Why did you follow them if you are not so involved? What are you doing in Athens?"

Sita could feel the sweat trickling down in between her breasts. "Anand and I are doing research into Italian and Greek artifacts."

"Very interesting," he smiled. "What have you looked at while you have been here, and what did you inspect while in Rome?"

Sita informed him of a list of places that they had visited in Rome, some very famous and others not so. She told Adonis that they had no time to visit any places in Athens yet, but relayed a few that they were interested in. To Adonis's mind all that she said seemed to be reasonable, but intuitively he was sure that she was not telling him everything. He'd check her answers for now. She wasn't going anywhere for a while and if there was something more as he suspected she would tell all later.

Anand was beside himself waiting for Sita to return. She had gone out hours ago to inspect a book they were interested in at the Municipal Library of Athens. Where was she? He could wait no longer. He locked up their room and headed for Carlo and his friends, because he feared that Sita being gone had something to do with them. He should have never got involved with their stupid search.

Without any respite Anand's mind would not stop envisioning horrible things happening to Sita. He had to find her. He could not lose her. She had nothing to do with this Brotherhood. "They must have taken her. How am I going to find her? Shit! Shit! Shit!" Anand was not one to swear or lose his calm, but this was intolerable, and his mind would not stop.

Meanwhile, the Italians were now sure that detective DiMarco was abducted. Heck, they had no idea what to do to locate him other than to go back to the Algiers Cafe, but that idea now seemed more dangerous than ever.

28

It was morning and Isabella was sitting in her preferred kitchen spot sipping her favorite drink, a cappuccino. Opposite sat her daughter also sipping a cappuccino. Joey had gone off to school, so it was just the two of them.

"He is getting more insistent that I go to Italy with him. I'm very tempted, you know, but if I were to say yes then I would be committing myself to a relationship with him, and I'm not completely comfortable in doing that. You know that I really like him, but his lifestyle scares me. First, he's been with a lot of women, and his overall disposition does not lend itself to stability."

Isabella listened to Maria spout all this without saying a word herself. She had heard all this before and was at a loss what to say to her daughter. In the silence that followed Maria's distressed expression Isabella thought about how normally self-possessed her daughter had been since she was a little girl. Watching her now, she was anything but. Speaking about Prem, she understood her daughter was caught between two very strong urges: the urge to risk following her heart or the urge to maintain a secure lifestyle for both herself and her son. Both desires were strong, and both were pulling her apart.

Isabella had chosen the more secure path to live out her life, although she recognized that in doing so, she was only half fulfilled. She had a wild and impetuous streak all her own which she suppressed. She had put this down to being a child of the early 1940's with society's taboos on being too adventurous, especially if you were a girl. Maria's generation was more free-flowing, although Maria, herself, tended to be more traditionally inclined. She did have her bold side; it just wasn't expressed often.

Prem seemed to be an illustration of his peer group. His wanderlust and daring nature seemed to fit right in with the 60's generation, and now his friendship with Maria was exciting her dormant risk-taking nature. Unfortunately, she was now a single mother and this did not go well with her ideas of going boldly where…holding back was a reasonable position to take. Isabella thought it also produced a sexual tension within her daughter that was creating confusion.

"I think you should go for it," Isabella blurted out after a long silence. "Leave Joey with me and go to Italy with him. See what's there for you. It could be an evaluation with a honeymoon thrown in. After a month in Italy, you will know whether he is right for you, and if it is not right you can cut it off without too much drama."

Maria simply stared at her mother with an open mouth. It was not what she expected.

Just about the same time all this was going on in Isabella's kitchen I was beginning to think that going to Italy was not in the cards. I didn't want to go there on my own and was becoming very pessimistic with the idea that Maria would go with me. My thoughts turned toward going back to the ashram in India.

I was reminiscing about the long walks I used to take while in Poona. I called those Poona walks the "Power Shuffle." The heat was intense and the only way to walk was to mimic a very slow-paced stroll no matter the distance one had to travel.

A particular walk came to my mind. It was a morning walk I took from my apartment on Boat Club Road to the commune in Koregaon Park. The distance from one to the other was a mile and a half or perhaps two miles. I used to walk it every day and on this one day I was experiencing a realization that everything in my life was the result of my own creation. This realization was the result of so many different ashram experiences that it is hard to pin it on any one of them. Let it be said that I was influenced by listening to Bhagwan's lectures; also through several group therapy insights. Furthermore, the generally loving vibe found in the ashram that supported me contributed to it.

As I was strolling, a profound sense of wellbeing arose, because along with the realization that I created everything came the realization that I was not stuck and could change it as well. The understanding made me feel so fulfilled that even dying at that very moment would have been more than okay. Everything was sublime during this walk. This feeling was heightened by the fact that I was in India with its abundance of uncensored life and death, both in equal measure.

It was with this thought in mind that my stream of consciousness turned toward India. I began to fantasize about going back there, feeling free and finishing my novel there. I saw myself writing in the gardens or the ashram café or perhaps on a rooftop connected to my flat.

Breaking my fantasy, Shanti called me from the other room. We were supposed to go to the Cambridge Central Square Zen Center together. Lately, we had been practicing Zen sitting at the Center every Thursday night. After having done so much more active and cathartic meditations both of us were more inclined to simply sit watching our breath go in and out while lightly focusing on the belly region Zen calls "the Hara".

Traveling to the Center I was reminded of the fact that the originator of this center was a master named Seung Sahn with whom I originally met some two or three months before I became aware of Bhagwan.

My introduction to him happened while attending a lecture of his in which he answered almost every question posed to him, "Keep Don't Know Mind." He could speak only a very few words of English at that time, but later after many years of my own meditation I realized that all spiritual experience is encompassed within those four little words. They point to the childlike innocence that holds no judgments, that holds no preconceived notions; and then again is always open to the here and now which opens the spiritual realm.

All this aside I was brought out of my India dreaming, but not my question of whether to go to India or not.

29

*M*arco and Dawn were a hit team used by the organization for very special occasions. This was potentially one. They were told to go to Athens and await further instructions, and so they found themselves in a luxurious hotel doing just that. Waiting.

The three Italians and Anand went back to the Algiers Café asking about DiMarco and Sita. Silence prevailed. Anand was especially beside himself lamenting his decision to come to Athens. Lisa was panicked in her concern about the fates of Sita and DiMarco.

The four of them left the café with Sal exclaiming that they would just have to wait. Their waiting was akin to being impotent. It was nothing remotely like the waiting Marco and Dawn were experiencing not far away.

Upon returning to their apartment they found a note under the door. The note was addressed to Lisa and in it was a simple two-sentence warning. "If you want to see your friends again, we suggest you do not go back to the Algiers Café. Just wait for us to contact you." It was not signed.

Simultaneously, when Anand entered his hotel room he returned to a disaster. The contents had been thoroughly rummaged through, with several things missing...including his prized possession. How would he and Sita finish their research? Shit! More importantly, was he ever going to see his wife again?

"What research are you really doing, Sita?" The tall man came very near her cheek from the back of the chair she was tied to. Sita did not want to answer this. She was agonizingly reluctant to tell her interrogator that she and her husband had been trying to uncover what they thought would be a true historical and world revelation. At the same time, she could sense that he knew that the answer wasn't ancient artifacts.

They were interrupted by others who wanted her interrogator's attention. He left her exhausted and alone.

'What could they do?' Lisa worried. Their friends were missing now for three days, and they were told just to wait. The secret society was surely behind all of this, and they could not even contact them to try and make a deal. Waiting was getting on her nerves.

Since the kidnapping Lisa had become stand-offish toward Carlo. Although she still felt warm feelings for him and a desire to be with him, she just couldn't see herself enjoying his company while her friends were in danger, or being happy while others were in despair.

Carlo had seemed to understand what Lisa was going through, although he also felt she was not being fair to herself or him. He did not push the issue, but did try to non-aggressively draw her in toward him. As time went by, he began feeling angry with the thought of somehow losing her before he even had a chance to be with her.

Carlo was not one to normally feel a sense of powerlessness, but dealing with Lisa and his inability to do anything to get Sita or DiMarco back he was indeed lost in impotence. He had thought about going to the Greek police, but swiftly put that out of his mind knowing that they had been at best ineffectual in the past, if not downright hostile.

At this moment he wanted to speak to Sal, but Sal was nowhere to be found. Lately, Sal was into taking long walks by himself, wandering the streets of Athens in what seemed to be an aimless pursuit of releasing his pent-up energy.

Although these three were becoming stressed out and increasingly fearful, it was Anand who was truly traumatized. He alternated between rage and depression. His beloved Sita was kidnapped, and he blamed himself. If he hadn't persisted in following his leads to discover the truth about vimanas, Sita would be safe and sound right now. If he hadn't been attracted to his friend's story and if he hadn't begun believing that it may have something to do with his own research, Sita would never have been abducted. His guilt was overwhelming. Oh, how he wished he could do things over again.

Sita was shaking. She had been blindfolded and put in a reclined chair. Gauze or some flimsy material was put over her face and then water was poured over her nose and mouth until she nearly passed out with no air. In fact, she did lose consciousness once thinking that she was dying. Long ago she told her captives about seeking out evidence for the truth of the existence of vimanas. They seemed mildly amused at her admission, but now they were asking her again and again just why she and her so-called friends were looking for the 'The Man Who Does Not Know'. She had been telling them for what seemed to be hours now, but in truth was no more than 20 minutes that the writing on the vase told them to do so. Suddenly, as it began it stopped.

Sita passed out and returned to awareness within what could have been minutes or hours. She was alone and thoroughly in shock. Still blindfolded, she heard the familiar sound of shoes scraping the floor coming toward her, and she braced herself.

"We have decided to let you go. You will go back to your friends with a message, and you will deliver it exactly as I tell you to or you'll wish you never heard of the Algiers Café. Do you understand me, woman?" The voice saying this was soft and menacingly cruel. "I asked you if you understand me."

Sita managed a nod of her head in the affirmative.

"Also, if your friends do not heed our suggestion things will go bad for all of you. Do you understand?"

Again, Sita nodded her head, yes.

Sita had soiled herself while being tortured and was a complete mess waiting to be released. Her hands were untied, but she was warned not to remove the blindfold. She was taken out of the room she had been sitting in for days and taken to a bathroom with a shower. Instructed to take a shower and put on new clothes handed to her, she was cautioned again to keep the blindfold on until no one else was in the room and to put it back on when she finished.

The shower was cold, but gave much relief. Sita was expecting one of her captors would violate her while in the bathroom but was relieved of that worry when nothing of the sort happened. When she finished, she blindfolded herself again and was taken in a car until she was dropped out of the vehicle and found herself a block away from her hotel room.

Entering the lobby, she saw Anand standing there. She burst into tears as did he. The hug was long, sad, and yet happy and full of too many emotions to imagine.

Marco and Dawn just happened to be in the lobby at the same time Sita entered it. They watched the scene unfold wondering who these people were and what their story was about.

30

"*They told me to tell you to go back to Milan and never to come back to Athens again.*" *Sita was talking to the three Italians and her husband. She turned toward her husband. "They said that they didn't care if we did any more research on our project just that it could not be done in Athens, and we should have no connection to the Brotherhood. We are all to forget anything and everything to do with 'The Man Who Does Not Know' unless we want early death."*

"Did they say anything else?" Sal queried.

"No, except that they warned me that I would be retaken if you didn't heed their demand and I would never see the light of day again if they were forced to do that."

"I am so sorry we put you into this Sita," blurted Lisa. "You should never have been involved in our affair."

Anand stiffened and looking at Sita told her that they would return to Delhi immediately. He was shaken to the core, even more it seemed than Sita, although she was in no way opposed to returning to India.

As they got up to leave, Carlo put his hand up and asked, "Sita, what did they mean by telling you that you could go on with your research? Why would that even be an issue?"

Sita looked at Anand. Anand turned a little red in the face, but simply said, "Let's go, Sita."

Sal got up from his chair, "Wait, why can't you answer Carlo?"

"That is between Sita and I. This has nothing to do with your quest. Why didn't you tell us just how dangerous your little adventure would be, and why did you use us as bait with this group of people? This is over for us now. We are going home, and I suggest that you do the same."

"But Sita, did they say anything about DiMarco? Lisa asked. "He is still missing."

Sita was quiet for what felt like a whole minute. "I was told to say nothing unless you asked, and I don't know why. God, I don't even know why they would think you wouldn't ask immediately, but those were my instructions. Anyway, they said to tell you that Officer DiMarco is not who you think he is, and it is better to forget about him. He will not be returned to you, and his life depends on you following their instructions to leave, and not come back."

With that Anand and Sita left the trio.

"We must leave at once," Lisa exclaimed when the Indians left. "This was a crazy idea, thinking that we could just come to Athens and find TMW. What can we do about DiMarco? I am afraid we may never see him again."

"There is nothing we can do!" Carlo explained. "We have already told the police here. The only thing we can do is go home by traveling through Rome and inform the Roman police what happened here."

Dejected, they all knew that the only course they had was to do just that. Their quest ended miserably, yet they were more concerned for DiMarco and the trouble they caused Sita and Anand than they were for the disastrous results of their search. They all knew that the search was over and resigned themselves to never finding the box, or the secret it held.

As I raised my head up from writing I fell onto a memory of surrender. I had been meditating for more years than I cared to remember by witnessing my thoughts and feelings, looking for an elusive enlightenment I had been enticed to search for.

I was living in Cambridge in a flat with my girlfriend at the time and her son. We had a boutique which doubled as a meditation center that was located just below the apartment. As was my practice at the time I found myself early in the morning in the boutique which the night before had been converted into a large open meditation room. All the clothing displays were on wheels in order that we could wheel them to the sides and create a large meditation space.

That morning sitting there in Zen meditation I decided to give up the quest and give up meditating. I decided to just sit without any objective goal in mind and I relaxed. As I relaxed more deeply into just sitting there in the room filled with sunlight my focus had a turn. I found myself couched in the is-ness of the moment, and the is-ness was not just something that things happened in, but was me. I was not there at all, only is-ness existed. It was all that was inside and outside what I had once termed as myself.

To say that this was a life changing experience is to not give it enough credit. From this point on in my life my attachment to what I had once believed myself to be, lessened and my sense of is-ness grew exponentially.

I was interrupted in my memory by Maria who came out from her apartment and sat next to me on the stoop. I could see that she was in some inner distress, but was more than disappointed when she informed me that she just couldn't go to Italy with me. She felt it was too much of a commitment to do so and just wasn't ready for it.

My protests that no commitment was called for reached deaf ears and after a very short time she went into the apartment to get ready for work.

31

*T*he trip back to Rome took about the same amount of time as the original trip to Athens. When they arrived, they sequestered themselves in a small pension for one night with the intention of catching a train back to Milan the following morning. They went immediately to the police station in Rome that they believed was the headquarters for DiMarco.

Informing the police officer who manned the front desk of the plight of DiMarco they were met with an incredulous stare by the young officer. "Please wait here," was all he said.

After only about a three-minute wait, out came the young officer with a short rather chubby man dressed in plain clothes. The man introduced himself as Officer Giuseppe DiMarco and asked them to step into his captain's office.

After the confused trio was led into the office with Lisa seated and her companions still standing, the man calling himself DiMarco spoke. "Now, what is this all about? As you can readily see I am not missing, nor have I been taken by any 'Not Knowing' organization. Please explain yourselves."

It was Carlo who explained the whole story to the real Giuseppe DiMarco and his captain. While doing this he and his two friends were in a cold sweat.

As he mentioned about being picked up by a police car by the man they all thought was Officer DiMarco, he was interrupted by the captain who asked what the alleged DiMarco looked like.

Sal chimed in and gave Paolo's appearance that was tall and thin, with dark complexion and deep brown eyes.

Later, the three of them were asked to look at some photos to see if they could pick out the person they knew as DiMarco. It was Lisa that reached for a somewhat faded photo. "That's the man."

"Paolo Garcia," the police officer in charge of the photo files announced.

The real Giuseppe DiMarco was told of the identification and sat down with the trio to explain that Paolo was a low-level criminal who often worked for various shady organizations, usually doing small jobs of dubious nature. He probably was asked to keep an eye on you by one of these groups, but it is a little surprising that he conned you into portraying himself as me and journeying to Athens with you.

"What were you doing in Rome and then Athens anyway?" DiMarco asked. Without hesitation Lisa told him their story saying to both Carlo and Sal "I don't want any more secrecy."

After hearing the story DiMarco commented that whatever they were looking for must be very important to one of the groups Paolo was associated with, but unfortunately this was all too sketchy for his department to get involved in. The only crimes that seemed to have been committed were stealing a police car and impersonating a police officer. For that, they will issue a warrant for Paolo's arrest.

He did promise to inform Lisa that if Paolo somehow returned to Rome he would be arrested. He would get word to her, but doubted that from all that the three of them told him Paolo would ever be seen again.

Sal was concerned with the idea that Paolo was gone forever because although he was outraged at learning that he had been duped by him he still had fond memories of the shared time with this friend he once thought him to be.

While waiting for the train back to Milan, Carlo was pondering the reason why Sita was told only to tell them about Paulo *if they asked her. He thought to himself perhaps they thought we somehow guessed that he was stringing us along, but then again, how could they figure that?*

The train to Milan was uneventful, and our three friends arrived there tired and despondent. They had failed miserably and did not look forward to the task of telling Juliana and the rest of the family of their misfortune.

Although the trio were depressed or angry for one reason or another, the family they came home to was more relieved than disappointed. Juliana was especially relieved that her children were safe and sound. "It is the best thing that happened. Now we can let this go, and I can let my obsession finish," was her response to their harrowing story.

Lisa and Sal went to work almost immediately. Lisa, to her old job and Sal was hired as an administrator for the Milan City Council. Carlo was exploring the possibility of going on another archaeology expedition with the University of Milan to Israel, although funding was still needed by the authors of the expedition.

The three of them were focusing on being back in Milan; although each was traumatized from the experience they just completed.

Carlo was suffering because Lisa had pulled away from getting closer to him. She had told him that she needed time to process what they were doing with each other. No amount of talking, flowers, or tickets to concerts would change the situation for him. She was depressed and lost much of her lighthearted spirit.

Lisa was ruminating over and over in her mind the fact that they left DiMarco, or whoever his name was, to a fate of probable death without even trying to do something for him. Whoever he was he didn't deserve that fate, and she condemned herself for not pushing harder to get him freed. She understood that she, Sal and Carlo had limited options when it came to

DiMarco and the Brotherhood and the powerlessness that came with that knowledge further disturbed her serenity.

Carlo was feeling hopeless when it came to his longing for Lisa. She just would not respond to him in the same way which made his longing grow and his frustration along with it. Although Sal's voice lacked conviction, Sal tried to comfort him by telling him that he was sure Lisa loved him.

Sal asked his sister to share what was going on with her, but was immediately rebuffed. She was not very communicative with him, nor the rest of the family. Carlo and her entire family simply reminded her of the abandonment of the imposter DiMarco.

As for Carlo and Sal they both were angry with the man they had thought was detective DiMarco and felt that he deserved whatever was done to him. Sal believed that he probably was killed, but Carlo wasn't so sure. He imagined that it could have been the Brotherhood that hired him in the first place and that his disappearance was only an exit to the situation he found himself in with his duped trio. After all, it probably was part of the reason they told Sita not to tell them anything unless they asked. It really didn't matter what happened to him.

Sal was also angry that his desire for material success as a possible outcome of their search was lost, and the fact that he was manipulated into liking the imposter detective felt like a violation of his good esteem. Although he didn't tell his sister, Sal also felt guilty for just abandoning his companion. He was torn between his feelings of lost pride and guilt. Regardless, life was settling into an old routine and would have stayed that way except for what happened on one dismal day three months to the day after their return to Milan.

32

Paolo had long ago given the Brotherhood all of the information they sought from him and for several months now he was just languishing in a dungeon cell somewhere unknown to him. He had expected that his life would be forfeited, but he was still alive. He began to believe that they just might abandon him in this prison. Why they decided to do that he had not the foggiest idea unless it was just another kind of torture. He understood that his gamble was now lost. Even if he somehow got out of this dungeon his life would not be worth much considering that the cabal would be hell bent to end it for confessing to his captors.

His everyday life was boringly regular. Breakfast was shoved into the hole at the bottom of the iron every morning. He was let out of his cage about midday to walk around a small outside garden. The garden was surrounded by 15-foot walls, the top of which had spiked nails. His daily walk-time was always supervised by two armed guards. This recreation time varied from what he thought to be an hour, or at the most two.

After his walk he was brought back to the cell now devoid of his morning food tray and was not fed again until the evening. His jailers never spoke to him unless they gave him orders to do something like get up or move or some such.

Only once in the past several months, was he brought to his interrogator and only then to be briefly asked who his handler was. This he did not know. "I never saw him. We only commu-nicated by phone." His interrogator's response was only a simple "I see."

He was beginning to lose any hope of freeing himself and began to fall into a deep despair. Throughout his life he had always been able to find a way through any difficulty and usually came out smelling like a rose in doing so. The thought of taking his life had occurred to him, yet he had not really reached that level of desperation.

While he was pondering his life, Marco and Dawn were still searching for him. They had not been so happy the past two months trying to find their target with the instructions to bring him to London. The organization had directed them to the Algiers Cafe where they began their search, but the trail quickly became cold. No one had any idea who he was and there was no one they could even get heavy handed with to get more information. They were left with surveilling the Algiers from afar to see if anyone seemed connected to the hunt. Boredom set in, but during the time spent in watching and waiting they began to glean just who was important at the café. Those who seemed important appeared to be suspiciously heavy-handed types.

They became sure that a tall skinny guy often accompanied by two goons was someone in charge, and eventually decided to grab him to see just what he might know about Paolo. This man was seldom alone except for once a week on Friday morning when he picked up coffee and a croissant. He didn't stay long and drove himself to an office in the newer part of Athens.

The two only had that short window of opportunity to seize him during his car trip from the Algiers Café to his office - after that the goons were always present.

It wasn't difficult, however, to make the capture. Using two cars to block and sandwich his Renault on a particularly small Athens street in an historic neighborhood, they used a dart gun to subdue him as he got out of the car brandishing his own gun.

Back at their apartment they revived him and began to work him over. His refusal to cooperate lasted a few days, but Marco could be very persistent. Sure enough, he relented. They then checked out the building where Paolo was supposed to be located and discovered that he was there under a heavy guard.

As Paolo was trapped in his depression, the duo was canvassing the building. They were devising a plan to spring their target from his cell. It wouldn't be easy, but Dawn devised the plan they thought would work.

First, they would have to get the skinny man to call up his soldiers to make the swap. Knowing that they were dealing with a well-oiled secret group who may be as dangerous as the organization that hired them was not in their favor, but then again, having one of their head guys was.

They would have to make themselves scarce after this affair, and believed "Basil", the thin guy's name, when he said that the Brotherhood would hunt them down. They were already in a mess and besides, the organization would protect them.

Basil was reluctant to call his people to arrange a swap - himself for Paolo - but what could he do? He would do it and get these assholes later. Right now, it was important that he survive. The swap was on.

It took place several nights later in an abandoned parking lot. The usual 'my captive walks toward you and yours walks toward me' was the plan. As Paolo began walking toward the car waiting for him, his mind was racing. "Fuck, the cabal is going to kill me. I need to run, but I am in the crosshairs of two insane groups."

He swiftly devised a plan thinking that his saviors may not know that he was in deep shit with the cabal. If that was the case, he could make a run for it, and deal with the organization later. He needed to play along with this charade long enough to make a break for it.

Upon reaching the car he found a man and a woman he had never seen before. They hustled him inside and immediately took off. "Stay low," the woman said. "They're going to come after us." Immediately, the man driving gunned the vehicle and they sped down the road. Paulo perceived that they had no backup – his luck. What was not his luck was that the woman held a gun to his head as she sat next to him in the back seat.

The plan Dawn had devised for their escape had them once again driving their car down a narrow street. They knew that they would be chased immediately after making the exchange and hired an unknown stooge to drive slowly between their car and their pursuers on that narrow street giving them time to make a get-away.

When Paolo heard the woman say to her companion "Did the block work?" Paolo immediately envisaged what they had done and moved into action. While she peeked out the back window he quickly reached out and wrestled the gun from the hands of his female savior, and before the man behind the wheel could finish his left-hand turn Paulo opened the back door and dropped out of the moving car rolling along the concrete in a way that would minimize any trauma to his body. He got up and ran for his life with a gun in hand. Paolo's reactions were always super-fast and this whole event happened faster than a hummingbird's wings in flight.

The car behind his previous get-away car stopped short but was blocked from seeing what happened while the two idiots who just helped him escape could not stop to pursue him. He ducked in between two trucks and down a side street and didn't stop running until he was to his estimation more than a mile away.

Now was the hard part. How does he get out of this city and indeed out of Greece? He had nothing, not even a change of clothes – no papers, no money, no friends. Whatever, he knew that he was always good at getting by on nothing. With his skills, he would improvise.

He started by smashing into a clothing store and finding cash and clothing. Then, he bribed himself onto a boat going to Barcelona. Three weeks later, that is just where he ended up; safe in a familiar neighborhood and thinking about what to do next.

As for his so-called liberators, Marco and Dawn, they also got away, but the organization was none too happy about them losing Paolo. They were again tasked with finding him and this time they were told to eliminate him. If they failed a second time it would not go well for their own survival.

Paolo realized that he had to connect with the Italians and along with them, find whatever treasure they were seeking. He needed that money to gain enough power to keep himself safe. After a short respite he had to go in search of them although he knew the organization would have eyes on them and his chances would be slim to none on succeeding. Still, he needed to start the search soon.

Marco and Dawn were already intensifying their search for him with their guns loaded. A chase within a chase had begun.

33

I was sitting on Maria's stoop talking to her. I was telling her that since she decided not to go to Italy I had decided to go back to India. How long I would stay there I wasn't sure, but I was ready to no longer pursue whatever we had going.

Regardless of my knowing that Maria never said or did anything that sealed us as a couple I felt as if I had just lost my lover. It was weird. I told her all this as I fell into her intense stare.

She sat there silently, just staring at me. We were sitting on the top stair - eye to eye. I noticed tears glistening in her blue eyes, but was at a loss as to what to do about them.

She put her hand on my face and held it there. Then she put her face closer to my face and slowly pressed her lips to mine. We kissed like that for just a moment. That short moment turned into a deep passionate full-mouthed kiss filled with longing. It was as if the tension between us needed to release itself and in that release our hearts became one. At least my heart was soaring. I simply could not believe that her heart was not doing a reciprocal dance.

After continuing with our passion for some time she got up and said, "Let's talk later after I'm finished with work or tomorrow. I need to go, but we need to talk more." With that she walked toward downtown. I watched her go down the street, turn the corner and disappear.

'What is going on?' I asked myself, but had no real answer. I would have to wait and realize that once again I was in limbo; without a plan, or even an idea of what to do next. Don't get me wrong, my mind was racing with all kinds of possibilities, but no real clarity.

It was a good thing that I have been in this place many times before. Remembering the first time I really rested in confusion I was brought back to a moment sitting in front of Bhagwan trying to explain to him all the craziness running through my head. "I am confused and crazy was all I could say." His answer was weird at the time.

"You are in a blessed space," he said. "Just watch it and don't try to figure it out."

Looking out at Chelsea Bay I did just that. I watched the mental chatter and went back to my story.

While Paolo was recuperating in Barcelona, Lisa was resigning herself to never being able to find out her grandfather's secret. She was chastising herself for pulling away from Carlo but still couldn't find the motivation to reconnect. She knew that she had feelings for him and that eventually she would reach out to him, but not yet. Hopefully, he was still there when she got around to letting go of her debilitating disappointment.

After having many discussions with Sal, Carlo decided to respect her need to be alone, although he did so with a lot of resentment and a fear of ultimate loss.

He recently contacted one of his school professors who was engaged to start another archaeological dig in Southern India near Madras. The professor wanted him to accompany him, and with no present hope of Lisa opening up to him he had accepted. The night before he was to leave, he went to see Lisa and say good-bye. He told her that he hoped to be back in six months and wished that she would be with him again.

Although she felt pain realizing he was going she couldn't bring herself to ask him to stay. With quiet tears she let him go thinking that it might be best for them both to have the time apart.

Sal and the rest of the family wished him a bon voyage seeing him off onto the ocean liner bound to take him to Bombay and from there to his new project just outside Madras. Lisa was not there. She was at work feeling rather despondent.

It was at the end of her shift while she was walking home that a rare and amazing event happened. As she walked by Café Triste which was situated at the corner of the street where she lived, she heard her name called out. Lisa turned to see who was hailing her and was shocked to recognize the old man she had encountered at the market in Athens.

He had the largest smile on his face and enthusiastically got up from his table to give her a hug. "Please join me." He said this more as a command than a request.

Lisa was taken aback by his forceful voice and at the same time, was a little embarrassed as she realized that she didn't know this gray-haired man's name. She remembered that she had never really asked him for it the first and only time they had met. As she was in the process of sitting down, she wondered just how she could have told him her story without even knowing who he was.

"What are you doing here?" she blurted out.

His smile got even larger after hearing her question. "Why, I have come to see you," was his response.

"But how do you know where I live? I am sure that I didn't tell you," she said with surprise.

"This is true," was all he said while letting her settle in her chair; simultaneously ordering a coffee for her. "I assume you still drink coffee?" he asked.

She nodded yes. Her eyes stayed fixed on his, willing him to tell her more. Instead, he asked her a question.

"*Tell me*", he continued, "*what would you do if you found the talisman you are looking for? I mean what would you do with it?*"

At this point Lisa's intuition was screaming at her to be very mindful of her answer to this question. First, why is he asking me this question and how should I answer him? Second, should I answer him? Immediately she knew the answers to both of these internal queries.

"*Let us say that I may be of help to you, but you must tell me what I want to know first. What will you do with the talisman if you find it?*" he asked firmly.

"*I told you that already,*" Lisa said cautiously. "*I need it to help me find my father's missing box. At least that was what I understand to be the case from the translations of our vases.*"

"*By the way,*" the old man interrupted, "*can I look at those vases, myself?*"

Lisa sheepishly looked down. "*They were stolen from us. Why are you asking me all these things anyway? Who are you?*"

"*I am the man you have been searching for. Now, tell me again what would you do with my precious talisman if I were to give it to you?*"

Lisa stared at TMW with disbelief. "*I really don't know.*"

"*Ah,*" he said, staring back at her. "*Finally, an honest and wise answer.*"

34

*A*nand and Sita were sitting on their veranda in the posh district of Boat Club in Madras. They were lamenting their difficulty of not being able to find any more clues to their research project on vimanas.

Vimanas are referenced in the ancient Vedas and refer to flying machines often in battle. Of course, mainstream scholars view these references as merely myth, but Anand believed otherwise and had for many years now convinced Sita of his theory.

His theory speculated that vimanas were indeed real flying machines which suggested that either ancient India was far more technically advanced than modern historians ever imagined, or that some outside power had influenced Earth and her inhabitants.

Studying the Vedas could be quite an eye-opening experience if they were taken literally. Unfortunately, the Indian couple needed some other corroboration to assure themselves as well as those that they might try to convince of their postulation. They had thought that they might find further evidence at the Vatican or in Greece's libraries.

It was not to be; they had not found anything more in either place. Getting caught up in the Italians' quest didn't help their cause either. They both were beyond grateful to have survived the ordeal with their lives. Yet, being back home they were disappointed with not uncovering anything more concerning their own quest.

Presently, they were back to searching for more evidence in India and Tibet. While sitting on their veranda they began to discuss an upcoming trip to Northern India.

"The last time we were in the monastery near Kashmir, we left too quickly," Anand told Sita. "We had read that important information on the source of the flying machines was held secretly in Europe, and we took off immediately for Rome. I think we need to look further into those Tibetan texts and perhaps visit other monasteries in the region before going elsewhere."

Sita had agreed with her husband and so they planned a new trip north. It would take them several weeks to get back to the monastery and then who knew how much time it would take to further extend their research. This time they made a commitment that they would not leave without thoroughly searching through the ancient scrolls.

It was later, on that same veranda perhaps a week or two from taking that trip to the mountains when they were shocked to see Carlo staring at them as he walked by with another older man by his side.

Carlo was just as shocked to see the Indian couple, but did not stop. Rather, he quickly looked away although he noted the address of the house. His new archaeological dig was about to become even more exciting. He was sure of that.

35

aolo was in heavy disguise. He had grown a beard and dyed his hair, even his eyebrows. Wearing shabby clothing and carrying a street broom he was indistinguishable from any street sweeper of Milan. He was turning the corner onto the street where he knew Lisa and Sal lived. As he slowly swept the curb, he kept his eyes down or so it seemed. He was keenly looking for anything out of the ordinary on the street as he was sure the cabal was watching his two Italian friends.

It was clear to Paolo that neither Lisa nor Sal would be very excited to see him, and he knew it would be near impossible for him to convince them that he wanted to help them continue with their quest, but it was his only option.

Right now, he had to get by the organization before trying to complete the other impossible task. Nothing seemed out of the ordinary, but that was only appearances. Perhaps, he thought, they were watching from one of the buildings across the street from their house. He saw nothing. The degree of difficulty to pull off his intention was going to be very high indeed.

After some time sweeping, he came to the other end of the street and turned the corner, no more aware of what he knew to be there than before.

While Paolo was doing his sweeping, Marco and Dawn had just entered Paolo's neighborhood in Barcelona. They would begin their search for their quarry from here. They were sure this was where Paolo must be hiding or at the very least had gone to ground for a time after escaping from Greece. They were confident that it would not take them long to find out if they were right or wrong about their intuition.

Sitting in meditation day after day as I watched my breath, aware of my navel, the thoughts and feelings passed by as if clouds in the sky.

All this sitting had decreased the level of drama I used to experience. No longer was I pushed and pulled to react to my thoughts and emotions. A subtle relaxation had crept into my inner world.

With this relaxation everything I once took with excess passion and fiery feelings was seen through the lens of cool witnessing. This witnessing allowed me to notice the little things of life more fully: the brush of a flower, the fragrance of my tea, the experiencing of another's emotional response without reaction, were all the outgrowths of it.

I was reviewing all these insights as I laid face down on the top floor of Jesus Grove. Jesus Grove was one of the ashram's many buildings and I was doing a Soma group on a section of that roof. Around me were many others all lying on their stomachs concentrating on the intake and outflow of their breathing.

All this I see in a memory as I am finishing the last sentence about Marco and Dawn. Why I am brought to this remembrance is a mystery to me, especially since I am writing about people so caught up in the drama of the chase. Perhaps, I am resisting getting caught up myself.

Yet, murder and mayhem are surely about to be enacted.

36

It did not take Paolo long to discover who and how the brother and sister he needed to reconnect with were being watched. The same night of his street sweeping reconnaissance he stealthily climbed up to the rooftop of an adjacent building to Lisa's apartment. There he scanned the building across the street and with his binoculars he spotted a telescope with a bird's eye view of the building and surroundings. The telescope was recessed from the window, not allowing him to glimpse it earlier.

He noticed two strong arm men were taking turns watching the Milanese making any attempt of him going through the front door basically suicidal.

Perhaps the rear entrance would be the better choice, but he soon discovered that way was also being watched from the rooftops on the other street behind the apartment building. It was a wonder that he was able to get to this rooftop without detection, let alone get into Lisa and Sal's residence.

"There must be a way to overcome all this surveillance," he thought. "There is always a way, isn't there?" he quietly spoke to himself.

All this spying had taken place well after that afternoon when Lisa had been confronted by Thaddaeus, 'The Man Who Does Not Know'.

Her honesty had done the trick as he decided to trust her with a few of his secrets.

"I have always been aware that there was someone in Europe who held the key and understood that my precious talisman was created to unlock it. You see the talisman is helpful in opening up a backup to the knowledge the keeper of the secret was supposed to safeguard," Thaddaeus emphasized.

"Now you are the keeper of the secret Lisa, but you seem to have lost the secret altogether. It is going to be very difficult to recover that secret now that you also have lost the vases. You see, without the exact wording on those vases you will never be able to decode the message hidden within them. Without this message you will never know where to look to find that place that holds the lost understanding."

"Fortunately, I have a pretty good idea who took your vases, but unfortunately if I am right, it will be impossible to get them back."

Inside, Lisa was feeling a rush of excitement that bordered on bliss and awe. "I have an exact copy of the translation at home," she exclaimed. "We wrote it all down so there is no need for the vases."

Thaddaeus looked at her for a long moment. "The translation is not good for this purpose. You need the untranslated words for the message to be revealed."

Lisa's brief ecstasy was deflated. She did not have that, however she quickly realized just who did have it and wasn't sure if they would give it to her after all that had transpired. She was going to have to contact Anand and Sita - this was not going to be easy.

37

It was less than a month away before our trip to Italy would happen. After our deep interlude on her stairs, she decided to go with me to the old country.

Maria and I spent many hours planning the excursion. We had also become lovers during this time, although we didn't spend many nights together due to her work and family obligations. Also, her personal code of conduct would not allow for us to make love in her house – according to her we would need to be married to do so. This had something to do with her mother and son being there.

The rules were okay with me, because now and then she spent some time in my bed and the connection we had there was rather blissful. Sexually, we were awesome together.

Planning a trip to Italy was entirely another matter. She wanted to wander all over the country staying a few days here and a few days there, while I wanted nothing to do with a hectic schedule. I preferred to only go to a few places in Tuscany and northern Italy, spending considerably more time in each place.

I especially wanted to spend a good bit of time in Milan with the idea of researching it for my novel's descriptive narrative. However, she wanted to only spend a few days with her family there and then get away from them. I was more interested in going deep into her family's history. My curiosity was such that I wanted to explore the apparent synchronicities I had become aware of between her family and the family I was writing about in my novel.

There were quite a few nights of heated arguments on whose plan would take precedence. Two Italians can really go at it.

Anyway, we had compromised significantly, and our plans were set for us to leave on an Alitalia flight some twenty-five days hence. We were going to more places than I preferred, but less than she wanted. The one thing was that we had agreed to spend a week in Milan. We would visit her family often while there, but not stay with them.

It was not as easy as Marco and Dawn thought to get any information about Paolo from anyone in his old neighborhood. It was a rough place, and they were immediately viewed with suspicion upon asking about someone who had grown up there. Word went out and they found themselves being continuously watched by a variety of street gangs that roamed his childhood territory.

The duo was not unacquainted with the workings of tough hoods. However, it took some time (longer than they had planned) to get to know just what groups had been allies of Paulo and what groups were not so enamored toward him. In the end it took a bit of money thrown into the palm of a prior enemy to discover that Paolo had indeed been in Barcelona after Greece and that he was no longer there.

No one seemed to know where he had gone, though. No amount of money, nor force was enough to get anyone to tell them where he was. Finally, they began to believe that he did not confide that knowledge to anyone; no matter how close they were with him.

Several weeks went by before they started checking the train and bus station for any clues that indicated where he might have gone. Nothing was found. They were not really surprised at their lack of discovery as he was professional enough not to leave any clear-cut tracks to follow.

"Where would he hide out?" Marco was sitting up in bed with his hands entwined together behind his head. "I would be going to the ground if I were him, but where would he go to do that if not in his old hood?"

Dawn was painting her toenails listening to her companion. After he stopped talking, she let her mind wander as she finished her last toenail. She looked up at Marco and said, "Perhaps he is not trying to hide. Perhaps he went back to his friends in Italy?"

"What? Why would he do that?"

"I don't know for sure. It is just a feeling I have. Call it a woman's intuition."

"But he was shadowing them for the cartel. They weren't his friends and what the hell would he want to contact them for anyway?" Marco responded. "He fucked up his work with them. What possible reason would he have for looking up those losers. It doesn't make sense."

"What if the Italians were on to something big and Paulo found out about it. Maybe he was planning to screw the cartel. After all he escaped from us bringing him back to the organization, and they now want him dead. Something is off and I just am getting this feeling we need to go find those damn Italians. We'll find Paolo there. I just know it." Dawn was intensely looking at her partner.

"Alright, let's go then!" Marco agreed.

Right at this point Paolo was formulating a plan to contact Lisa and Sal. He had been watching the brother and sister for several days now and saw that they were under constant surveillance. Whenever they left their house, they were blissfully unaware that they were being followed by a group of operatives. "They need me," he thought.

To get in contact with them, he needed to pick just the right place to somehow intercept them on one of their journeys away from their house. He decided that it had to be when one of them was in the market and it had to be during the busiest time. He considered contacting Sal first, but realized that even though Sal might be easier to deal with, it was his sister who he needed to be convinced of his sincerity.

Even if he persuaded Sal to believe his desire to help them achieve their goal, Sal would not be able to get his sister to believe it. On the contrary, she would just reignite in her brother any doubt or fear they had toward him. In truth, he wasn't sure just how they would receive him although he was guessing that it wouldn't be with open arms.

Besides, Paolo thought, Lisa was more often in the market and more easily approached using his plan. His target assured, he only had to wait until she hit the flower stall at the height of the market's most trafficked time.

He did not have to wait long for his chance because the next day as he followed Lisa behind those tailing her, he could see that she was indeed going to the very market he predicted.

He rushed ahead. There was a place where the flowers were tall stalked, preventing anyone from spying on her for just a moment. Those flowers were also conveniently in front of an alley which ran away from the market.

As he hid behind the flowers he waited for Lisa to pass by. At that point he knew those following would lose sight of her for a moment. He reached out and grabbed her arm, and pulled her toward the alley. At the same time he threw a hood over her head and warned her not to make a sound or face being killed.

Paolo was always quick with his actions, but his abduction of Lisa was truly remarkable even for him. Before a half a minute passed, he had turned the corner of the first alley off the original and removed her hood. As he pulled her along, they vanished away from the market area. Heading down another busy street, he directed her to look straight ahead until he pushed her into a church.

As he surmised, no one was there. Facing her he saw fear in her face, and then rage. Lisa said nothing. She only looked with such intensity it made Paolo tremble within.

"Sorry," he began, "It was the only way I could get to you without being seen by the cabal. Do you have any idea that you are constantly being watched?"

Paolo spoke fast as if he needed to drown out her thoughts of hitting him. He knew that he had just a moment to get her to hear him out, although he was also of the mind that she might just be pleasantly surprised he survived Athens.

Before he could utter a word, Lisa spoke. "I know who you are Paolo and I need you to leave me alone."

"What?" Paolo frowned "How do you know that name?"

"I am not telling you, but I also know that you work for a secret organization and have been spying on us for them. I can't believe that you had us all fooled, except for Carlo. He was right about you all the time and now you're back. Whatever it is you are planning to do, it won't work because we are through with our little venture."

Lisa turned to go, but he stopped her.

"Wait! Please, let me explain. I am very sorry for leading you guys on, but I had to, or they would have killed me. Lisa, I stopped working for them after going with you to Athens, and they are now chasing after me."

"Well, that's too bad now, isn't it?" Lisa said with steel in her eyes

Paolo knew it would not be easy to get Lisa to trust him and to continue with her quest, but her discovery about him was completely unforeseen and presented a possible insurmountable hurtle. He implored himself to think fast.

"Look, Lisa, you all left me in a dungeon to die at the hands of that 'Not Knowing Society' – the least you can do is give me a chance to explain why I came to you. I can't do it here, though. The cabal's men will be looking all over for you by now and

I'm a goner if they catch me. Please give me a chance to tell you more of my story, please."

In truth, Lisa was glad to see that her friendly enemy was still alive. The old man said that he got away, but that he wasn't sure what happened to him after his escape.

"I know that you visit your friend on Via Lecco. Please visit her in the evening the day after tomorrow. I will meet you in the hallway there and I will explain further. Bring Sal and Carlo if you must although that would be far more dangerous. Come Lisa, I beg you. If you don't, I really am a dead man." Paulo opened the church door and let her walk away.

The Spaniard sat in a pew going over what just happened. He knew that he just took an enormous risk by letting her go, but what else could he have done? Although he still had designs on making a profit out of this venture he realized that he needed to get hold of whatever secret Lisa's family had in order to stand a chance of getting out of this mess with his life. That secret was now his only possible bargaining chip for his safety.

As Lisa walked away from the church, she was sure that she would not be meeting Paolo again. She was a little startled, however, she felt glad that he was alive and made it safely away from his captors. Part of her believed that she was well within her rights to think he deserved to be still imprisoned by the 'Not Knowing Society', but she realized that she had bonded with Paolo as a friend even though he was anything but.

Be that as it may, she had no intention of having anything to do with him again, especially after all she had learned about him from the old man.

38

Bhagwan sat in his lounge chair in Buddha Hall as regal as any king. Every day he would enter the lecture hall to give a talk on a variety of spiritual traditions and teachers. Every time he would sit in a living room chair the exact same way lifting his right leg over his left sitting cross legged. He would maintain this position for as many hours as he would speak. His lectures would last two, three, and sometimes four or more hours. He would never move his legs once he positioned them until he was finished and rose to leave the hall.

His only movements were made with his arms, hands, and head. He always moved in a very slow, deliberate and graceful way. The way he presented himself was truly other worldly and I often thought that he was something beyond human.

His manner of speaking was also most hypnotic. In and of itself it was a powerful technique to foster silence and stillness in the listener. Speaking slowly with long pauses between words, his discourse would often help me fall into a mind-stopping gap. Silence so pregnant with peace and bliss would more and more be the result of these ventures with this other worldly being.

On top of all of this, Bhagwan was more than occasionally seen with a glowing aura all around him. The word 'enlightened' comes to mind, but by this I quite literally mean that he was lit up.

Some of the most blissful moments I can remember in my life came while listening to this Indian guru talk without any ums or ahs between his words, and without any teleprompting or props. His lectures were more like singing than speaking. Where exactly did he come from? Of this, I am not sure, but I was sure that I never saw or heard anything quite like Bhagwan even to this day.

The only thing I can think of to describe all this is magic. Magic was all around this being and this again was indeed other worldly.

Before leaving Lisa that day at the café, Thaddaeus had shown her the talisman she and her friends had been seeking. It was a simple key that he said could open whatever box, locker or door that held the secret knowledge that her family had lost. He told her that he would not give it to her unless she somehow was about to discover and decipher the original message in the original language that was found on her lost vases.

Thaddaeus also told her about Paolo. He explained that Paolo worked for a very powerful agency that sought nothing short of world domination. They had their hands in every major event that took place on the planet and had infiltrated all the major governments, corporations and military agencies all over the world. He told her that the organization was far older than even his society which could be traced back some 2500 years.

The fact that this cabal was involved with this whole adventure of hers meant that the quest was more than just dangerous, but probably impossible to be carried out. "Maybe you should just forget the whole thing," he suggested. His tone appeared to be so gentle when he proposed this to her. She thought maybe he was right and for a moment or two felt relieved that she could just do nothing. Then she thought of her father, her brother and especially her mother knowing that she just couldn't give up so easily. Now that she saw the talisman and had achieved in part the second phase of her journey it was not the time to throw it all away.

Instead of going home from her confrontation with Paolo, Lisa went to her brother's workplace to find him.

"Sal, I just was kidnapped by Paolo," she informed him.

"That bastard!" he replied. "Are you alright?"

"Yes," she replied. "He wants to talk to us, although I didn't give him much of a chance to do so. He does know, however, that we understand just who he is and who he works for. He seemed a little surprised at that, but still asked to meet with us clandestinely. I told him, 'no.'"

"What does he want to talk about?" Sal asked.

"He didn't say because he told me that you and I are being followed and that if he took the time to talk with me then he and I would both be in danger. Have you seen anyone following us?"

"No! To tell you the truth, I haven't been really looking"

"Well, he said we have been so let's be on the lookout. I don't like all this. Could it be that even after we have stopped searching that damn mafia is still watching us. I don't like this one bit. Let's be very careful Sal. Let's be very careful indeed."

"Maybe the best thing to do is meet with Paolo and find out what's going on, Lisa. I know that we don't trust him, and I know that he's an asshole, but if what he says is true, we need to get more information. Especially now that we plan to go to India and find the lock to whatever TMW's talisman is supposed to fit."

"How can we believe anything he says to us?" She was worried.

"We can't," her brother retorted. "But, even if he lies to us, we can get an idea as to what we will need to do next. After you leave, I am going to see if we are really being followed. By the way, how did he propose to meet with us without anyone seeing?

Lisa told him, after which they devised a plan for Sal to go to the roof of his work building and watch carefully to see if Lisa was being tailed. She was to walk away very slowly down an alley next to the building then take a right down another alley and quickly down another walkway. Sal would have a bird's eye view of his sister while anyone trying to follow her would be forced to stand out while doing so.

They were to meet up at home and further decide whether to meet with Paolo.

Just as Sal was trying to spy on anyone following his sister, Marco and Dawn were getting on a train bound for Monte Carlo where they would stay overnight before going onto Milan. Within two days they would be in position to complete their assignment if Paolo was where they believed him to be.

While I was reminiscing about what it was like to sit in Buddha Hall with Bhagwan, my stream of consciousness wandered to thinking about other spiritual teachers. During that same time period there were quite a few other gurus from Asia all spreading a similar message to the western world.

To their disciples I imagined that these masters all look like they came from some other worldly realm. Perhaps I thought, they did.

39

Maria and I are off to Milan. I am very excited to be with her and about exploring the city I have only experienced through my imagination.

Touching down at the airport I realize that we are in the center of a thoroughly modern metropolis. We take a cab heading for the Porta Venezia area of Milan near where her family is located.

Maria had told me that the last time she was in the city was when she was in her early teens and that she is also very anxious about reconnecting with her relatives.

We end up in the Starhotels Ritz that turns out to be within a building of modernity nestled within a medieval neighborhood. The contrast is quite impressive to say the least, although as Italy goes, Milan appears to be a bit humdrum.

I have only ever visited southern Italy. Rome, Florence, Sorrento, the Chianti region all of which have a flair for the artistic and ancient. Milan is rightfully thought of as the business capital of Italy and it reflects that architecture and look of any modern city in the world.

Don't get me wrong, the cathedral in Milan called the Duomo di Milan is quite a spectacle with its hundreds of sculptured figures on just as many spires and sporting a square that rivals the Vatican's.

Next door to the Duomo is a mall called the Galleria Vittorio Emanuele II. It is one of the most impressive outdoor covered malls in the world. Its 19th century facades are as tastefully artistic as those in Florence or Rome. The activity there is every bit as busy as the most toured parts of Italy.

We are to spend a week here and I can't wait to visit Maria's family and ask about the family legacy she tells me they maintain. I am hoping that they can share it with me, although Maria has said that they have protected this secret since as long as any of them remember. Perhaps, I am being too optimistic to believe they will let me in on any part of it simply because I date their niece/cousin.

Anyway, even if I cannot get direct knowledge of whatever the family has been entrusted to carry forward, I can still obtain some information on the way they have preserved their secret over the centuries, if indeed it is that old.

Our first evening in Milan we simply went out for dinner and returned to our rooms to frolic and sleep.

The next day we went sightseeing and shopping. It was not until that night that she and I went to her uncle's home where I was introduced to some twenty people all of whom were related to Maria.

The family consisted of two uncles, two aunts, a grand aunt, and some fifteen cousins with children. It was a lively group to say the least and I felt right at home considering my Italian background. Her family seemed to take to me, until I found myself later that evening in the library of her Uncle Gino.

"So, Maria tells me that you are interested in our family secret," Uncle Gino started the conversation.

"Actually," I responded, "I am not so interested in your secret, but in the fact that I have been writing a book about a family who lived in Milan during World War I who also had a secret they were entrusted with for many centuries. What is disconcerting is that I began writing my book long before Maria had told me about your family history. The idea that your family holds a secret, dovetails remarkably well with my writing. The coincidence is remarkable. So much so that it makes me curious as to how I could have come up with the story in the first place. I have begun wondering if I had somehow read Maria's mind and put it in my novel. Do you think that is possible?"

"It depends," was all that Uncle Gino replied before we were interrupted by Maria and her cousin Alba.

"Uncle Gino, is Prem pestering you about the family heritage? He thinks that somehow, I am giving him mind signals that are turning up in his book. Can you enlighten him on this silliness?" Maria was being very playful with her uncle while I was shocked at her dismissiveness of me. She had never made light of my theory before, always supportively listening to me and taking me seriously. It hurt.

Her uncle remained silent for a long pause. "Don't be so condescending about your boyfriend's idea. Many stranger things have proven to be true. I for one have a desire to read what you have been writing about. Will you allow me to do so, Prem?"

Up to this point in my narrative I had refused to let anyone read even a page. I felt that I was not far enough along in the story to do that, and I wasn't sure how good my storytelling was. I could see everyone looking at me as I hesitated to respond.

"I will do so under one condition!" I answered. "If you feel it has any connection or even similarity to what has gone on in your own family's tradition you must be honest with me and tell me."

"Of course," was his immediate reply.

The next day I handed over to Uncle Gino all that I had written.

"Sal, you seriously think that we should meet with Paolo in Genevieve's hallway. It sounds not only crazy to me, but dangerous as well," Lisa was probing her brother.

In fact, after her initial reaction of not having anything to do with Paolo her curiosity kicked in and she was leaning toward that very decision.

"Yes," Sal said assuredly. "We must do it and find out what he is after, because although we know he worked for that organization that is a threat to us we have no idea what brought him here at this time and we need to know. Especially, before implementing our plan to go to India."

"Paolo said that he would meet us there tonight. We can expect to be spied on after what you discovered from the rooftop. At least, he wasn't lying about that."

At six in the evening, they strolled over to Lisa's friend's apartment together. This was somewhat unusual, but not entirely so since Sal had accompanied Lisa several times before to visit Genevieve.

They assumed that they were being followed, but could not figure out by who. They did not grasp the idea of multiple people switching off to do so. If they even thought about the lengths the cabal would go to keep a watch on them, they just might have aborted all their plans.

Reaching Genevieve's building they entered the front door and stepped into the hallway. Their friend lived on the third floor. No one was in the front foyer, so they began climbing the stairs.

Paolo had scouted out the layout of the building the day before and planned to bring the siblings up onto the roof through a skylight entrance located in the hallway located on the top floor of the building.

He was more than pleasantly surprised to see his two, what should he call them… friends or enemies? He was recessed in the shadows of the third-floor landing in front of Genevieve's door.

When they all met, he immediately put his index finger over his mouth signaling quiet and indicated that they move up the stairs and finally up through the skylight entrance to the roof.

On the roof he corralled them to stay in the center, away from the edges. There he spoke, "Please keep your voices down while we are up here."

Sal began, "You son-of-a-bitch, what do you want with us, Paulo? I can't believe you led us on for so long and that I was always defending you to Carlo. You played me, you played all of us, but fuck you. I only wanted to come here to tell you that and now that I have, I don't really care to stay."

"I don't really care why either of you came," Paulo recanted. "I am just glad you did and now that you're here, please give me a chance to explain myself."

"Who, or what do you work for first?" Lisa interjected.

"Okay, okay, I worked for a worldwide organization that is known by many names: the cabal, the organization, or the reptiles. None of those names are really their name and as a matter of fact I don't know their real name as they never told me. The truth is that I just did contract work for them as I have had many employers over the years. I'm a freelancer."

"They asked me to follow you and to inform them of all your doings from the minute that you arrived in Rome. That's what I did until you decided to go to Greece."

"Yah, we did decide to do just that, but we would have never been able to go without your money. Why would they want you to take us to Athens if you were just following us? This makes no sense." Sal was getting agitated.

"They let me take you to Athens because they didn't know that I paid for you to go there. I never told them that you didn't have the money and I convinced them that I had you believing I was the Italian cop and through that guise I could more easily keep track of you."

"Why would you do that?" Lisa started to raise her voice.

"Please speak softly. I am in great danger, even more than you are," he said looking side to side.

"After getting to know you a little bit through the Officer DiMarco disguise, I decided that I wanted to know more about this secret your family has been keeping for centuries. I thought I could use it for my benefit."

In the process of Paolo's incarceration, subsequent flight, and hiding he realized that the only way he could protect himself was to go on with this quest. The only way he could do that was with the siblings and the only way he could convince them to let him help was to tell them the truth, or at least most of it.

"What benefit?"

Paulo wasn't sure which of the siblings asked the question, but he knew that how he answered was crucial as to whether they would believe him or not.

"I thought I could steal it from you and use it as leverage to gain more power with the cabal."

"You fucker!" Sal made a move to leave.

Lisa held him back "No wait! Are you here just to antagonize us?"

"No! I'm not here for any such reasoning. I am here because I need your help and, I believe, that you need mine," Paolo insisted.

"No way we need you Paolo," Sal retorted. "You fooled us once and that's all the chance you get. You'd be the fool now if you think that we could trust you again."

Lisa felt the same as her brother, but there was another part of her that needed to follow through with Paulo's statement. *"Why do you need us and why do we need you?" Lisa asked.*

"Look," Paolo began, "the cabal is after me and they are not looking to give me any medals. They want to eliminate me. I got caught and I spilled the beans on them to the Greek Society and they won't tolerate that. The only thing that might save me is if the information you are trying to retrieve is potent enough to give me leverage against them. Even at that I am taking a major

gamble that your secret is enough to do that, but it is the only chance I have. As for why you need me, I think that is obvious. You are over your heads dealing with this organization. You weren't even aware that they had you under surveillance. How do you think you can follow through with your quest when they are dead set against it? I know them and the world they play in. With me you have at least a possibility to achieve your goal. Without me you might as well give it up and believe me I do not want you to give it up."

"You presume too much," Lisa answered. "Our family secret is just that; a secret not to be shared, especially with the likes of you."

"Hear me out, please. The cabal is so hell bent on stopping you from retrieving your father's box that it must be very damn important to them. I believe that what it may contain could be so important that it would seem reasonable to them that you shared its content with me since I helped you get it. If they are led to believe l know of what the secret is I could threaten them with releasing it to the world. To do all this, however, they must know that we succeeded in getting it back. Furthermore, you are also in danger if you continue looking for the box which I am sure you are. Once you continue to look, the contents of what's in the box may be the only thing that will save you as well. If they even suspect that you are continuing with this search, they won't just continue watching you. No! They will cut you down like they did to your father."

"What do you mean? Our father died in an accident," Sal was still fuming.

"Yah, if you believe that then you might as well believe in Santa Claus. Right, Lisa?" Paolo grinned.

40

It was not until two weeks later that Carlo could get away from his work preparing for the archaeological dig when he attempted to visit Anand and Sita. He was sure that they would not receive him with open arms, but he felt compelled to try to smooth over the fracture they had in their friendship.

Finding their house was rather easy. Their bungalow was large, and in it he could see movement, although it took some time before anyone came to the front door to answer his knock.

The person who finally came was neither of his former friends, but a young girl who seemed to be domestic help. She spoke in broken English and indicated that the owners were not home and that they went away for an indefinite time period. Carlo asked where they had gone and was told only that it was some place in northern India or Nepal. They couldn't be contacted because wherever they went it was remote enough to afford no easy access and no modern method of communication.

Carlo left a note with the young woman. In it he explained that he really wanted to connect with them and that he was so very sorry that they had to leave each other in such a tense and uncomfortable way. He apologized for all that happened in Athens and hoped that they would meet with him while he was in India. He told them that he was traveling about 150 miles outside of Madras toward the north and that he planned to be in India for six months, if not longer. The small village that he would be near had a telephone in the tavern. He left the number with her hoping that they would be so gracious as to give him a call whenever they returned from their journey.

Thinking that he had done everything that he could to try to reunite with the Indian couple, he left their house more than half feeling that they would choose to not contact him at all.

Carlo had written about all this to Lisa and Sal. It was precisely because Carlo had seen the Indians and knew exactly where they lived that the siblings felt emboldened to travel to India to seek them out and hopefully persuade them to replicate the writing on the vases in their original language.

"Let's go, Lisa," Sal prompted. "We don't need his help. We can't trust him anyway."

Their whole meeting with Paolo had taken about forty-five minutes which was truly a short period of time for her to visit with her friend. She had time to think.

"Paolo, I want to know about this cabal you are talking about. I was told that they are a very old and very powerful organization, but just who are they? If we are to possibly trust you again you can start by being more informative. Just who are they?" Lisa asked.

"They have lived in the shadows so long that it is impossible to tell you who they really are," he began. "Just know that they are the puppet masters behind the working of the entire world. Their people are a part of every major government, political and spiritual group on the planet. They control the media, entertainment industries, and own most of the resources of this planet. Their reach is beyond measure and their power appears to be limitless. I am beyond crazy to have tried to challenge them in any way, although now I have no recourse but to do so. The truth is if I were you, I would leave well enough alone and go back to my simple life. Our chances of succeeding are slim to none."

Lisa frowned. "If they are all that you say they are, what could my family be guarding that is so important to them? It *must be something outrageous. Also, how did my father's secret survive all these centuries intact if this cabal is that powerful?*

"I have no idea, in answer to both your questions." Paolo replied. "I can only guess that somehow they did not know that your family was the guardian of whatever it is they are now guarding."

"Let's go," Sal insisted.

Lisa looked at her brother and then turned to Paolo. "We are not ready to trust you Paolo and are not going to work with you. I am sorry." At that statement she got up from the roof's flooring and stood next to Sal getting ready to leave.

"Look" Paolo pleaded "I know I deceived you and have no right to ask anything of you, but I really need you to help me and besides I'm sure you still want to uncover your family's secret. Please think about it some more. I will be at the Café Triste the next two evenings if you change your mind or want to talk further. Go there and I will connect with you. No need to see me there. I will see you and arrange a secret meeting."

Lisa and Sal left Paolo on the roof and went down the stairs and out of the front door. As they left the building they turned to go back home when they heard what sounded like gunshots coming from Genevieve's roof. Frightened, they looked around and upwards, but saw nothing. It seemed nobody was watching them, but again shots rang out from above.

Lisa turned around to go back into the apartment building, but her brother grabbed her by the arm and pulled her away.

"We gotta go, Lisa. Now."

They began running home more than half expecting to be shot at themselves. They arrived home without incident, however they were both freaked out.

"We should have gone back to Paolo." Lisa felt nearly hysterical.

"Are you crazy, what could we have done? I'll tell you, nothing." Sal rambled.

"Do you think they killed him? As much as he was horrible to us, I don't want him to be killed. Please let him be okay." She was getting more frantic.

"Paolo can take care of himself. He probably got away like he did before. I don't want him to be killed either, but right now I am more concerned with our lives. This shit is getting serious."

"What are we going to do now?" Sal continued.

41

igh up in the Himalayas, Anand and Sita were guests of the Tibetan lamas who lived close to Dharmsala, India. Borders in these majestic peaks were never clear, nor taken seriously by the inhabitants. Tibetan Buddhism was centered in Tibet, but roamed all over Nepal, India and Bhutan.

Our couple was sitting in a monastery seldom visited by outsiders and were led there by the text of books they had found in the original monastic library they had encountered in Nepal. The Rosho Monastery was supposed to hold the secret of the flying machines that the ancient Hindu books spoke about.

Anand was unsure what he would find, but he believed the library would give them the next clue in their search to prove that the ancients were far more technologically advanced than the world ever possibly imagined.

The scrolls they had encountered in Rosho Monastery were more than exciting. Vimanas were described in several of these rolled texts not as allegories, but as actual physical planes or at least something like planes. The writings were produced by people who explained in detail what flying in them was like. They described the ground moving swiftly below them and of seeing the terrain of the land in a way only possible if that person was seeing it from above.

The writers further detailed what it was like to pass other vimanas in mid-flight. It was incredible to read all this and both Indians were more certain than ever that their theory was correct.

They were unable to discover what would be an acceptable form of proof for their hypothesis. What they needed was to find actual drawings and drafts of these machines with their locomotion and power source to prove to the scientific community that the designs really worked.

They had hoped to find these drawings here, but once again were only led to believe that the schematics they desired were held somewhere in Europe. The library in the previous monastery had mentioned that what they sought was in the western lands which suggested Europe. That is why they had gone to Rome in the first place.

Here again the scrolls mentioned going to the West, but they said it more clearly and indicated where to look. It read, "Instructions on how to build vimanas can only be found by seeking the Holder of the Truth, and the Truth Holder is obliged to hand it down to his eldest son in succession throughout the countless centuries. The Truth Holder and his family hold the secret."

"What do you make of this?" Anand asked. "Could it be, Sita, that this is connected to Lisa's lost secret?

"It is hard to believe, and all this is way beyond coincidence, yet something inside me knows that the two are indeed connected." Sita replied.

"I hope we are wrong, my love, because if we're not then we must go back into the cauldron of chaos that surrounds our Italian friends. I was hoping that we were through with that danger.

Speaking of danger, Marco and Dawn were arriving at the Milan Central Train Station right around the time the two Indians realized that their fate was still intertwined with Lisa and her family. A woman met them at the train who told them that Paulo was spotted the night before on a rooftop. They had tried to eliminate him right there and then, but he had gotten away.

She further told them that he had contact with the two Italian siblings he previously was mixed up with that same night. "Your instructions" she said, "are to get Paolo and both siblings and end their interference." Dawn smiled in approval at the woman before leaving the station.

The deadly couple figured that the brother and sister would be easy. They had their address, and they were so out of their league to do anything to stop them. All they needed to do was scout out their living quarters and make their break-in and entry look like a robbery that killed everyone inside.

First, they had to erase that pest Paolo. Later, they could do the mass killing and flee Milan.

A trap needed to be set and its bait was the Italians with whom Paolo would assuredly try to contact again.

"We will need to keep an even closer eye on these two Milanese, then finish this job and go on vacation.

In my travels I began to become an excellent tarot card reader. The actual event that opened me up to my intuition and the tarot happened, of course, through the vehicle of a lover.

Mary was a woman I had met while in grad school right after I became acquainted with Bhagwan. She was a very pretty, round-faced blonde who stood no more than 5 feet tall and was a projection of my mother. Of this I was sure since my mother was a blonde who stood slightly less than five-feet tall. The physical similarities were just too striking to be ignored.

Although I was originally attracted to her friend, I became enamored with Mary. She was not my first girlfriend, but most definitely my first love. Upon my returning from my first trip to India the two of us moved into an apartment together. After two intense years of ups and downs in our relationship she told me that she had fallen in love with a coworker.

I was devastated. Her declaration to me was completely unexpected, but I could see the love in her eyes for the other man when she spoke her truth.

For two and half years I had been meditating and listening to Bhagwan. At that time and even now what I had gleaned from the master was that freedom is a higher value than love. My freedom, her freedom, and freedom itself, is a higher value than love because it was the milieu in which love could be born. Without freedom love could not exist, but without love freedom is.

With this understanding I knew I could not stand in her way from pursuing another love no matter how much I loved her myself. After that very first conversation when she told me about her other lover I decided to move out of our flat, and I told her so.

"Just give me the three weeks left in this month and I will find another living arrangement and go." I told her.

As it turned out her lover was not often available during that last month we had together, so we found ourselves spending a great deal of time with each other. Seeing this fact, I asked Mary if she would spend those last three weeks doing all the things we had planned to do before this sad discovery. "We can complete our relationship if we do so," I pleaded. She agreed.

And so, we did. We went to see the play we both loved. We ate a candlelight dinner on top of the tallest building in Boston. We spent a night by the sea on Cape Cod. All this was ridiculously romantic and all of it broke my heart into smaller and smaller pieces.

Because of the whirl of the intense emotions brought up within the short period of time of our parting I lost contact with my logical mind for a while. The world became only a heart. Feelings were all that existed. As I tried to tell some of my closest friends at the time, "Feel the world, don't think it."

Of course, everyone looked at me as if I had just gone over the edge. Going over that edge was the very thing that opened my intuitive being for it was shortly after I had moved away from my lover that I started to read the tarot for others. I saw stories in the pictures and those stories inevitably were true visions for whomever I was reading for. It was as if a door opened in my heart that my head was previously unaware of and that door led to another kind of knowledge beyond intellectual-knowing that up to that time I had been clinging to.

The Italian siblings discussed Paolo with their mother and uncle. Uncle Guido was adamantly against having anything to do with Paolo. Their mother was less sure although in the end, she too decided it would be foolish to trust the Spaniard. Since Sal was locked into his belief that Paolo was 'no good' and would remain that way it was only Lisa who hesitated to completely close the door on their former betrayer.

At the least she felt that she and her brother needed to meet him one more time, if for no other reason than to make sure he was still alive. If they go to the Café Triste and receive no contact, then he probably died on the roof. God knows what they would do if that was the case.

Although Sal argued to the contrary, Lisa was sure that if the cabal had killed Paolo their trip to India was finished and, as a matter of fact, their whole quest was over.

While she was telling her family that it would be difficult to maneuver without help so long as the threatening organization was watching them, she became increasingly aware that the word impossible should be substituted for the word difficult.

Although she did not tell anyone in her family, she knew quite well that they had to trust Paolo once again because he was right - without him they had to simply give up.

She knew that neither she nor Sal was ready to stop searching.

That very evening Sal and Lisa headed for the Café Triste, but before they ever made it to the Café a sedan blocked their passage while crossing a street corner. It was Paulo.

He shouted to them to get in the car. They quickly did and sped away, leaving their nemeses too shocked to be able to pursue them.

No one spoke while Paolo raced through the streets of Milan toward some unknown destination. After driving for fifteen minutes, they found themselves on the other side of the city in a cemetery park.

Paolo turned the car off and turned to his companions. "So," was all he said.

"We came because we were afraid you were dead," Lisa exclaimed.

"Against all odds I managed to still be very much alive, but those odds won't last long if we don't discover your secret. I am convinced that the two of you will also not last long either if we don't leave Milan immediately, especially after this stunt of picking you up that I just pulled."

"Are you with me?" he asked.

The siblings answered at the same time, "Yes. No."

"Well, which is it?" For the first time either sibling could remember Paolo looked scared.

Lisa and her brother turned and looked at each other for what seemed a long time until Sal turned to their betrayer and quietly said, "Yes."

"Thank you." Paolo sighed with relief. "I am sorry for my abruptness, but we cannot stop to get anything you might need. We are going now and will pick up whatever we need on the way."

With that, Paolo headed for the Austrian border. They had a long ride before them.

42

Though very attached to my manuscript I gave it to Uncle Gino. It had been a week since Maria and I left Milan. I felt naked without it. More than I ever imagined, I frequently worried about losing it as I had done quite a bit of writing up to that point.

Uncle Gino had promised me that he would keep it safe and that he would finish reading it before we returned from our tour of the rest of Italy.

As expected, Italy was magnificent. Furthermore, our ease with being together while traveling was beyond marvelous. We found ourselves relishing the budding compatibility often found when two people really fit with each other.

The only hiccup that came between the two of us happened when I confronted Maria about feeling dissed when she seemed to belittle my theory that there was some connection between her family and my storyline.

She told me that it was only in jest when she did that, but I was thoroughly convinced that she was not telling me the truth. We never resolved this, but simply agreed to disagree. Other than this one disagreement we were enjoying each other's company more than either of us ever imagined.

Maybe the fact that Maria had no other obligations distracting her from just relaxing with me was the reason for our bliss. Whatever it was, I was happily growing closer to her.

"*Fuck,*" *was all Dawn could say after losing Paolo so quickly.* "*That little fucker is beginning to really get under my skin,*" *she complained to Marco.*

"*He sure is a fucker, and now we will have a hell of a time finding him.*" *Marco replied.* "*At least we have a car and license plate to check, although if I know that bastard, he won't use that car for long. No time to stop and smell the roses. We need to get on it now.*"

As the group began their sojourn to Anand and Sita, the Indian couple were leaving the monastery to return to Madras. They had assumed that their best shot of pursuing their quest was to try to get in touch with Carlo. The last time they saw him they were astonished to see him walking past their house. Maybe they could track him down and if not, they would have to go to Milan to find Lisa and Sal.

Although they both had a lot of apprehension about following their lead, they began to feel a sense of excitement with the idea of getting closer to what they were trying to prove.

"*You know Sita, if our friend's secret proves what we believe to be true, it would be really great. The only thing is, if that is the secret then why all the cloak and dagger stuff? It would be mind-blowing to the world that the ancients were significantly more advanced than we thought them to be, but to have two secret societies willing to keep it from everyone seems a bit too crazy. There must be more to what they are hiding, don't you think?*"

There was no answer from Sita, just the rumbling of the train's wheels rolling on the track.

It took two and half days, journeying from their Himalayan peak to downtown Madras. Getting off the train both Indians were thoroughly tired and looking forward to reaching their abode.

As the couple were arriving home, Paolo, Lisa, and Sal were nearing the border of Austria. They stopped in Venice to get supplies and second-hand clothes for themselves. While driving little was said. Seeing Paolo's palatable fear had diluted any resistance from the siblings as to Paolo's idea that the cabal's kit gloves had come off. The threat of Paolo's attempted assassination meant they also had not long to survive without taking immediate action. Although Sal maintained his doubt even as they reached the border, both agreed to participate in Paolo's plan.

All Sal could think of was what had they gotten themselves into with a man they couldn't trust. He felt trapped.

When they stopped at a small town in Austria to rest, Paolo came out with a plan of what to do next.

"We need to go back to Athens and find the head of the 'Not Knowing Society'; kidnap him and get him to give us the talisman. It is the only chance we have of going forward. And I know it is a crazy plan but...."

Lisa realized that she had never revealed to Paolo that Thaddaeus was the man they had been looking for. Was now the time to do so?

"How in god's name are we supposed to trust you?" Lisa asked Paolo.

"Yes, Paolo, how the hell are we supposed to trust you?" her brother chimed.

"There are no assurances I can give you. All you can do is take a risk. Besides, what exactly are you going to do if we just split up from here? I for one will just try to hide out in Afghanistan or India, but the organization has people everywhere so I think it will be futile. I'm afraid it will be futile for all of us. It's disturbing, but you have to take a risk.

"Then we need to go to Madras, India," Lisa informed him. And then she explained who Thaddaeus was and what they needed to do in India. First, they needed to go to Istanbul where Thaddaeus told Lisa she could contact him if needed.

They went through Romania into Bulgaria and crossed over to Turkey at Turkirdag. The journey took a day and a half with an overnight stop.

The shining city of Istanbul located by the crystal blue waters of the Mediterranean Sea was a short distance from the Turkish border.

Arriving at night they found a small hotel and settled into one room. Money needed to be conserved and they didn't plan for a long stay in the city.

The next day Lisa went alone to the library where Thaddaeus had directed her to contact him. She was simply to ask for Berat, the Bookworm. Not knowing Turkish, she asked in English as Thaddaeus had instructed her.

"Come back in an hour," was the reply.

She waited in a section of the library that held international maps. She pondered over a map of India. It was a very large country and the fact that they had to traverse most of it to get to Madras did not add to her confidence or belief in a happy ending.

She could sense his presence before she really knew that he was there, but from behind a row of bookshelves out walked the old man she recognized as the head of The Unknowing Society.

"I did not expect you so soon, Ms. Lisa," he greeted her. "Have you already found what is needed?"

She explained to him what had happened and where they must go to get the information. When she came to the part about Paolo's return he raised his eyebrows, but said nothing. She finally explained that she believed the Indians had drawings of the original writing, but was not completely sure about it. In any event it would take some time for them to return with the pictographic writing. She asked him where he would be in four to six months.

You play a dangerous game Miss Lisa, although I see that you may not have much choice. On the other hand, I am willing to offer you and your brother the protection of The Society if you wish to discontinue this perilous quest. Of course, you will need to let Paolo go his own way. After all, he created this mess for himself. You may not find your family's secret, but at least you will be safe and then after a while the cabal may simply forget about you.

"Thank you," Lisa said with sincerity. "Your offer is very tempting, but Sal and I are not ready yet to give up. We must continue with our plan."

"Then you must be very careful, especially around Paolo. You must use his dark abilities, but do not get sucked into trusting him. If you get the information, I would suggest you find a way to cut ties with him and return to me free of such a burden. I will be in Turkey for the next two months and then in India near Tibet. The place is called Dharamsala. I will remain there for the following two months. From there I will travel to Bombay before returning to Athens." He told her the contact info and wished her well.

She noticed something she had not seen before, a clarity and a peace emanating from the man in front of her. For the first time in many months, Lisa felt a sense of encouragement and relief in his eyes. It occurred to her at that moment that she could possibly succeed in her task.

43

*P*aolo stole another car in Athens, and they quickly departed for a very long and treacherous trip that brought them through Afghanistan and into India. Finally, after crossing most of the length of the Indian subcontinent they arrived in a town near Carlo's archaeological site.

The following day they went looking for Carlo, and eventually found him in a tent snuggled in a sleeping bag. They woke him up and greetings all around were made with Lisa and Sal. Paolo was a surprise they wanted to introduce to him later.

Eventually, Lisa asked her brother to give Carlo and her some space. He left the tent promptly with an eye toward finding Paolo.

"So, what's going on?" Carlo eyed his questionable lover.

"We came to get information from our friends in India," she said.

"I don't really want to know about that now, Lisa. I want to know what is going on between the two of us. When I left Italy, you didn't even come to see me off, and now you're seeking me out to get something from Anand and Sita. I've left you alone for some time now hoping you would let go of whatever was bothering you and come back to me, but I sense nothing of true love within you for me. What happened to you?"

"I don't know Carlo. When we left Athens and the whole venture seemed to fall apart my feelings for you changed. I thought that I only needed some time before they would return,

but it seems that they have not. Perhaps it was the romance I fell in love with in that foreign city, or maybe it was the letdown I experienced when we were forced to stop the quest. I am so sorry Carlo, but I just don't feel the same as I did in Athens. Maybe if we give it more time I will change again."

"I don't believe this, and no, I won't give you more time," Carlo replied. "I will give you Anand's address, but I do not want to continue on this foolish quest with you any longer. Please leave and send Sal in. I will write down the address and give it to him."

"Carlo please don't be angry with me and let's not separate like this," she implored.

"Go Lisa, just go," he turned away from her.

Lisa reluctantly left and sent Sal into the tent.

"Lisa just told me that you are angry with her." Sal began.

"Your sister just told me that she doesn't love me anymore. She even hinted that she possibly never loved me in the first place. It seemed only to be a romantic infatuation, if that. Angry, I am so angry. Why the hell did she come here to tell me that? She could have written and asked for Anand's address. I don't know why your sister is being so cruel. Anyway, here is what you want. Sorry, Sal. I am not angry at you, but you just happen to be here. I wish you success on your journey, wherever it may lead."

"Did Lisa tell you anything that has happened in the last two weeks?"

"No, and I don't really want to know either. So, don't tell me, brother."

"But Carlo, you need to hear this. We...."

"Stop, Sal. I really don't want to know. I need to get back to my work. If we ever meet up again you can fill me in on the details, but only if I'm feeling more inclined. Thanks for every-thing Sal, but now you better take your sister and go."

Later, address in hand Sal met up with Lisa and Paolo ready to take off for Madras again.

Sal's face was noticeably turning red as he said, "Shit, shit, shit, Lisa what did you do that for? Are you crazy?"

Lisa sat crying in the back seat of the stolen Athenian car. Nothing came out of her mouth, nothing in that moment would.

They drove onwards to find Anand and Sita.

As Paolo was driving toward Madras, Sal was sleeping in the back seat while Lisa was in deep thought quietly gazing out of the window.

"You want to talk about it?" asked Paolo without looking toward Lisa. There was no answer. "Look, I don't know anything about your relationship with Carlo, but it sure looks like you could use an ear right now."

"What would you know about such things? You're just a con man who doesn't seem to have a clue about how others might feel," she returned.

It was not so much her tone that hurt him, it was the fact that she was mostly right.

"Sorry," Paolo answered.

At this point Lisa looked at him while he was staring at the road. For a moment or two Paolo looked like a lost little boy.

They found the Indian couple's house after several hours of wandering. Streets in Madras could end up becoming empty fields while street signs were few and far between. The Hindi directions they received were more confusing than helpful.

Eventually, the task was done. They found themselves standing in front of a modest bungalow with a lovely porch. Sitting on a lounge on that porch, was Sita staring, seemingly lost in thought.

Paolo sighed with the thought of the cold greeting he might receive. Lisa, surprised with herself, felt a loving sense of nostalgia seeing Sita silently sitting there. Breaking both women's separate revelries, Sal jumped out of the front passenger's seat and shouted to Sita.

44

In one of the very many Vatican's galleries Maria pointed out to me several masterpiece paintings that had some strange figures in the skies overlooking Middle Age village scenes. Without a doubt these figures looked like saucers in the sky. As we looked together at the strange objects we started a conversation on whether we thought UFOs were real or not.

I thought they were, and she did not. "But look how many people claimed to have seen them," I said.

"If they were real, then why haven't they landed in plain sight for all to see?" she asked. "I won't believe in them until I actually see one for myself."

The conversation continued without either of us moving from our positions and lasted for quite a few minutes until I changed my thinking.

"Have you ever heard of vimanas?" I asked my lover. When she replied in the negative, I gave her an explanation of the vehicles reported to have existed in ancient India in one of their great religious texts.

"Maybe these European masters of the Age of Enlightenment somehow knew of the writings of the great Indian sages who lived 2000 to 3000 years prior to them. Seems highly unlikely," I said. "But who knows? The historians would be quite amiss if this was true."

"That would be strange, and who really cares?" she added. In this way we closed that conversation with me more interested in the possibility of vimanas than she was.

In the famous gallery of Uffizi in Florence we also saw two paintings that depicted these weird flying disks within them. *Very strange,* I thought.

Naples, Rome, Florence, Tuscany, Venice and the lake regions done in a three-week period was quite a whirlwind, but it was a great adventure for us and probably the most romantic trip I ever took. By the time we were heading back to Milan from Lake Como we were very much enamored with each other and looked forward to going home in this state of being.

Sita looked up to see Sal bounding up her walkway. She was shocked and a little flustered. Her departure from Sal and the rest of them was not exactly on good terms. The fact that he was here when she and Anand had just decided to travel to Italy to find him and his sister was beyond serendipitous. Before engaging Sal, Sita yelled into the house for Anand, and then upon turning her head saw both Lisa and "Detective Giuseppe".

Since the Indians had no idea about Paolo's real identity, they greeted him with smiles he was not expecting. In truth, their reconnection with him was warmer and more inviting than they had for the Italian siblings.

Nothing was said about Paolo as they sat around the dining room table. As the tea was poured the initial awkwardness was broken with apologies by Lisa for needing to disturb them again.

"I am truly sorry for all that you both had to go through and wouldn't have come all this way to bother you now, but I hope you have something that we need," she said.

They proceeded to listen to her story and everything that had happened since they had been together. During the part about Paolo being a member of the cabal both Indians looked aghast and dismayed, especially Anand. However, they did not interrupt

Lisa as she continued to describe Thaddaeus and the story that he needed the writing on the vases to be untranslated.

"This is why we came all this way," Lisa explained. "I am hoping to god that you still have a copy of the untranslated writing. Please, tell me you do."

In response Anand started, "Before we go into that we need to tell you that if you had not come to us just now, we would have gone to Milan to find you."

"What? Why?" Sal blurted out.

"It has to do with our own research," Sita began. "We have not been forthright in telling you just what we have been looking for, although you knew we were looking in the Vatican for clues to our quest. Now we believe that what we are interested in may have a direct connection to your family's secret. Unless our intuition is a complete error, we are in some ways looking for the same thing."

"And what is that?" asked Paolo.

"Given what Lisa just told us about you I am reluctant for us to reveal that just yet," Anand responded. "I want to know just what you are doing here Paolo. I understand what Lisa just told us, but your motives seem suspect to me. I'm not yet convinced that you are not still working for the group that hired you. Why would they be pursuing you? Wouldn't it be more likely that this is just another lie to help this cabal?"

"Ask Lisa and Sal. They tried to kill me in Milan." Paolo said.

"You could have set it up with them to make it look like they did. After all, you knew that you needed something really convincing to get us to let you back on this quest," Sita retorted. "Lisa and Sal may have let you back in for whatever reason, but I for one am not and I doubt Anand is either."

"Ditto," Anand agreed.

Everyone in the group stared at Paolo.

"What can I do to convince you?" he asked.

Lisa finally turned to the others and shared that since they left Milan, Paolo has been very helpful with getting them here. She ended her dictum with "Without him we probably would not have made it."

"That may be the case, but I don't feel comfortable sharing our research and much of anything else with Paolo right now. Paolo, are you open to leaving us alone for a while so that we four can talk this over?" Anand asked.

With a nod Paolo got up and left the house telling them that he would be back in an hour.

After he left, they discussed him and quickly came to the agreement that they would leave him out of the loop for a while, and maybe even longer. That decision took only 10 minutes to be reached, and soon they were on to more disclosures.

The couple explained their research, and the reason why they concluded that the Italian's family secret just may contain what they had been looking for, namely proof that vimanas did exist as true flying vehicles in ancient India. This knowledge led the siblings to discuss with Anand and Sita the possibility that they might be right.

"Your theory seems a little far-fetched, but if it gets you to help us further with the search, we are all for it," Sal exclaimed.

Sita left the room then and upon reentry proceeded to present a paper bound thin booklet. She opened it revealing the original writing of the vases they had lost. "I am not sure what we will get out of these, but let's study them before handing them over to the Greek. I can't trust this Thaddaeus of yours either. After what they did to me in Athens I am not so trusting as you two seem to be," Sita said.

"I feel the same," Anand contributed. "Before we make a copy to bring to TMW, let Sita and I study the writing more carefully to see if we can get anything more out of it. We can set you up with a small house owned by a friend of ours just down the road and you can visit Madras for a week or so. Maybe we

will discover something and be able to do this without any help. Then again, maybe we won't and have to find the Greek. Please remember not to share this with Paolo for now.

Unbeknownst to the group members, the cabal had planted one of its members to quietly watch the Indian couple. Their precaution had just been exceedingly rewarded. Not only did they find Paolo, but they had just about all the members of this renegade group together under one roof.

The word was sent to headquarters and shortly thereafter Marco and Dawn were rewarded with the news. Having lost any trace of their targets' whereabouts they were happy to be able to finally get down to business and finish this job.

45

The second time I had returned from the ashram in India I weighed less than 125 lbs. Normally, I was closer to 160 pounds, but a bout with Hepatitis A took its toll.

When my family and friends saw me alight from the jet that took me home, I am sure they were aghast at what they saw. They were confronted by my appearance as a ragged tired mess of skin and bones. Yet, inside of me I was anything but a mess. Rather, I had a series of transformative experiences that catapulted me from a consciousness focused almost entirely on the material reality I was taught to believe, into an awareness of an existence that consisted of magic and wonderment unhinged from the strictly material.

Lying on my bed with a high fever with no energy I was ready to die in the most blissful manner. It was as if death was floating over me and would gently release me from this movie. I enjoyed the movie, but it appeared to my inner being that all that is, is all that is without any compulsion to label it.

I fell into a fitful sleep and was literally transformed into a world more substantial than my waking one. Sitting on his chair, Bhagwan informed me that I was not going to die yet and that, as a matter of fact, I would be very old when I reach the culmination of an enlightened awareness. He said to me that my task was just to relax and have fun. From this space I woke and again there was reality as I had known it.

Sure enough, although I was all on my own with this fever and delirium I managed to get up and walk from my flat towards the greasy spoon Indian restaurant a block away. After taking no more than a dozen steps a rickshaw sped by me, suddenly stopped and out popped this angelic female who took one look at me and ordered me into her vehicle. After getting the few belongings out of my flat, she took me to her own apartment and planted me in her bed whereupon she nursed me to some semblance of health. I had known Amrita as Govind's former lover from the first time we were in India; now, she was my savior.

Without her I have no doubt that there would be no words on this page forthcoming nor breath in my lungs. No one knew where I had lived, and I had lived far away from the ashram at the time. As I just said, I was ready to go as Buddha so aptly put it – *"...beyond the beyond."*

Furthermore, I was having dreams instructing me as if I was taking a university doctorate degree in awareness. One dream portrayed to me my love for my girlfriend at the time. This scene quickly changed to an undefined image and Bhagwan's words ringing in my ears saying, "You have known one type of love, but I will show you a greater love." As I woke from this sentence the words merged into the call of a tropical bird. They were in such sync that I was disoriented for no short amount of time.

Again, another dream that was a recurring childhood horror dream revisited me. Just at the point of terror in the dream when I normally would wake up sweating, I remained sleeping listening to the bone chilling sound that I feared and that sound became a voice yelling 'mind, Mind, MInd, MINd, MIND' louder and louder until I woke up laughing never to have the dream again.

During this illness it was as if I was experiencing a serious download of information and that understanding allowed me to break through barriers of mind and heart that had limited my world since a very young age. Perhaps the illness allowed me the space to be vulnerable enough to perceive this new awareness.

Whatever, reaching my parent's home I was in terrible shape on the outside while glowing within.

The trio who had reached their comrades in India were in terrible shape, but ecstatic within at the relief that what they came to India to find, they had indeed found. They were even more joyful that they might not have to look for the further answers they sought by retracing their steps across Europe.

Unfortunately, although Anand tried to mix and match the original Pali characters every which way he could conceive, he had no luck in making any sense of the writing other than as his original interpretation.

They would all have to find Thaddaeus who should still be in Turkey, yet he said that he would move to Dharamsala, India in about a month. The five seekers discussed what to do. Should they go to Turkey now which would take them a week or two, or wait and find the head of 'The Not Knowing Society' in Northern India. They decided to wait. Sal and Lisa were tired of traveling, although Paolo thought it a bad idea to wait weary of staying too long anywhere for fear of the cabal finding them. The Indians for their part just came back from a long trip so they were not eager to depart either. Besides, everyone other than Paolo didn't believe that the cabal would find them so quickly.

Several days after the decision was made Marco and Dawn had arrived in Madras. They were given the address of those they sought and were laying out plans to finish their assignment. It would be easy and quick, and they would eliminate everyone without much trouble. The next day they scouted out the house where they all seem to meet and observed that there was no real security nor did these amateurs seem very security minded. Of course, there was Paolo, but they did not expect that even he would put up much resistance from their surprise attack.

On the third day after their arrival, they waited hidden outside of the target house. Their plan was simple: break in the front door with guns blazing shooting everyone in the parlor where they all would be congregated. The parlor was just left of the entrance. Then after confirming everybody was dead they would immediately flee Madras. Both enforcers used Glock eight chamber handguns with Marco having two, one in both his hands.

Just as expected, it was just past 10:30 in the morning when everyone of their marks arrived. Dawn said to Marco that this was just too easy and then, "Let's go."

Marco entered first, shooting the lock off the door and bursting through the entrance into the room only to stumble over his own feet while firing his weapon. The first shot went into the parlor, but the second shot found him turned around. That shot went toward the door where Dawn was coming in. It hit her right in the third eye. She didn't even have a chance to get off a round of ammunition.

Marco was on the floor trying to get up quickly, but Paolo, fast on his feet, was there before he could recover, and with a lamp in his hand smashed Marco's head.

When Paolo looked around, he could see Lisa kneeling by her brother who was shot in the stomach. Sita was hysterical, Anand was white as a sheet, and Lisa was so shocked she could only stare at Sal.

Paolo took control. He came over to Lisa and after taking one look at Sal realized there wasn't anything they could do to save him. Although he was still breathing, he would not be for long. Turning toward Anand he grabbed him by the shoulders and with a firm, but low voice told him that he needed to keep it together. We need to get rid of the bodies and tie this guy up pointing to the unconscious Marco.

Paolo knew that he should shoot the son-of-a bitch that shot Sal, but still couldn't get his head around killing someone if he absolutely didn't have to. So, Anand and Paolo secured Marco while the women did everything they could to tend to Sal who was bleeding out rapidly. Crying wildly, Lisa watched as her brother managed to open his eyes to take one final look at her before exhaling for the last time.

46

er grief was beyond anything she had ever experienced. Even with all the other prior losses in her life there was nothing that compared to this. Lisa sat wailing as she cradled her brother's head in her lap. What had she done by trying to find some stupid family secret her grandfather hadn't even entrusted to her? If she hadn't been so crazy Sal would have never even been here and would be alive right now. This was beyond anything that she could endure.

Everyone knew that there was nothing to do to comfort her, and besides, they had so much to do and so little time to do it. They all had to either call the police, or get rid of the bodies and do something with the guy tied down on the floor.

Anand and Paolo were arguing. Anand wanted to call the police. "This is my house. We can't just dispose of the bodies, Sita and I will be in no end of trouble. Besides, we can't just discard Sal like he's a nobody. You're crazy for even suggesting it."

"But you don't understand," Paolo retorted. "We need to get out of here as soon as possible. The cabal will come down on us like a ton of bricks and so swiftly that we will not have any time to breathe. My little trick wiring the doors is not going to save us the next time. We were just lucky he didn't see the wire. If you call the police, we will be hung up for days here and they will have this guy (pointing to the man on the floor) out of prison in no time." A little baksheesh and they will let him go, while we

will be asked to stay here so the police can investigate. We will be sitting ducks."

"Lisa, I am so sorry about Sal, but we must bury him and the woman in the back gardens, clean this place up and leave as soon as we can. We just don't have time for anything else – not even grieving," Paulo insisted.

It was hard. It was impossible, but she knew Paolo was right. They needed to straighten up the home and bury Sal and one of his killers and go. No time to even think.

"Paolo's right Anand, we need to get far away from here and fast," Lisa said this in an unrecognizable tone. She would need to somehow say goodbye to her beloved brother.

Since they had to wait for night in order to dig two shallow graves and dispose of the bodies, Lisa did have time for grieving. Too much time, in fact. The depth of her feelings felt overwhelming.

Somehow, she managed along with Sita to clean up the blood and rearrange the house. They washed Sal's body and wrapped him in one of Sita's saris to give him some semblance of a proper send off. Both women looked like the walking dead as they did all this. Lisa felt dead inside – her beloved brother was gone.

As the women were doing this, Anand and Paolo secured Marco more thoroughly. They started arguing what had become assuredly the most difficult problem they had to solve…what to do with Marco. They managed to get his name from the Portuguese ID he had on him. Out of sight from the others, Paolo slapped him around a few times. He tried to get information from him, but Marco would not budge; Paolo had no stomach for torture. After they gagged him, they tied his hands and feet ready to do whatever they were going to do with him.

He couldn't be brought to the police for obvious reasons, and he couldn't just be left tied up in the house. Neither did they just want to let him go.

Anand came up with the idea of leaving him in the desert they would have to pass through on their way out of India.

"We can put him in the van and when we get to the Kutch desert, we can go off road and leave him somewhere in the middle of it. We'll give him a canteen of water and who cares what happens to him after that. Even if he does manage to get back it will take him quite a while to do so. By that time, we may be able to find what we are looking for and get this damn organization away from us." Anand was talking fast, obviously still in shock.

Nobody liked the plan, but none of them had any better ideas so they bundled Marco into the back of the van, tightly secured and covered him with a tarp.

That night Lisa said words over her brother as they all buried him alongside some horrible woman who tried to murder him. The Indians closed the house and sent a message to the servants that their services would not be needed for a while. They instructed the servants not to come to the house until they were back. This message was highly unusual as they had never given such a directive before, but they thought that even though it might give rise to some suspicion their staff would follow the instructions.

That same night they headed west toward the southern coast planning to turn north at the Indian Ocean and ride the western shore of India through Gujarat and the Kutch desert. They needed to find the head of 'The Unknowing Society' and discover where to go to find this secret that seemed so important that people would kill and torture for it. Turkey was their destination as they didn't have the luxury of waiting for Thaddaeus to come to India any longer.

Anand drove with Sita occupying the front passenger's seat. Lisa and Paolo were in the back. Everyone was lost in their own thoughts avoiding eye contact, nor engaging each other in any way. Occasionally, Sita and Anand would say something to each other keeping their conversation limited to directions and where and when to make stops. Lisa sat silently with her face turned toward the window. Paolo kept looking at her, obviously wanting to do something, but could not figure out what that something might be.

Paolo seldom felt awkward in his life as he always seemed to find a flow in any situation that arose, but he was really feeling an internal turmoil sitting in that back seat. Hours went by without any relief to his angst.

Anand broke the tension with a swear. "Hell," he shouted. "What secret could be so important that they would kill to keep it so? I just don't understand. Even if it has something to do with our research, why would someone try to kill all of us to stop it? Why? There must be more to what we are looking at." He said all this while looking at Sita.

Paolo spoke, "None of you truly understands what you're dealing with here. The cabal will stop at nothing to get what they want and if what they want is this secret information to not be revealed to the public then we better find it soon, or we will all be joining Sal. There is nowhere we can run to be safe. Our only power is the threat that we can reveal what they don't want us to."

Nobody responded as the silence only deepened.

It wasn't until the third day of traveling just before they were to enter the desert that Lisa turned away from the window and angrily looked at Paolo asking, "So how many times have you killed for the cabal, Paolo?"

Paolo was taken aback. "I don't do that. I only do odd jobs that have nothing to do with killing people."

"I don't believe you," suddenly, she was seething. She started swinging her arms at her backseat companion. Paolo managed to get a hold of her and tightly held her.

"It is all your fault that Sal is dead. This would never have happened if you hadn't come to Milan. Sal would be safe at home

if you had stayed in the hole you escaped from." Concerned, Sita drove the van off the road as Lisa cried uncontrollably.

Paolo never remembered feeling remorse since he passed the age of eight. As he held her, he found himself second guessing himself. Her grief was getting to him. His feelings were tumultuous and as she finally started to relax out of exhaustion while in his arms, he became frightened of what he thought of as an inappropriate tenderness he felt toward her welling up.

As Lisa became calmer and Paolo released his hold on her everyone again became silent. This silence was soon interrupted by Anand telling Sita that since she had turned off the road she might as well drive overland onto the desert floor. Soon they would need to rid themselves of the excess baggage they were carrying.

Sita felt uncomfortable. "Isn't there anything else we can do with him?" she asked. "It seems overwhelmingly cruel to just drop him off in the middle of the desert."

"He killed my brother, and you think it is cruel that we give him water and a chance to live? Fuck, that's a lot more than he gave Sal or any of us," Lisa returned.

"There is nothing else that we can do Sita," Anand added. "Besides, he looks like a tough guy, and he just might make it out of here alive. If so, maybe we should be more worried that he might try to kill us again."

Of course, Marco was listening to all this. He was more than pissed with himself that he tripped over the wire and was doing his own mourning for Dawn. How could he fall for such a simple trick? In his defense, the wire trick was usually done when no one was around and not strung up when the house was full. It didn't matter. He messed up and he lost Dawn because of it.

Dawn and he were not lovers. She preferred sex with women, but they were partners. All the same, they had worked together for many years. He loved her in his own way and these fuckers got him to shoot her. They would all die by his hand for that.

He knew that they planned to leave him in the desert, but his military background prepared him for surviving under the harshest conditions. He would get out of this and would meet up with them again. Then, they would wish they had killed him when they had the chance.

And so, they left him deep in the desert, and planned to head north out of the country then through Afghanistan and toward Turkey. The quicker they got to Istanbul the better it would be for them. They would stop in Agra and steal another car. Paolo would not hear of them wanting to continue using Anand's vehicle. They needed to be as stealthy as possible.

47

We arrived in Milan and were tired. Our whirlwind tour through Italy ending at Lake Como was magical, but the pace was exhausting. After arriving we stayed in our *pensione* sleeping twelve hours straight, and after that we made love for what felt like another 12 hours. A whole day went by without leaving the flat, and the next day when we finally ventured out, we went for a very leisurely breakfast and spent the rest of the day sightseeing, capping it off with a candlelight dinner near the Piazza del Duomo located in the 18th century mall named Galleria Vittorio Emanuele II.

It was not until the third day back in Milan that I had any thought about contacting Uncle Gino to discover what he had to say about my unfinished manuscript and if he considered it strange that its content seemed to relate so closely to his own family's secret.

Sitting in his study I felt very relaxed watching Gino as he sat behind his massive desk, and yet I was also eager to learn what he construed of my perceived synchronicity.

"I understand your wonder at the similarities of the two storylines, but I am very convinced that it is all just a coincidence. Maybe if you were to relay to me where you plan to go with the story then I might see it differently," he said.

For several reasons, I had no intention of telling him the progression of my tale. First, I wasn't completely sure where the story was going as I was writing it, as they say – "off the cuff." Secondly, if I did give him some of my ideas as to the direction it was heading, I feared that he might overly influence me in one way or another. I couldn't tell him anything, but asked him if I could send him periodic updates to the story as I wrote them.

"Perhaps, it will become clear as to whether our stories are somehow in sync the further along I go with my manuscript." I suggested.

He enthusiastically agreed to this process. Furthermore, he started sharing without any prompting on my part the fact that his family has been protecting their secret for longer than he knew. His speculation was that they held it for hundreds if not thousands of years. I wonder what, could it possibly be that was entrusted.

"Right there?" I asked. "Doesn't that seem very amazing that my story's secret and your family's secret could both be kept for such an amazing length of time?"

However, he would not budge and thought it only amusing that they did. It was at this point I began to feel that maybe Uncle Gino wasn't being completely honest with me. Something in his eyes told me to be more discerning about what I was being told.

When I was alone with Maria later that day, I asked her about her uncle.

"Would your uncle knowingly deceive me?" I inquired of her.

"To be honest," she answered, "I don't know my uncle well enough to answer your question. Perhaps, this information he is holding onto is more interesting than any of us in the family have given it credit for being."

Two days after that conversation Maria and I got on a plane bound for Boston. As I got on the Alitalia flight, I remembered hoping that Gino would be more forthcoming if my continuing manuscript did indeed coincide with whatever he was holding close to his chest.

During the long ride from Agra to Istanbul there was the continuation of long periods of silence. However, because of Paolo's persistent inquiries, Anand and Sita became more talkative about their own research. They began to doubt their hypothesis that Lisa's secret had anything to do with their work. The fact that whatever had been held by Lisa's grandfather could be so potent as to cause such murder and torture didn't equate with what their research was hoping to reveal.

Sita with Anand's approval told her companions about their belief that the ancient Hindus must have used sophisticated flying machines and thus must have had a far more technologically advanced civilization then anyone previously imagined.

"Of course," Anand contributed "this is mind-shaking information and will force the world to review what it thinks it knows about history, but it isn't that revolutionary to cause your cabal to go to such extreme lengths to keep it secret, is it?"

"I don't know," stated Paolo. "It is quite an amazing speculation on its own. What if it is only part of the story that is not being told? What if there is significantly more being withheld from the eyes of the world? For example, where would your ancestors have gotten the knowledge to make such advanced weaponry? I'm not so sure that your original instinct that somehow the two are connected is all that wrong."

Lisa was now going through periods when she was very silent for hours at a time contrasted with angry episodes toward Paolo. For short but very intense episodes she shouted to all in the car, "What does all this matter, and who cares? I've been thinking that we should turn around and go back to your house, call the police and give up this horrible endeavor. We could get a message to this cabal that we won't seek their precious secret any longer, give my brother a proper funeral and save ourselves from getting killed."

There was stone cold silence in the car. It was so silent everyone could hear the shallow breathing taking place as all eyes went toward Lisa.

"Look, I can't do this anymore," she broke the tension. "My brother is dead, he is dead, and I'm to blame. Ultimately, it was my persistence to have this adventure and it's destroying me to continue as if nothing happened."

After a moment it was Paolo who responded. "Lisa, I know that you blame me for making you carry on and I know that I worked for the people that shot Sal. I know I am not the person to ask this of you, I have no right, but if you back out now you are sentencing me to death. The cabal may let the rest of you go, although I somehow doubt that, but they surely will not give me that consideration. You don't owe me anything, and as a matter of fact it is I who owes you for giving me this chance. I am doomed if you don't pursue this to the end."

"You're right Paulo I don't owe you anything," she said as she turned her head to stare out of the window.

The tension was thick as a London fog as they drove further north. Finally, they stopped at a small hotel. Returning from the hotel lobby, Anand spoke as he handed a key to his wife for the room the women would share.

"Perhaps we can sleep on this and decide what we are going to do in the morning." With that the men retreated to their room while the woman did the same.

"Shit," Paolo said to Anand as they entered their room, "I am truly fucked if she gives up on this. She has a connection with Thaddaeus. He won't give me the time of day if she is not involved."

"You know Paolo, you have spent so much time on your private island thinking only about yourself that you reek of

smallness. I know you are in a hell of a predicament, but grow some real balls and stop thinking about just yourself. Lisa is in utter distress, and you have done nothing to relieve that. As a matter of fact, you have done so much to exacerbate it. I will support whatever she wants to do. You just might have to use your considerable resources to elude this organization of yours without her help," and with that Anand went to bed.

As the two women were lying in their respective beds ready to sleep, Sita who hadn't said a word to Lisa since Lisa's outburst, softly relayed her thoughts to her companion.

"You know, Lisa, it is not your fault about Sal. You are not giving him respect when you say that it was because of you that he is dead. Sal, I can assure you was as much on board if not more so with your hunting down this secret. It was his family and his grandfather, too. I had more than a few conversations with him where he expressed his eagerness to make this journey knowing the dangers involved. As I recall, he understood those dangers somewhat better than any of us. I must ask you this. Do you want to further disrespect your brother by giving up and making his death mean nothing at all?"

Tears were pouring down Lisa's face. Sita got up from her bed to hold Lisa's hand as she poured out her sorrow.

Finally, after quite some time, Lisa told Sita that she was so afraid. Sita told her that she also was full of fear, but that she felt they needed to finish what they had started, and that all of them were grown-ups making their own individual decisions to go with her.

Just before going to sleep Sita added, "You know, Lisa you have to contact Carlo and tell him what happened – he deserves to know. I am not sure what happened between you two, but I have a feeling you may need him right now. Promise me that you will send a telegraph to him about Sal and where we're going."

Lisa simply nodded her head.

Lisa reluctantly acknowledged this new phase of her journey as they continued north out of the country.

During the two-week trip to Istanbul all of the passengers joined in speculation of just what they were possibly going to find at the end of their adventure.

Anand and Sita agreed that they thought Lisa's grandfather was entrusted with such knowledge that it could drastically change the course of the world. They concluded that it must have something to do with the rediscovery of power and technology – a technology they believed that could explain how the pyramids were built, how ancient underground temples could hold vast stone crypts, how our ancestors could be so accurate with their mathematics and astronomical calculations, and so much more. Anand was sure that they would uncover information to show that those who supposedly were thought to live in a Stone Age culture were people vastly superior in knowledge - more superior than our present civilization. He speculated that this secret was kept hidden for centuries because either humanity could not handle the knowledge, or maybe the various groups wanted to keep the power it could generate to themselves.

Although Lisa agreed with most of what Anand theorized, she was not so sure about why it was kept a secret. Perhaps the population at large was kept in the dark because although some groups had the knowledge, they didn't really understand how it worked and they just thought no one would believe them.

Paolo pointed out to Lisa that if the latter was true then there would be no need to keep the information secret at all costs. No one would need to be killed if they just thought they would be ridiculed. She conceded the point to him. Still, she was not completely convinced by any argument as to why whoever had the knowledge kept it hidden.

Paolo was curious as to what Lisa's family was supposed to do with whatever information they were protecting over the centuries. Paolo asked Lisa, "When was your family supposed to reveal what they had? If they weren't meant to reveal it, what good was having anyone entrusted with it in the first place?" He directed this question toward her as if she somehow knew the answer. She didn't.

Lisa, for the most part, did not participate with all this speculation, although even she became part of the conversation when theories of how dangerous the box they were trying to rediscover might be.

"How dangerous could it be?" She challenged them. "The box was small, and I doubt it could hold that much material to be as ominous as you are all fantasizing. "My own feeling is that it contained wisdom of some sort. My mother told me that whenever my grandfather said anything about that box, which wasn't often, he spoke with such reverence that she was sure he thought it was sacred."

Obviously, no conclusions were made, but it seemed to break some of the tension they were all under just by engaging in conversation.

48

When I first became acquainted with Bhagwan Shree Rajneesh, he talked about how every world master, of which he was one, had twelve non-incarnated masters guiding them on their sojourn into the physical plane of existence.

These twelve other worldly beings and the one incarnated guru made up a team focused on sending a particular message to the people of planet Earth. This message was to be delivered first to a particular group of people who could resonate more easily with it and then through these people to the world at large. This was the real trickle-down theory.

He told us that this has been happening for thousands of years. It happened with Lao Tzu, Krishna, Buddha, Zarathustra, Jesus and countless others.

As I review this information now it appears to me that this technique of sharing wisdom may not have worked as well as it was intended to. Almost all of these teachers seemed to have only created religions with rigid creeds far removed from their original insights. Most of these religions did maintain something of the original teachings, but missed the mark on much of what the masters had wished to convey.

Knowing this I've wondered why they even needed their twelve non-incarnated beings to help them in the first place. It seemed to me that they would have done just as well on their own. Maybe, it was just one of those mystical stories that gives some sort of magical credence to the orator. Perhaps again, the man I call Master, was just using a psychological technique; the kind of trick the ad agencies use on the general public to sell their wares.

Then again, maybe this world is much more magical than it appears to be and that groups of wise beings are all around us pointing the way. Maybe it takes more than just one individual here and there to be able to truly enlighten even a small group of disciples. With that in mind, would the council of thirteen, so to speak, create a magnetic field of enough power to send waves of wise understanding into this dense place we call Earth. I really didn't have any idea if this was true, but the thought of it created more credibility to my mind.

I was once again sitting on my favorite stoop back in East Boston. Just the sun, myself and Chelsea Bay. Maria was at home in her apartment. We had an uneventful flight back and a most unforgettable journey through our roots. I imagined that we would settle into a comfortable relationship on Bremen Street, although that was yet to be seen.

They arrived in Istanbul after a two-week journey in their third stolen car. Paolo was amazing when it came to stealing cars, although all his companions had no less than several anxiety attacks apiece over the thought of being stopped by the police in the various locations they had to travel through.

No time was wasted with contacting Thaddaeus. This time Lisa found him at an open market deli where he said he would be every Wednesday at 1pm. By no coincidence they arrived in the city at 11:00am on Wednesday morning. None of them wanted to waste any time in making contact.

Lisa was still having second thoughts about the whole venture. She considered what Sita said to her and felt the truth of it, but she also feared that it was again selfish of her to put any more lives in danger. Feeling torn, she had sent a message to Carlo displaying her anguish about Sal's murder. Furthermore, she informed him of where they were going.

Feeling the pressure of all three of her companions wanting her to pursue the goal, she fretted about the consequences. Still feeling conflicted she went to meet Thaddaeus.

From the moment when she sat down in front of him, Thaddaeus was aware of a difference in Lisa. "What is wrong?" he asked.

Without any hesitation she told him all that had passed since last they met. She found comfort in this man she hardly knew, and she wondered how that was possible. Believing that she should have reservations about this man who headed a dangerous society, she couldn't help but confide in him. Somewhere in the middle of her story Lisa's eyes filled with tears and the flow was unstoppable. Thaddaeus sat holding her hand as compassion filled his face.

When she finished and began composing herself the old man across from her sincerely asked "Do you still want to keep going with this? If you want, I can follow the clues and take this whole thing away from you. You can go back to your family, and I will make it known to the cabal that I am the one they need to stop, not you or your friends. After all, I have a very extensive organization myself. There are only a few of you. Just say the word."

Lisa looked up in suspicion. "Who are you really Thaddaeus and what does your group do?" she asked.

"I cannot tell you that, my dear. Besides, it would not be safe for you to know these answers. So, what do you say? Would you like to stop all this, and give me the transcription from the vases and go home?"

Although tempted, she realized that she could not do what he asked. Something inside was holding onto the need to know her family's secret. Something inside was feeling that she was the inheritor of her family's burden. She was the guardian and the *protector of her grandfather's legacy and although she yearned to protect herself and those around her, she knew that she could not give up the quest.*

"I cannot do that, and I need to get your assurance that you will give me the key and the knowledge of where to use it." she told the old man.

"My apologies, my dear," he said. "I had to be sure that you would go to great lengths to discover your search's end. I had to know that you would not give up. I can see now that you have the courage and the spirit to find your lineage's trust. I will, indeed, give you the talisman and point you in the right direction to find what you desire."

With these words Lisa reached into her coat pocket to give him the words on the vases as written in Pali.

"No need for that, Thaddaeus said. "I have known all along where the key is to go."

"What!" Lisa cried. "You mean we didn't have to go to India where my brother was killed?" Horror was written all over Lisa's face.

"Did you think this journey would be easy?" he responded. "Do you think it will get any easier? This is what you signed up for, my dear. Do you still want the lock the key turns in?"

"I thought you were a kind and thoughtful human being," she fired back at him. "Now, I can see that you are just like the cabal, maybe even worse."

"Lisa, you should go home and forget all this. You are not cut out for what you may discover. I am not just a kind and thoughtful human being. I am the head of an ancient foundation dedicated to protecting truth and wisdom. This is something you should have explored with me before ever going forward on your fantasy quest. In your naivete you marched off. Go home!"

Thaddaeus got up to go. Lisa was tempted simply to let him go, but that something inside wouldn't let her.

"No, please wait," was her response. Echoing Sita's words to her she told him that she could not let Sal die in vain and she couldn't abandon her family's legacy.

"This does not change my anger toward you, but I need to know. Please tell me where the key goes," Lisa insisted.

'The Man Who Does Not Know,' stared at the young woman in front of him as if he was undecided what to do next.

"I can protect you and those you're with only in a limited fashion. There is no protecting you on the last part of the journey you need to take. That part of the journey is a treacherous trek, and you will be allowed to only take one other person with you. When it comes time for the decision as to who to take you will need to choose wisely for both of your sakes. For now, you will need to go back to India — to Dharamsala. Once there, I will explain further. Tell your friends that they can come with you there under my protection, but from that point you will have to go on with only one of them and they will have to find their own way back."

As an afterthought he said, "By the way, your friend Carlo has arrived in Istanbul and is staying at the Amir Hotel. Don't look so surprised. I know everyone who is involved with you. Unlike you I do my research thoroughly."

49

*I*nstead of immediately returning to the crew Lisa began walking the streets of Istanbul lost in her thoughts. Why had he sent her to India knowing there was no need? She got Anand and Sita involved again for no real purpose. Sal would possibly still be with them. Thaddaeus said that he had to make sure of her resolve, but that was just a lie. Her mind was a mess. Nothing seemed to make any sense. Now that she got all these people involved, possibly even Carlo, they were going to have to go on their own to God knows where. All this was just foolishness, and she began to feel that whatever she would do from here would be even more dangerous than it had been already and would probably end up being wrong. She felt lost.

She sat on a bench overlooking the city's beautiful river. Should she really go on with this crazy venture? Could she? Finally, after several hours watching the river float by she went looking for her friends.

They were waiting for her at a café with no end of worry. She was very late, and relief permeated the group when she walked in.

She told them all that Thaddaeus had said and how afterwards she had wandered the streets pondering what to do.

Every one of them had their own perspective which she listened to. Paolo, of course, said that there was no other solution but to go on with their search. This was echoed by Anand, although he suggested it with as much anger as Lisa had about what had *needlessly transpired. Sita was the only one of the three who was hesitant. She asked Lisa if it was really all worth it, considering what may happen if they continued.*

There was a knock. Paolo answered it, finding Carlo on the other side of the door. He walked past Paulo and stopped dead center in the sitting room where they all had gathered.

Seeing Carlo, Lisa lost it with memories of her brother, Carlo and herself beginning their trip to Rome. She went crying into Carlo's arms. "He's dead Carlo, my brother is dead." Carlo just held her for what seemed to be an eternity. The rest of them stood there, watching silently.

Looking around Carlo pleaded, "Please tell me what happened."

It was Sita, not Lisa, who began the descriptive narrative telling Carlo all that had happened while they were in Madras and during their subsequent journey. Sometime while Sita went on speaking Lisa disengaged herself from her ex-lover and sat down observing him take in the whole story.

When Sita finished Carlo turned toward Lisa and asked her what she was doing in Istanbul. "You need to give up this insane journey before you end up with Sal. Let me take you home," he pleaded.

"We can't do that," Paulo interjected.

Carlo moved from his stoic position to face Paulo. "You bastard, who the fuck are you to say that? If it wasn't for you Lisa wouldn't be in this mess." He swung at Paulo's head. Paulo ducked and sent a jab to Carlo's chest which connected and landed him on his ass. Paolo moved in to continue, but Anand and the two women put themselves in the way to stop the scuffle.

Carlo quickly got up from the floor threatening to throw another punch, but Lisa shouted for him to stop. The two young men eyed each other for a long moment, but broke off tension when Anand asked them to stop with the childishness as they all had to work together. "If Lisa wants to continue this journey, that is her choice," he said. "She has been considering it for some time now. It is her decision, not yours, Carlo, or any of ours."

"So, what the hell was Paolo saying 'no' for if it's Lisa's choice?" shouted Carlo.

"He doesn't want me to give up and neither does Anand, nor do I believe, does Sita," Lisa answered. "They all have their reasons to continue. Carlo, do you think I should really go back home?"

"Yes. Whatever their reasons they're not worth your life, nor theirs for that matter. I don't care what your grandfather was holding onto - it's just not worth it." Let me take you home. Besides, your mother has a right to know that her only son is gone."

"While I was walking by the river, I thought the same as you Carlo. Yet, I have decided that I must continue because it is what Sal would want me to do. I'm sure of it. Even if I were to die, I must try to recover my family's secret. Carlo, will you come with me, with us? I know I have no right to ask this of you, but I really would feel better if you said yes."

"Christ, Lisa, you're crazy." Carlo paused for a moment. "Of course I will go with you. Someone has to keep you safe."

"I'm not going to let anything happen to her," Paolo interrupted.

"You're the problem, Paolo. You should just leave," Carlo retorted.

At this point the two men aggressively moved towards each other until Sita intervened saying none of them were going to let anything happen to Lisa or anyone else. "We are all in this together," Sita declared.

After they explained the plan going forward to Carlo, they all decided to take off in Carlo's vehicle in the morning. Carlo asked Lisa to come stay with him at his apartment, but she declined. They agreed to meet up in the morning.

I put my writing down as I was interrupted by Joey coming out from his apartment to join me on the stoop.

"What's up?" I asked.

"Nothing, will you throw the football with me?" Joey pleaded.

We ended up passing his football back and forth for an hour in the school yard next to his building.

Since I had returned from Italy with Maria, Joey and I began spending quite a bit more time together. As the relationship between Maria and I continued to deepen, I began having dinner more often with Joey, Isabella, and Maria. Everything about the relationship was going smoothly, except for my connection with Maria's uncle in Milan. I had written to him several times sharing the progress of my book and inquired if he saw any common threads with his family's secret story. I heard nothing in return.

At dinner that night in Maria's kitchen sitting with her family, I questioned her about why her uncle was seemingly ignoring my correspondence.

She had no idea, although she herself had received several letters from him and her aunt replying to letters she had previously written to them.

I began to suspect that he was withholding information that made his family secret and my story's secret very similar indeed, though I wasn't quite sure why he would do that. Perhaps, when he begins to see how my story is unfolding, he will be more forthcoming.

The day before they were to arrive in Dharamsala the conversation between all five seekers turned to the same subject they had been discussing throughout their trip. What could possibly be the information that the cabal was forcibly trying to hide from them?

Lisa told her companions that she felt that Thaddaeus didn't know what they would find. She said that he hinted that his society had its own ancient secrets that might very well have something to do with what her grandfather had been entrusted with. He just wasn't sure if they were the same or even related. Regardless he wouldn't share anything he knew and only shared that if the world knew half of what happened in antiquity people would be shocked, angry and extremely fearful.

Anand and Sita explained that they were certain that the ancients were far more advanced technologically than our historians tell us or even knew.

Their statement led to a discussion on just where that advanced technology came from. Carlo thought that maybe it came from more ancient humans that we know nothing about, but whose traces were destroyed somewhere back in time. Surprisingly, Paolo agreed.

Lisa and Anand leaned toward the theory that we were visited by some other beings from outer space who gave our forebears help to create the advancement.

Sita was alone in holding the view that many of the indications they had been reading about in the Vedas were describing extraterrestrials and that these beings were literally part of what we know as human history.

When they all turned to the subject as to why the cabal would want to keep any of these suppositions so secret, and why they would kill to do so, the conversation got chaotic.

Anand became angry; yelling that there are always people who simply want to feel they know something everyone else is in the dark about. It gave them a sense of power.

Sita shared that maybe there is something about the knowledge that is dangerous for human society to know about.

"Bull," Anand retorted. Everyone was taken aback to hear Anand being so abrupt toward Sita, when he customarily always spoke to her in a loving and gentle tone.

Seeing the others' reactions, Sita defended her spouse telling her companions that their opposing views were a bone of contention between the two of them for some time now. "Anand is very sensitive to the hurt that has rained down on humanity through the withholding of secret knowledge."

"It created a milieu of distrust that grows exponentially as time goes on and destroys the social fabric. You can see it throughout the world today. All this war, poverty, and division is the result," Anand explained.

Carlo was of the belief that the technology was still around somehow and that the cabal didn't want to share it because it was the foundation of their considerable power in the world. "Who knows what stuff they may have at their disposal," he said.

Paolo agreed with this notion although he laid out a scenario that in less technological times, like in the Middle Ages, their secrets would have made them seem invincible and with the current growth in machines and engines they would be hell bent in doing everything they could to hold the rest of the planet back.

Lisa did not speculate, saying only that she thought there was no reason that justified killing someone. While making that observation she asked about how big and widespread the organization could be.

Paolo answered her, "As far as I know they are everywhere, although I am not sure if they are just one big group or many splinter groups." He had heard information that they were in all the Americas, Asia, Africa, Europe and even in Australia. He finished by saying that they pretty much ruled the world, although very few people know about them.

At this point Lisa turned to Sita and said, "Perhaps this cabal is made up of the aliens you think are part of history."

That was the last word before the group broke apart for the night.

The next day they arrived in Dharamsala.

50

Fifteen miles outside of the city, the group trekked up to a monastery where they were greeted by six monks who were maintaining the enclave while the rest of the monastic population were involved in a two-week retreat inside the locked meditation hall.

The welcoming committee placed each of them in a separate cell, with the women placed in a separate part of the building away from the men.

Thaddaeus told Lisa he would meet them at the monastery before giving her further instructions about the next part of the journey. They waited for him to show, but after a week of waiting the group started to become frazzled.

While Sita and Anand were reviewing whatever books they could find in the monastery's limited library, Paulo and Carlo continued their fighting. This was difficult for Lisa to prevent.

After ten days, even the Indians were antsy as they had exhausted their reading material and began to doubt that the Greek would ever appear. The group received no help from any members of the religious order and indeed these meditators didn't seem to know anything of what Thaddaeus might have been referring to.

"What do we do now?" Carlo asked. The five of them had not been together in one room for over a week.

"We wait," Paolo answered.

With daggers coming out of his eyes, Carlo ignored Paolo other than to look at him.

"So, Lisa, are you ready to go home yet?" Carlo asked more pointedly.

Lisa looked around as if pleading for an answer from the rest of them.

Anand shrugged and Sita lowered her eyes while Paolo told her that she knew where he stood.

"I need to stay longer. This must be a test he is putting us through, especially me," she surmised.

Another week went by at which point the Indian couple decided that they should return home. They had been worrying more and more about the situation they left at their house. Did any of their staff check up on the place even though they requested that they didn't? Unlikely as it should be, they feared someone might have found the graves. They just couldn't wait around this ashram any longer and needed to do whatever damage control that might keep them from being in trouble with the authorities.

They left that day with hugs and some tears. During that day Carlo was pressuring Lisa to do the same, and she was beginning to make it a real consideration. This left Paolo the only one not ready to budge.

"Please Lisa, stay a day or two longer," he pleaded.

With the departure of her Indian friends, Lisa knew she would not be able to keep Carlo and Paolo from hurting each other. She decided that she had to make a clear and definite decision that day. She couldn't understand why Thaddaeus would just leave her here, but she couldn't wait much longer so she told both the men that she would stay just two more days after which she would get Carlo to take her home and wished Paolo the best wherever he would end up.

The Greek told her that the journey wouldn't be easy, but she never dreamed that he would simply abandon her.

The following day nothing happened, and Lisa told both men that she was packing, and they should as well. She had given up although she would not leave until the morning of the day after tomorrow. She held no hope of going any further on this quest.

The next night after Lisa went to bed with the idea of leaving first thing in the morning, a soft knock on her door woke her from her troubled sleep. Cracking open the door, she spied 'The Man Who Does Not Know' patiently waiting on the other side.

"May I come in?" he asked politely.

She opened the door wide and let him in. Before she could utter a word, he put his index finger to his closed lips indicating that she was to remain silent.

"Say nothing. Just listen. Tomorrow night you are to leave this place and walk on the path the monks indicate to you. You will follow this path with some instruction until you come to a monastery which will appear hanging from a cliff. There you will contact the abbot who will give you some information and instruct you further. Tonight, you will need to make the decision as to which one of the two young men you will take along with you. The other must be sent away and will be out of your contact until you complete the journey in these mountains. Choose wisely as your safety and the safety of all your friends may very well be at stake with this choice.

51

Toward the end of my experience living in Bhagwan's commune in the USA one of the disciples had written a question to Bhagwan after he began speaking again about having a close encounter with a UFO on one of the ranch's large fields. She asked what he thought about the existence of extraterrestrials. His answer was short and rather curt.

Paraphrasing, he said that other beings from other worlds did indeed exist and were on the planet, but that it was no concern of his disciples as we were there to know ourselves. The extraterrestrials were doing their own thing and it really had nothing to do with us.

I remember thinking at the time that his answer was too limited and that there must be more to it than just they had their own agenda while we just had ours.

Lisa had thought about who she would pick to accompany her when she first arrived at the monastery. She had thought about it a lot, but had not come to any conclusions. However, she was so convinced that the Greek would not show that she forgot about his directive and with some relief let the problem go.

Now it seemed that Thaddaeus had at least in part made the decision for her. Obviously, he thought she had to take one of the guys along. She had no idea why, but she was leaning in that direction anyway. The only thing was, she was seriously considering Anand as her fellow traveler and now that option was off the table.

This was going to be difficult. Her first reaction to taking Paolo along with her was a definite NO. She still was angry with him and trusting him was very difficult. However, he was the better choice for several reasons. He was more capable in this violent world she found herself. She believed that he would be better if a crisis came up and she was convinced that a crisis would arrive before her journey ended. In short, he would be more protective of her, and she would feel less guilt if he ended up in harm's way since he put himself in the position all on his own. She reminded herself that Paolo seemed to be in this only for himself. What would happen if they found the lock the key fit and discovered the secrets it held? Would he just leave her and try to profit on those secrets without her?

Carlo loved her and since she had spurned him was it even fair for her to ask him to go with her? She was still confused about her relationship with him. Something inside had given up on it, but she was not sure what that something was. She felt a subtle guilt when around him, but again was unclear what that was about. She really needed to sort it out, but now… she had to decide.

Her ex-lover was someone she knew she could trust. He was smart and capable in so many ways. Would he be up to the task of dealing with any danger they might encounter on this next part of the adventure? Could he deal with the cabal and protect her or would she just be getting into a situation that would kill them both? Funny, she still felt protective of him. She would never forgive herself if something happened to him. Then, she would be responsible for two people she cared about dying.

She slept little that night. To complicate her decision even further she was fearful how the one not chosen would react.

Morning arrived all too soon, and she was still not sure which way to go. The two men had a tentative truce between each other, and she wanted to do anything but make this decision while sitting with them. However, there was no way out. At breakfast while all three were around the same table she decided to decide.

"Thaddaeus came to me last night and told me what to do next. He said again that I must pick one person to accompany me on this next portion and since it is just the three of us here it must be one of you. Please understand, I cannot pick both of you. Otherwise, I would."

Paolo spoke immediately, "You must pick me. I am the only one who can help you if we get into trouble."

"That's bullshit." Carlo stood up while shouting this.

Paolo responded and before a moment's breath, they were on each other. Each man swung in earnest. Paolo finally grabbed Carlo in mid-swing and wrestled him onto the ground where they rolled over each other punching and grabbing.

Lisa screamed for help and this time several monks came running to break up the two men. Lisa then ran out of the room exclaiming, "I can't believe this."

Later, she visited each of her companions separately. She admonished them and asked them both to accept her decision. She consoled each by informing them that she would share everything she found with the one who was left behind when she returned.

Later still, she asked both men to come together in the dining area where she pulled out two pieces of paper, one of which had an X written on it. "The one who picks the X comes with me while the other has to wait for us." Crumbling the papers without anyone seeing which paper was marked with an X, she put a paper in each hand and held both hands behind her back. Turning to Paolo she asked him to pick. "If you get the X I go with you, otherwise I go with Carlo."

Without hesitation Paolo picked. It's in your left hand. Bringing that out from around her back she opened it. It was blank.

Looking at Carlo she said that they were to leave tonight with gear the monks would provide. Turning toward Paolo she said, "I was warned Paolo that you are not to try to follow us — they will know. Please just tell me where I can reach you when we finish this."

Very, very, reluctantly Paolo told her where he planned to be in Dharamsala. He then got up and left without saying good-bye.

52

*O*n that first day after being left in the desert, Marco found a little shade. He slept in that shade the whole day venturing out as dusk set in. He knew that his only hope of surviving was to head west and so he oriented himself via the stars in that direction. His survival skills were honed during his days as a French Foreign Legion member. The fools left him enough water and he rationed it well. He was sure that he would walk out of this hell, although after the third day of walking and not finding enough vegetation holding desert water, he began to question his confidence.

His water had run out after the second day. Toward the end of that third day the terrain changed enough to bring him into an area with cacti that had some juice. Just as his thirst was becoming unbearable, he spotted the plants that would keep him alive.

Even though he slept during the day in the shadow of large boulders, his whole body felt the sting of the burns he sustained from the sun's radiation.

Several more days heading west came and went. More cacti with life supporting water gave him the surety he needed to keep going. He was starving, but knew that he could maintain this condition for at least another week before a deadly weakness set in.

After eight days, Marco could not believe that he still had not reached some sort of border to his environment. He was weaker *than he thought he would be and was beginning to hallucinate. This was not good, and he began to doubt that he could continue much further.*

On the arrival of the tenth night he began to rise from his resting position, but he faltered. He couldn't get up and knew that he was in trouble. He thought, "Fuck, how could a bunch of amateurs take me down?" He didn't want to die but he was resigned to it, and in some ways, more troubled by the way he would go out. Closing his eyes, he stayed by his rock in a prone position.

Throughout the night he bounced back and forth from simply resigning himself to his fate and wanting to seek revenge as a way of correcting his error and sloppy work that allowed his friend to die.

His eyes were encrusted with cooked tears. In the morning he managed to open them a slit, only to see another mirage. Although this mirage was different. He saw a small group of desert wanderers with camels coming toward him. He knew it could not be possible.

Sometime later he woke up in a tent and began to realize that his mirage was far more real than anything he could have imagined. He was found!

After his initial sigh of relief his next thought was to find his enemies.

Maria and I had been back for about four months. Everything was going great as far as I was concerned, until I began noticing little changes in our relationship.

At first, they were very subtle. Maria's mother who would usually eat dinner with us seldom came to the meals. I also started to realize that Maria was not talking much about her family any longer; especially, about her family in Europe.

When we returned from Europe, we often spoke about her family. I frequently brought up the topic of her uncle. She was very forthcoming until this gap happened. She became reluctant to talk to me about Uncle Gino, or about any correspondence she might have had from her family.

My relationship with Joey was still the same. We connected especially around sports, and he confided in me easily. Even though I never thought of having a child of my own, I truly enjoyed being Joey's big brother or even may I dare say his stepfather.

The one thing that never happened was a response from Uncle Gino to my letters. I kept wondering why. I kept feeling that somehow my story might be hitting too close to home. I obsessively began pondering how that could be.

Paolo left Dharamsala and went to Delhi. He had no connections there but theorized that he could lose himself amidst the bustle of the city for a time and it was advantageous that it was not that far away from the area where he left Lisa and Carlo.

He understood why Lisa took Carlo with her instead of him, yet he knew that her choice was a mistake and one he hoped would not be disastrous.

His real concern, however, was why they had not heard anything of the cabal in the four weeks since the killings at the Madras house. By now, he was sure that they must have eyes on them, although he had not seen any evidence of their presence yet.

One thing he knew is that they would be coming soon. He only hoped that Lisa and Carlo were far enough away in no man's land and that Thaddaeus had enough support through his organization to protect them for at least a while.

Before leaving the monastery, he thought about secretly venturing onto the path they were to follow, but because of the monk's warning he chose not to.

I hate to sit and wait, he thought. That's why he convinced himself to check out any writings he might find to show him the monasteries located in the area that the Italians traveled toward. He might be able to take another route and keep a watch on them from afar.

53

Upon entering the path that was led by the monk they hiked continuously upward that first day. Late in the day they entered the snowline and continued up from there. Both Carlo and Lisa thought they would reach the other monastery that first day. They found themselves on the side of the mountain as dusk approached and the monk informed them through hand signals and gestures that they were to set up camp for the night.

They each had a single person tent and their own individual camping stove that they used to create a campsite while the monk indicated that he would be fine spending the night outside under the very cold stars. After setting up their makeshift camp they cooked some vegetable stew previously provided to them on the individual burners and they settled down for the night.

The monk woke them the next day at first light. They began packing up and without any food started climbing the mountain.

Looking at Lisa, Carlo showed worry on his face. Lisa for her part managed to keep herself composed, but within she was as concerned as her companion. How far did they have to go she wondered, as she managed to plod onward, step-by-step.

The monk did not speak as he led them onward.

Early afternoon that second day they seemed to reach a plateau as the incline disappeared and a horizontal trek began. On this flatter path they stopped to have some cold provisions they were given. The high pass through the mountain wasn't long, and they came to an overlook that presented the view of a deep valley below them. In the middle of that valley, they could see what they knew to be a large building, although from their perspective it looked tiny.

They began their descent to what was obviously their goal. The snow was quite high so the procession was slow and they didn't get very far before the monk gestured for them to stop and set up camp, meaning for them to spend a second night outside in the mountains.

At this point both of them were cold and exhausted, and if they hadn't been aware that their destination was not far they would have been troubled indeed.

As it was, they had hardly spoken to each other throughout the trip, basically keeping their conversations limited to their present situation and surviving it. At times those long silent periods became uncomfortable for both ex-lovers.

It was a blessing when they finally reached the monastery situated high in the Himalayas.

Upon arrival they both were brought to the abbot. He directed his monks to show them to their sleeping cells where they both promptly plopped down in exhaustion. Neither of them woke up until the next morning.

Morning came and after a small bite to eat they anxiously waited to be brought back before the abbot. They sat together in Carlo's cell as Lisa came to him looking for some connection.

Carlo was the first to speak. "You don't have to say anything. I am just glad that you chose me to come with you rather than that slime ball Paolo. The truth of the matter is I don't understand why it was a question that you would pick him. What has he done to convince you to trust him?"

"I don't want to talk about Paolo right now," she interrupted. "I want to talk about you and me."

"*You have already made 'you and me' abundantly clear,*" he blurted out.

"*Carlo, I know you're angry with me and you have every right to be. I closed off to you and still haven't given you a clear reason why. That's because I still don't know why myself. Something happened in Athens and maybe I need to talk it out with you more to understand it myself. Right now, I can't stay closed off to you and I don't want you to stay closed off to me; especially in this situation. Can we be open to each other? I promise that we will talk about you and I more fully whenever we complete this crazy trip.*"

"*I don't know, Lisa, I am still hurt, and I am still in love with you. While I'm drawn to help and protect you, I am also angry and confused. It's hard to stay open with all that is going on inside of my head,*" he admitted.

"*Please, Carlo, I need you. I don't know where this trek is leading to, and I am scared for both of us.*"

At that moment, one of the monks came to get them. He indicated that they should follow him. As they got up to do so Carlo grabbed Lisa's hand, squeezed it, and then let it go.

The abbot was sitting in meditation at his personal altar when they were ushered into his room. Along with their guide they both stood and waited for the head monk to finish his inward journey.

It took about five minutes before their summoner got up and turned to face them.

"*Welcome to our humble home,*" he started. "*Please plan to stay here for two days before going further into the mountains where your quest will take you. While you are here, I ask you to be respectful of our daily schedule. I will not ask you to meditate with us nor do any other of our daily routines other than have meals with us every morning and evening. It has been suggested that you should pass your time reading some specific scrolls from our library. Lama Dhyan, will help you with that since the writing has to be translated, and many of the drawings need to be explained. He will also help you with any of your physical needs while staying here. May the blessing of a thousand Buddhas be upon you."*

With that they were dismissed into the care of the lama who then led them away to a large hall that held many desks and chairs arranged in the form of a Star of David. He motioned for them to sit and proceeded to leave them there.

The two Italians immediately began talking. "What do you think is happening? I mean, I wasn't aware that we would have to go on further from here. How many monasteries will we have to go to?" Carlo said this all without taking a breath.

"I have no idea what's happening," was all that Lisa managed to respond before opening the door. Lama Dhyan returned carrying more than several scrolls that he gently laid down on the desk before his two charges.

Lisa jumped just a little when the previously silent lama opened his mouth and in a deep baritone voice explained to them in completely unaccented Italian, they were to start by reading the manuscript he began opening. He explained that he would read it to them since the writing was in ancient Sanskrit.

At first, they were perplexed because the first few paragraphs were nothing but devotional Buddhist chants. It wasn't until the middle of that scroll that they began to realize that they were about to listen to something few on the planet had ever been gifted to know.

The monk's rich tone began to explain that what was about to be presented came from prior writings much more ancient than the one he was presently reading. These prior musings were in fact very ancient indeed as they indicated that they stemmed back thousands of years in the past. As he went on the idea of thousands of years became clearer to mean tens if not hundreds of thousands of years in antiquity.

Lisa and Carlo often shook their heads in disbelief as the lama went on reading.

Tens of thousands of years or more in the past, the earth was populated by humanoids not unlike but at the same time quite different from present day Homo sapiens. The writings painted a picture of multitudes of these humanoids roaming the hills and fields of ancient Earth and that among them were others who came from the stars. These others were not gods as one would often hear about through tribal legend, but other types of intelligent living beings who quite literally came from other parts of the galaxy.

The scroll painted a picture of several very technologically advanced types of creatures that originated on more than one location in the Milky Way. It did not tell exactly from where any of these creatures came from, just that they did not originate from Earth.

Although they clearly were portrayed as not gods as anyone would imagine a god to be, they were so highly advanced in technology that they might as well have been gods, especially when compared to the primitive humanoids populating the planet at the time.

Lama Dhyan at this point put down the third scroll he had been reading and asked his wards to excuse him as he had a duty to perform in the meditation hall. They were instructed to study the drawings found on the three manuscripts he had read until he returned.

"What do you make of all this?" Lisa asked her companion.

Carlo responded with a shrug and turned to the drawing left for them. Some of the drawings were pictures of what appeared to be star constellations of which he could not possibly understand. Then there were drawings that looked like vehicles of some kind. These brought to his mind their two Indian friends and their research.

"I bet you Anand and Sita would love to see these pictures. Maybe they could make more sense of them than I can," he continued.

Finally, he began studying what looked like depictions of cities of some kind. They were very unlike any city he was aware of. First, they all were made in a circular fashion. They were several concentric circles that had what looked like moats between them. Land surrounding water surrounding land. Then the buildings were made quite differently from any he was used to seeing. There were buildings completely spiral in shape and some with extremely high peaks coming to a point. Many of the buildings looked transparent as if they were completely made of glass.

"Some of these buildings, Lisa, look as if they would be impossible to make," he said.

She could only agree with him as she too was at a loss as to what to make of all the pictorial sketches.

They studied them for over an hour until a monk called them for tea.

After tea, Lama Dhyan came and brought them back to the library where he continued with his bizarre history lesson.

He began reciting from a new set of scrolls that explained that before these ancient humanoids they had been introduced to, there were other even more ancient peoples roaming the earth going back many millions of years. Of these the texts only said that their civilization was advanced beyond the understanding of present-day man.

This information was given in the writing to help explain to the reader that life on earth has gone through a vast number of cycles throughout the planet's existence.

The next bit of wisdom came as quite a shock, especially to Carlo.

Current man was created by the ancient astronauts from other worlds using the humanoids existing on the planet and their own DNA. They would combine the two different strands in various and multiple ways; experimenting with creating different types of hybrids until they finally settled on what we now think of as modern man.

Both Italians asked the lama what was meant by DNA. He told them that he did not know, but he was told it would be discovered in the coming years.

It was becoming late, and the lama put away the scrolls before taking the duo back to their respective cells. He did not even allow them to stay together, but insisted that they retreat to their own spaces until called for supper.

Supper came and went without having much of a chance to talk since meals were taken in silence. It wasn't until the morning when they met after breakfast in the library with the lama that they had a chance to say something to each other.

At this point, Lisa asked Lama Dhyan what they were being given all this information for. Both Italians turned toward him expecting some response. None came as he laid down the scrolls in his arms and picked one up and opened it. The history lesson simply went on.

Lisa and Carlo learned that the other worldly beings had produced their hybrid off-springs in order to be slave labor for their needs. They needed a more intelligent humanoid to do their bidding. In general, this was everything from farming, mining, as well as caring for their children and households.

At first, they made them in such a way that they could not reproduce, but somewhere in time these aliens had a falling out within their own group and splintered off from one another. One of the splinter groups thought it more efficient if the hybrids could reproduce and replenish their stock and thus that ability was given to some of them.

What the aliens did not intend was that they should multiply so quickly, but that is exactly what happened. As the history goes on for thousands of years humanoids did grow to much larger numbers than their makers intended. The story stopped here for tea again and did not continue until the afternoon.

The afternoon session started with Lama Dhyan explaining that in the morning the duo was to leave the monastery and trek on to their next destination.

After this instruction the lama continued his reading. For long periods of time the new man was left to develop, but the aliens from time to time would add modifications into their creations to help develop more physical, mental or spiritual characteristics. It went on this way with man developing into more aware and knowledgeable beings until their numbers truly frightened some of the group that were against making reproductive beings in the first place. They decided that they needed to destroy this creation and amongst themselves decided on the method to use to accomplish this feat.

The lama stopped his narrative and bid them a safe and prosperous journey as he would not see them again.

After dinner they were again led to their respective cells and in the morning issued travel clothing and provisions to go back into the mountains.

Leaving the monastery with a different monk as guide, they began a journey that first descended and then ascended the peaks surrounding them in majestic splendor.

The first day was mild with brilliant warming sunlight and camping out was more pleasurable than they previously had remembered. However, the second day the clouds gathered, and a sudden storm dumped many inches of snow, obliterating the path they had just traversed. It did not seem to disturb the monk's sense of direction so onward they went.

In the late afternoon of the second day they were ascending toward a mountain pass that was in view. As the snow stopped, a loud pop rang out from a position above them. They all looked up, and just as the monk screamed for them to take cover a second pop arose. The monk fell into the snow that quickly turned red with his blood.

Carlo and Lisa were crouched behind rocks looking at each other recognizing their inevitable end.

"There is someone shooting at us from above," he yelled to Lisa.

54

Recently, I was spending less time with Maria and her family and I began to feel an aversion to sitting on her stoop. The vibe I sensed there was not very welcoming. A few times I asked her if something had changed with her feelings toward me. She acted as if I was crazy, but I could not ignore the unsaid messages I was getting, even though the sex we were having was still more than great.

An aloneness settled in that I only experienced once or twice in my life. The aloneness one can feel when being together with another or others is the most profound sense of being alone there is.

While on one of my many trips to India, I found myself living far away from the ashram in an area of the city away from others of the community. I became very ill there. Lying on my bed all alone and not sure if I would live or die, I entered the first deep state of aloneness I can remember. The space was not frightening and in fact it brought up a mystical connection with the whole of the universe.

This aloneness I was going through now was not very comfortable or enlightening even with the occasional great sex. I needed to confront this immediately.

With that in mind I went to Maria's house without calling or informing her in any way that I was coming. It was early in the morning, and I knew that she would be there.

She answered the doorbell and asked me what I was doing there so early. I told her that we needed to talk.

There was a reluctance to let me in when she asked if it couldn't wait until later, but I insisted and she came outside.

Sitting together on the stoop I told her that I needed to know what was going on. This time, seeing the resolve in my eyes she did not deny the problem, but what she had to say was quite shocking to me.

"My uncle is the problem," she admitted. "He has told my mother and I in no uncertain terms that we are not to encourage this relationship, and that if I continued to do so he would have to cut us off from the family."

"What?" I was incredulous.

"I don't know what to do," she continued. "That's why I have been distant lately. I have been corresponding with him asking him why he is so insistent on this, but I have not gotten any satisfactory answer. My thinking was that I could just bide my time and that this would all go away, especially if I got some distance from you, but that is not working. Prem, I don't know what to do. I don't want to lose my family connection, but I care about you and Joey cares about you." Tears were welling up in her eyes.

"This has something to do with the secret your family is keeping, doesn't it?" I asked.

Her response was that she honestly didn't know as her uncle would not tell her what it was about. After some more speculation, she admitted to her belief that I was right.

I then shared with her that I thought that somehow, I was hitting a nerve with her uncle through my story. Not being able to explain how or why, I became convinced that what I had been writing dovetailed closely with what Maria's family was involved in and now her uncle wants her to cut ties with me all together.

"That's impossible," she kept saying.

Yet somehow, I knew that it was. I began to want to understand more of just how the impossible could be possible.

"Look Maria, I am falling in love with you. I think you know that, but I don't want to be the reason you become estranged from your family. If you really think it best, I will leave you alone, at least for a while. I'll leave you alone until I finish my book. You decide."

"I don't want to," she began. "But perhaps if we take a little break my uncle will come around. In the meantime, I will insist that he tell me what this is all about. Although so far, he is not willing to even tell my mother. By the way, she also thinks it has something to do with this cursed task my family has carried over the centuries."

"Maybe you could finish that book of yours quickly," she said as she kissed me and then got up to go inside.

I began to write in earnest at my own kitchen table from that point onward.

Although they were pinned down, they seemed to be protected from being hit while behind the rocks. They heard several more pops and a couple of pings on the rock barrier they were behind, and then nothing until darkness settled in.

"We've got to move from here," Carlo whispered, and with that utterance he got up and raced to another rock covering up the trail. Nothing happened, and he beckoned to Lisa to follow. In this way they moved further up the trail until they rounded an outcropping that shielded them completely from the view.

They continued to race up along the trail, not stopping until they had advanced a half a mile forward. There they found a small cave hidden on a ledge above the trail. The opening, of which was covered by bushes. They entered it.

Above them a well provisioned Marco was situated on his own cliff shelf searching for his targets. He realized that they had moved from their original position, and knew that it wouldn't take long for him to find them. Anyway, they couldn't get far on the mountain trail without him seeing them. He had tracked them using the intelligence that the cabal had given him. Now, his revenge would be secure and his job over.

55

*A*nand and Sita reached Delhi within a week after leaving the monastery. They intended to go straight home, but luckily met a close neighbor in the market just outside their neighborhood who asked them what happened at their house.

Apparently, the house had been swarming with police for the past several days. The constables had not allowed anyone entry into the house, nor would they answer any questions about what they were doing.

Sita deflected the friends' concerns with a fabricated robbery story, and then they found a restaurant to discuss what to do.

"I'm afraid Anand," Sita sighed. "We can't go back to the house."

"We must go back," Anand returned. "Otherwise, we will be running forever."

"If we go to the police, they will arrest us, Anand. Even if we can convince them that it was done in self-defense, we will be restrained one way or another for a long time. I can't do that. Besides, how do we convince them that she tried to kill us when we buried the two bodies and left? We must run."

"Oh Sita, where can we go where they will not find us?"

"We must go to Dharamsala and find Lisa. We can only clear ourselves if she discovers the secret and gives us an explanation as to why all this mystery and intrigue happened. It is the only *chance we have. Please." They were on the next train back to Dharamsala.*

Marco traveled cautiously up the path. He did not want to risk revealing himself to those he was pursuing. It was snowing and he could see some of their tracks, but the snow would soon cover them. Still, he was in no rush. After all, how long could they last on the side of this mountain without much in food or water?

Soon their footprints were completely covered so he kept to the path skillfully marked by the lamas who had been using it for centuries. Even though he was moving slowly, he went right by the cave the Italians were sheltered in as the level of snow made it much more difficult to see.

Lisa and Carlo huddled at the cave entrance where they could see a very small portion of the trail. It was from this vantage point that they saw Marco going by their position and continuing further up the trek.

They had no idea it was Marco. All they could see was someone in furs with a hood over his or her head, and the rifle their pursuer was carrying.

"We're safe for now," Carlo said, "and hopefully he continues on the road forever. I wish I had a gun," he continued. "The only thing we can do is wait here until dark, and then go back to the monastery we came from."

They had enough food and water for a day or maybe a day and half if they rationed. The trek back to the monastery would stretch their resources, but they could make it.

Lisa looked into Carlo's eyes and tears formed. She wrapped her arms around his shoulders and cried. He held her for what seemed to be forever. He felt such deep love in those moments and such deep sadness because of that love.

Lisa did not let go of Carlo for a long time and when she did, she brought her lips to his and kissed him without thought. She was pure emotion in that kiss, feeling a sense of finality and longing she had not realized she had been holding back since Athens.

That night they zipped their sleeping bags together and their body heat soared as they made love for the first time not knowing if it would be for the last time.

In the morning Lisa woke first with her head propped up on one elbow. She stayed that way staring at her lover until he opened his eyes.

"I have been such a fool Carlo," she softly cried. "My fear of hurting you and possibly losing you was so great that I even fooled myself into believing that I didn't love you. Can you ever forgive me?"

Carlo answered her with only a tender kiss that led to a passionate embrace that led to fierce coupling answering the question and affirming the first wasn't the last. It was passionate and tender, but it was not long.

Afterwards, Carlo got up and told Lisa that they had to go quickly.

He looked out at the small section of the path they could see and saw no movement. "We need to start back now if we stand any chance of making it back at all, but we need to eat something first."

Before leaving their sanctuary, they ate a chapati and beans and downed a mouthful of water. The snow had ceased falling during the night and was fresh and clean on the trail below.

As they came upon the trail Carlo exclaimed, "Damn!" He could see that there were footprints coming from up the path going back to the monastery from which they had come. Their pursuer had backtracked sometime during the night or early morning. Now, they were forced to go forward onto the next monastery wherever that might be.

"We don't know if we have enough food and water to make it to the next monastery," Lisa worried.

"The monks provided us with what we have, and I am sure they would have given us enough to make it. We only spent an extra night so if we ration, we will make it if whoever is trying to kill us doesn't catch up to us again. Let's hurry," Carlo responded. They started on their way.

In his pursuit of the couple, Marco began to feel confused. He had traveled through the night to catch up to them, but realized they couldn't have gone so far without him seeing them. At that point he doubled back. Where were they? The snow was clean. He knew he must have missed something. He reversed course once again going out toward the original trek while scanning more carefully the area surrounding the path. He spotted the cave the second time around and approached it carefully.

His rifle ready, he breached the cave entrance only to find some fallen food on the cave floor. They had been here. Sure enough, he discovered new footprints in the snow that were not there when he first backtracked. He knew that he would find them and finish his goal of killing them. Determined, he quickened his pace.

The writing process has an ebb and flow to it. At times words come out with great urgency and with an ease that truly amazes me. At other times the process is like slogging through thick mud with every word posing a challenge to overcome that is just as amazing to comprehend.

Lately, the latter has been my experience. It seemed that writing at my kitchen table just wasn't as easy as sitting on Maria's stoop. I put this down to being the case simply because I enjoyed looking out at the sparkling sun shimmering on Chelsea Bay. Whatever the reason, I did miss sitting on those steps, but with all the tension developing between Maria, her family and I, I just couldn't go there.

As I pondered the situation with Maria and her family, my mind wandered with questions about what was going to happen between her and I. She was definitely not happy with her uncle and his insistence to break us apart, but at the same time she was acting strangely around me. I realized that her family had a great influence on her decision. Her mother seemed to be deferring to her brother.

If their secret was anything like what I had imagined to be in my book I could understand why, but my feelings were still very hurt despite that understanding.

I must continue to write and finish the story just to bring some resolution to my relationship and possibly some understanding as to what exactly was going on with its weird connection to Lisa's family.

56

It took the better part of the day, but Marco finally spotted his targets. They had a significant lead on him and were too far ahead for him to be able to take a shot. It wouldn't be long now, although he worried that they might be getting close to the next monastery.

Marco's view of them kept appearing and disappearing as the trail was winding. He hurried his pace realizing that within fifteen minutes what he feared would come into his awareness, and just as he had suspected, his fear became a reality. Walking around the bend, he got a good clear sight of the two Italians. Further ahead, the serpent-like trail progressed downward. Less than a mile away in the valley there was another monastery; their obvious destination. He was still out of rifle range, but if he moved faster, he believed he could start picking them off in another two-hundred yards.

Lisa felt an overwhelming relief when she glimpsed the monastery below, but that quickly became terror as Carlo looked backward toward the trail that they had previously passed and eyed their pursuer fast approaching them.

Mountain passes in the Himalayas can be very narrow and if you go over the edge, it's over. Lisa and Carlo were coming up to such a pass. There was no cover for them to hide from the shooter. They couldn't go back, and their only chance was to get by the treacherous path that lay 150 yards ahead. The difficult stretch was about 500 yards in length before it widened and presented some natural cover for them.

All these calculations went through the minds of the hunter and those being hunted. They weren't going to make it unless the shooter was completely inept, and Marco wasn't.

"We need to move as fast as we can," Lisa shouted. "Stay low and look at your feet. Maybe we can make it."

Lisa was in front, and she hit the precarious trail first. Carlo was right behind staying as low as he could and moving as fast as he could without overrunning his companion. They were fine for the first 100 yards but then a shot rang out and Carlo felt a sting in his left leg. Luckily, he was able to maintain his balance as the bullet must have only grazed him.

"Go on," he screamed. "Try to make it."

"No," she shouted "There is no way and I'm not leaving you to die alone. I love you."

Then a second shot rang out, but to the surprise of the two Italians they were not hit nor was there any bullet spray from the rock around them. Looking back, they realized that the shot was aimed at their purser and seemed to come from above them. Bullets began to ricochet around their nemesis who tried to return gunfire, but soon turned back down the path to seek cover. They were now out of his range.

Although in some pain Carlo was able to forge ahead. They both scrambled along the path heading down toward the monastery below. As they made their way, they heard several more shots ring out from what seemed to be two different firearms. Then there was silence.

The path widened and Lisa helped Carlo walk as he was losing blood. Lisa was scared for his life, but there was no need. After resting for five minutes she managed to use part of her shirt to make a bandage and stop the bleeding that was dripping from a very shallow nick on his thigh. They were going to make it, but what just happened was a mystery. Who saved them?

Another two hours and they were at the door of a temple cut out of a mountain shelf. Two sides and the roof were mountains with only a sculptured façade. They were let in and helped by several monks who dressed Carlo's wound and fed them before bringing them to the abbot.

Most people on our planet have no idea of what *being* is. Although they are *being* every moment of their existence while living, they are asleep. At the most they glimpse it here and there as an awe-inspiring experience, such as watching a particularly beautiful sunset or having a particularly intense orgasm. However it only remains an experience, not an understanding that this is who they are.

I am walking by Revere Beach on a cloudless day imbibing the twinkle of the sun on the ocean and no longer am I witnessing the scene, but I have become it; not even knowing that I have become it – 'is-ness' as usual.

I remember spending countless days sitting in Buddha Hall at the ashram and listening to Bhagwan attempt to draw his audience into a state of *being*. As it was, only a few of us could go there with any awareness, although in time many of his disciples, I hope, became familiar with their presence rising into it more and more in their everyday life. I wonder if Lisa and Carlos having such a close brush with death realized their 'being-ness' and were transformed.

The abbot received his two guests in the library. He sat quietly watching them as they entered and took their seats across from him.

"Something has changed in you Carlo," he knew his name.

"How would you know that?" Carlo asked.

"I can see it in your aura," was the response. *"Who are you?" The monk queried.*

"When I got shot and I was sure of my own death I ceased to be, only everything was there, and I was that which was

everything. I can only say that I am, which doesn't make any sense I know, but that is all I can say."

"It makes perfect sense," explained the abbot. "This 'knowing' is what many of us in these temples strive to attain, and it is the basic realization of the extraterrestrials you have been introduced to in the last monastery."

"That did not happen to me," Lisa interrupted.

"I know," the monk said. "Someday it will, and when it does you will not just understand, but will be what these enlightened other worldly beings already are."

"What do we do now?" she asked.

"Someone is obviously looking out for you. There is nothing we can do at this moment, so you need to continue with your search. There is more for you to learn here and there is one more destination to journey to in order to finish it," was his response.

The couple were given food and shown to their respective cells. This time the cells were next to each other and when left alone they came together in Lisa's room.

"I can't do this Carlo. This is crazy."

"I wish I could be happy with saying 'I told you so' but it's not doing it for me right now. It's too late to do anything except go forward and trust our host to help us out of this mess. Do you have any idea what just happened? Obviously, the cabal is trying to kill us, but who interrupted their attempt? Could it be the Unknowing Organization?"

"I have not the slightest idea, but I hope we find out before we must leave this place," Lisa answered. "Both our would-be murderer and savior are probably still out there unless one of them killed the other. If that happened, I hope to God it was our pursuer who lies in the snow, but with my luck it is probably the other way around."

As she was uttering these words Marco was able to fall back down the trail to find cover from whoever was shooting at him. It couldn't be anyone from the monastery his targets managed to reach. The monks didn't own guns. Who the fuck could be way out here and how would they know he would be? It didn't matter. He had to get away from his disrupter and set up another ambush for when that sonofabitch couple would re-emerge from the monastery. For that he would need to climb, but he couldn't move until it was dark enough to go unnoticed.

Paolo had been waiting on a ledge in front of the monastery for a day and a half. It was lucky that he chose to pick this monk retreat and not the first one the Italians visited. He knew that they would never make it without his help so the first thing he did in Dharamsala was research maps showing the likely monasteries his friends would be trekking to. It was obvious where they would be going; it was just a matter of where to catch up to them.

He was lucky, but he had to pat himself on the back because he was better than lucky. He also had to admit that it was really a great decision on Lisa's part not picking him otherwise he could not have secured his rifle and pistol. Without him, whoever was out there trying to finish this would have. Furthermore, he realized that he would have been the one on the path defenseless and by now dead. His ability to stay alive and get what he wanted was indeed due to luck, but more so due to his skillful maneuvering.

From his vantage point Paolo could see that there was only one enemy out there. He or she had moved back down the trek and was now behind excellent cover and could move further to a place he would be unable to know about. He needed to withdraw closer to the monastery and keep vigilant as to where this shooter might pop up again.

While taking his new position Paolo thought about going into the monastery and announcing himself but nixed the idea. First, he might screw up the search by breaking the rule which only allowed Lisa one companion, and then it would be more advantageous to protect the two Italians if his location remained unknown to whomever was out there.

Unexpectedly, Maria's cousin wrote her a message that she wanted to visit her and her mother and that she would arrive within a week. She asked if they could pick her up at the airport and if she could possibly stay with them while she was in Boston. Although it would be cramped, Maria could not say no to her family so she would work out an arrangement to put her cousin up in the crowded apartment.

"Why do you think she wants to come now?" I asked on one of our more infrequent visits with each other.

"Not sure, but I can hear you thinking that it has something to do with that mysterious book you are writing," she answered. "You know, you're probably right. She never expressed an interest in coming here before. Damn! How could it be possible that what you are writing has anything at all to do with my family? How is it possible it could have anything to do with its secret or anything else my family is involved with? It is just so ridiculous, yet it seems to be testing me and this relationship in general."

Maria had never opened up this much about the stress she was under due to her family's coldness to me and my venture.

"The other day, my mother was on a roll and told me that in no uncertain terms her brother was dead set against our relationship because it was a threat to our family's legacy, and she asked me to end it. When I asked her how it was a threat, she said that she did not know, but her brother was adamant about it and that she could only surmise that it had to do with his secret. Then she went into an explanation that her mother had sat down with all the children at one time or another and told them that they had to listen to their elder brother when it came to helping him keep the family's great task. Neither her nor her other siblings were told what that was, only that they had to help maintain the family secret."

"My mother implied as well that it was my responsibility to help Uncle Gino uphold this legacy. Prem, I just don't know what to do. I'm falling in love with you, but this family thing is very important, maybe even more important than our relationship."

"Please don't decide anything yet." I asked. "All this pressure on you tells me that what I have been writing is very close if not spot on with your uncle's ancient secret. This cannot be a coincidence and the weirdness of it is beyond anything imaginable. If I am writing about coming out with something that is existentially real, maybe it is time that it is to be revealed to the world. Let's wait and see what your cousin has to say."

They ate and slept fitfully that night. Upon waking they both refused food, but took tea and asked to be led to the abbot who saw them immediately.

"I will take you to our library, myself," he said upon receiving them. "I need to share more of our scrolls with you. These will take you at least two days to review and digest."

They found themselves in a room filled with rolled up parchments. Once again, they were presented with scrolls that needed a translator to decipher the writings in Sanskrit.

The abbot proceeded to read.

The aliens had come here hundreds of thousands of years ago, if not millions of years ago. The book was unclear as to this point. It was so far back that it was a moot point how far back it really was. There were many aliens that arrived over millennia of time. Some of these species were aggressive and self-centered while most were friendly and compassionate.

Most shared their technology with the creatures of this planet and as stated before genetically sculptured those creatures to eventually become present day Homo sapiens.

Many alterations were made and discarded until we have modern human beings. At this juncture the abbot added that soon scientists will unearth a multitude of human types that history never knew existed; all completely different species, yet all human in one way or another.

He continued, that for the most part all the aliens understood the universe to be alive and conscious - a being in and of itself. In their view the basic structure of existence was one of wholeness or oneness.

The pages further explained that our sense of separateness is an illusion that is maintained by our physical brains coupled with a form of hypnosis that makes the underpinnings of how physical reality works.

They explained further that the cosmos was nothing but vibratory energy and that everything in it vibrated at various rates of oscillation. Depending on the state of a being's personal consciousness level the energy itself is perceived differently. Whereas, a human may see a chair, some of these aliens vibrating at a different frequency may see a ball of green light or fluctuating wave pattern, or even something beyond our limited imagination.

Furthermore, humans are not necessarily trapped in physical reality as they are accustomed to it, but have the power to vibrate differently and begin to see the universe's energy patterns in a completely different way.

The scrolls suggested that life is everywhere. We are not alone and have never been alone. We are not even remotely unique, and we are not separate from that which we perceive around us.

This point seemed to be an important one. The abbot took another parchment and continued more deeply on this theme of not being separate.

Imagine as you sit here reading these words with whomever is in the room that it is a completely whole activity, the text challenges the reader. All who are in the room are interconnected with each other. The book is nothing but an aspect of you, the reader. Just as you, the reader is an aspect of the book itself. Everyone listening to what is being read is contributing to the consciousness and energy that is expressing itself in the moment. You are all the players in the room whether appearing inanimate, animate, or in any other way. They could not exist in this moment without you, nor could you exist in this moment without them.

The abbot stopped his reading. "We need to take a break."

The day had gone by as if in a moment. It was supper time.

57

The alien idea had not come to me at first. This was to be a novel with only a criminal organization as the protagonist, but other worldly images kept popping into my thinking so much so that they found their way onto the page.

During that period, I was spending less time with Maria. The writing became more difficult, but in the past few days since we began seeing more of each other it has been flowing quite regularly. Especially, since I have been writing on my favorite stoop again.

It is funny to watch the ebb and flow of the creative process. Perhaps, Maria acts as my muse. Her cousin is due to arrive tomorrow, and I am pouring whatever I can into this book until then.

That night the abbot collected his guests and once again brought them to the library. Instead of bringing out scrolls, however, he asked them both to sit quietly with him.

He directed them to sit on cushions provided across from him as he sat cross-legged on his own. They created a soft triangle together. He closed his eyes in meditation saying nothing else to them. After looking at each other they followed his lead and closed their eyes as well.

Carlo almost instantly became weightless. Just as quickly, his constantly chatting mind was silent. In that silence, he found himself looking down on the three of them, himself included. This did not appear odd or out of place for some reason, but rather natural.

He was no longer separate from what lay before him. He was all three people he was viewing, as well as the cushions, the library; everything seen and unseen. It was not even accurate to say he was these things. In truth, there was no one existing to realize this, yet a realization was happening.

This all felt to happen in an instant before Carlo opened his eyes and was greeted with a smile from the abbot and a face of wonder from Lisa. "I had hoped that you could get a glimpse of what I had been reading to you this day," said the abbot. "As it is I can see that my friend here had more than a glimpse. Perhaps before going to bed, you could share with Lisa your experience and tomorrow we will continue with the reading."

With that said, they silently stood up. Lisa and Carlo returned to their adjoining cells without saying a word. Carlo entered Lisa's room, and sat on her bunk.

"What was that all about?" she asked.

"Before I say anything, how long did we sit there?" he asked. "Also, tell me what you saw when we sat down with the monk."

"I didn't see anything, although it was pleasant to sit in the quiet of his presence. It was very relaxing, more relaxing than I have felt in a long time. We sat for a long time, perhaps forty or fifty minutes. What did you see?"

He then attempted to explain to her what had happened to him and how it made what they had been told in the reading crystal clear. He could not put it into words, but he managed to impress upon his companion the enormity of what they were being told.

"Let's put it this way," he said to her, "these aliens had a view of this existence way beyond what we are used to perceiving."

The next day once again they found themselves mid-morning in the library with the monk and scrolls in hand. The reading continued.

The singularity is an infinite possibility and using one of its possibilities called vibration begins to oscillate at different frequencies to create the illusion of many-ness just as a prism shining white light into it presents the appearance of many different colors. The universe began by creating two reflections, love and fear. Then these two reflections refracted into various other expressions. Love showed itself as compassion, trust, gentleness and caring; while fear illustrated itself as despair, loneliness, anger and aggression. To make the experience even more interesting, love could be expressed sometimes as that which is usually the refraction of fear and vice versa. Love was hidden in all fear and fear was hidden in all love because they were just one thing anyway.

The lama began reading from a scroll that seemed to be a continuation of what they had learned in the first Tibetan sanctuary.

The two factions were at odds with each other. The faction that wanted to get rid of their creation because it had gone wildly against its intended purpose. This posed a threat to the dominance of the aliens who were against the other group that wanted to save their creation and allow them to prosper in their own fashion. In short, one group was more rooted in love and the other in fear.

Each group acted in its respective ways. The destroyers diverted a comet in order for it to ram into the planet. This created floods, chaos, and killed most of the Homo sapiens living on the planet. The other group instructed a sufficient number of people needed to repopulate the planet on how to survive the tragedy. This became the story of the great flood in the various books and oral teachings throughout the world.

It was then explained that this was only one representation of the ebb and flow of the two primal vibrations of the One being throughout the millions of years in the life of planet Earth.

Those who survived began the race anew. They started as primitives once again while being helped later by the loving group of extraterrestrials. Thus, history as we have been taught was born.

The aliens had both mechanically advanced technology and psi technology. A new text provided further explanations. There were machines that helped them travel across the universe, levitate objects, move whole planets, cure diseases, create energy out of nothing, traverse long distances by walking through doorways, and much, much, more. Furthermore, they explained that much of this could also be done using psi energy, or in other words pure thought. To use psi energy a person had to be vibrating at what they termed a certain density. It seemed that many of these other worldly creatures could transcend the laws of physical reality at will.

The higher the density achieved, the closer one came to the infinite potentiality of the singularity until one merged totally with it. The consciousness that merged with itself however never lost its unique vibratory expression because that expression was forever part of the One being itself.

High density beings could do amazing things as if they were gods, and these other worldly beings were of that nature having existed for longer than anyone could imagine.

The scrolls talked about the great stone structures found in many areas around the world, such as the pyramids and Stonehenge as being built using a combination of these alien technologies. So much of our history was revealed as being directly or indirectly influenced by visitors from beyond. The history that we were taught was mostly a lie.

During the mid-afternoon session drawings of flying machines and levitating machines were shown to them to examine. Both Italians commented to each other on how much Anand and Sita would have loved to have seen these schematics. Lisa asked if she could take some of the diagrams to show her scholarly friends, but was told that she would not be allowed to do so.

By the time the abbot got up to escort them to the evening meal, Lisa and Carlo were thoroughly exhausted from having their previous perception of what life was blown away. When most of one's preconceived notions are challenged to be completely wrong, one's very ground of being is shattered. They were both trembling upon entering the dining hall.

The pair ate dinner quietly with the rest of the congregation and then went off to their cells. When it appeared that no others were in ear shot Carlo knocked and then entered Lisa's cubicle.

Before Carlo could say anything, Lisa wrapped her arms around her former lover. "Just hold me, Carlo."

They stayed entwined for quite some time. Eventually, they let go of each other. Lisa whispered, "I needed to feel as if I wasn't going crazy." She then kissed him so passionately that his response only ended when they had both climaxed in unison.

While lying there looking up at the ceiling Lisa asked, "Why are they telling us all this? I don't understand. Do you think that this is the family's secret my ancestors have been protecting all these years? If so, why was my family singled out to protect it when it is so readily available here and through these monasteries? I don't understand."

"The only thing I know is I'm sure glad you picked me to go on this part of the journey," answered Carlo. With that, another passionate kiss and they both felt a warm glow when they woke up together completely enveloped in each other's arms. They somehow had fallen asleep on Lisa's very narrow cot.

That morning, before starting the continuation of the readings, they were informed by the abbot that this was to be their last day in the monastery and that they had one more trek to make to one other temple deeper in the Himalayas.

"Your stalker has been found and we know where he is. He is being watched by another who is above him. They are both

waiting for you. We plan to send you out through a secret exit neither is in view of. We will make sure neither follows you if by some chance they discover you are gone from here," was the lama's response. "Now, we need to finish with the reading.

And so, he read to them about eons of connections between the extraterrestrial visitors and the humans that they had a hand in creating.

For more millennia then can be remembered there has been a war going on in this galaxy of ours. This war has two factions – those aliens who cling to fear and separation exalting the sense of self-centeredness and those aliens who are rooted in love and all that love vibrates as compassion, sharing, and giving.

For thousands of years the aliens have used planet Earth and its inhabitants as a stage to play out this struggle.

While there are aliens who want to control Earth's people for their own self-aggrandizement, there are those who want only to bring people closer to unity consciousness. The purest form of love is not just a vibration, but the very essence of the singularity in its wholeness. Hence, the war is often depicted as between the dark forces and the light forces. Men and women are the pawns used in the battle for eons and eons. Yet this battle is included in the wholeness of existence and is but a play allowing for existence itself to become more aware of itself.

It is the human beings on this planet that also need to become more aware of the drama that they are playing out and that is being enacted around them. The scrolls attempted to show that existence itself knows itself through the various consciousnesses of the human beings and many other aliens, animals, plants, crystals, and what we term inorganic matter that makes up the world as we know it. Consciousness is one appearing to be many through the prism of the dimensions and inter-dimensions that refract it from its essential essence.

"This is making my head spin," Lisa stopped the monk from going on with his reading. "I need to take a break."

"Me too," Carlo chimed in.

"We are almost through, and we are running out of time before we need to stop, but I will give you a moment." At that the abbot left the library promising to return shortly.

"Carlo, do you get all this?" Lisa asked.

"Definitely not all of it, but the general gist seems to be that we ordinary people have been controlled by aliens and elite humans whom they supported for a very long time, and that we are still being controlled to this day. At the same time, there are other aliens fighting against this control. I think that's it." Carlos returned.

"I agree that is what I heard, but somehow all that is a play between a singularity that is akin to our very consciousness, and that is way over my pay grade." She responded. "You're the one who experienced a feeling of oneness, do you get all of this?"

Just then the monk returned. He walked over to one of the shelves holding scrolls and picked out one small very ancient looking manuscript.

He began his interpretation:

There will come a time when the people of the world will learn of this secret and at that time the planet and all that is on it and in it will be ready to join the more advanced races of the galaxy and beyond. They will be ready to become aware of this truth and ready to understand it. There are a few keepers of these secrets with the means to convince the world of their validity. When those in this group become aware of what has been going on it will be time to reveal it to the rest of their brethren.

The abbot rolled up that which he was reading and replaced it back onto the shelf.

"Please eat and go to your cells to sleep. We will awaken you very early in the morning and you will travel to your last destination that is higher still in these peaks. 'The Man Who Does Not Know' told us to tell you that you will soon find the key you have been looking for."

"You will need to be careful even though we will detain those that are looking for you. The organization that is trying to prevent you from obtaining the key is large and knowledgeable with tentacles reaching everywhere… even here. Goodnight and good luck."

They were dismissed.

After dinner they went to their cells, but Carlo insisted on sleeping with Lisa even though the cot was not made for two bodies. "I will not let you be on your own, nor do I want to be alone. This may very well be the last night we spend alive," he said as he held her.

58

*P*aolo congratulated himself for having provisioned well before he headed into these insanely high peaks. At night even in the summer months the temperature could dip below zero degrees Fahrenheit. His last night out on the ridge he occupied was one such night. His clothing was made for such nights, and he had come with enough food and water. He may need it depending on how long the two Italians would hold up in the monastery and for how long the hitman planned to wait for them.

He had kept his adversary within his sights for quite some time, but realized as the morning sun rose that whomever it was below him had moved. This discovery did not upset Paolo because he had a commanding view of the entrance to the monastery. No one was going to be able to get in a position to fire on his friends without Paolo being able to take them out first.

All that being known, he wished that the couple would leave their safe enclosure soon and hopefully with the key they were after.

The shooter undoubtedly went back down the trail and hopefully gave up his quest although the Spaniard doubted that to be the case. In any event he would maintain his vigil on the ledge until he saw Lisa to the finish line. He really didn't care what happened to Carlo, except that he couldn't show Lisa his apathy toward her former lover.

Similar to Paolo in his determination, Marco followed his instincts and had backtracked down the previous trek. He too provided well for himself and had brought climbing gear that clearly was needed.

After spending a day and a half sheltering in place and waiting for his targets, Marco realized that he would need to first eliminate whomever it was that had him pinned down from above.

He reasoned that even if he lost the couple when they left the temple, he could pick up their trail again without losing much time. For now, he was going up to get rid of this pest.

Maria's cousin arrived that next day. Claudia was a cute petite woman with dark brown eyes and an olive complexion. She looked more southern Italian than Milanese. Bouncy and spry her smile gave the sense of fire and ice – a formidable being.

This woman's intensity showed up immediately at a dinner with Maria and I that was scheduled at her request the second night after she landed. I had made a reservation at Riso's Restaurant where we were sitting.

Claudia gave me the courtesy of first ordering drinks, but after that she peppered me with questions. "How is your book coming?" She asked.

I told her that currently it is going very well, although for an extended period in the last few months it was going slowly because the words and ideas weren't coming easily.

"Why was that?" she said while raising her eyebrows.

My answer reflected the fact that I missed writing on the stairs of Maria's apartment and the fact that there was tension between us due to Claudia's father's antagonism toward me.

"How is it flowing now?" she asked with an awkward smile.

Explaining that the storyline was pouring out of me now, I sighed with a great sense of creative overflow.

"Why do you think that is happening now?"

"It has a lot to do with writing again on my favorite stoop outside Maria's apartment and the fact that we are in less of a struggle now."

"Is that so?" Claudia commented.

"Woo, Claudia," Maria interjected. "Hold off with the interrogation."

Claudia's intense stare focused on her cousin, but was interrupted by the waiter coming to the table to ask us for our menu choices. This allowed a bit of time to break a rising tension I knew would only be revisited before the meal was finished.

I changed the subject after the waiter took our order to delay the inevitable. Questioning Claudia about how the family was back in Italy and what she was doing with her life gave us all a respite.

My diversion tactic did not last long before Claudia brought it back to the main point. "You didn't explain why writing near Maria and the family on your favorite stairs had such a beneficial effect on your progress."

"Don't know, I just feel comfortable there. Why is that so important?"

"My father wants to know if Maria didn't give you the idea about the family you write about by telling you first about her own family. Maybe she helped you with the whole story."

"I told your father when I was in Italy that Maria told me nothing," I said to Claudia.

"He finds that very hard to believe," Claudia answered.

Maria sat at the table stunned in silence until she said to her cousin – "I never told him anything until after he showed me some of his writing and then I only said that it seemed a coincidence that his main theme parroted our family situation so closely." Maria was angry.

"Perhaps, Maria, you said something to Prem during a lover's chat or just in casual conversation that you don't remember."

"No, I didn't," she responded louder than intended.

Finally, I interrupted them and demanded to be told what this whole questioning was about.

"Your story is way too close to the story of our family. Daddy thinks that somehow you have been given this information. It is just not possible for you to be able to write with such accuracy about what has been kept secret for so long. He told me to tell you that he demands that you stop writing this story."

"Hell," I quietly said. "All this is crazy. It's ludicrous that Uncle Gino would think that any of what I have sent him came from Maria. She doesn't know anything about his secret. Heck, I bet you don't know anything about it."

"No, I don't, and I don't want to know. I do know that it would be dangerous to reveal it to the world at large and I know that you need to stop telling your story before you reveal whatever the secret is."

Both Maria and I sat there shocked. Claudia then turned to her cousin and said, "Maria, Papa doesn't know that I am here. He thinks I am in the Alps, skiing. I came here to try to protect you from getting hurt." Turning toward me she continued, "And to protect you, Prem…from getting killed."

Marco was now high enough to be able to look down on his enemy. All he had to do was traverse sideways until he could find him and take him out. Of course, that was true only if whoever it was trying to ambush him was still where he had been.

59

Bhagwan was asked if aliens were visiting us. I heard him reply yes, but that we should leave the aliens alone and let them do their own thing. Even if they land in our fields, we should not bother with them.

According to fellow sannyasins I had talked to, aliens did land in our fields. One of my female friends told me that one night as she was walking home by a large empty pasture, she saw a circular vehicle humming in the middle. She had always wanted to see an extraterrestrial craft and was excited by the sight. When she went toward it however, she got more and more the feeling to stay away. She did.

On another occasion a disciple was asking the master if there were going to be any significant changes on Earth that could kill many people. His answer was rather disturbing as he told us that there would indeed be tumultuous changes happening in the future. He went on to say that many would die and that the very rich already had the means to leave the planet when that happened.

I wondered how that could be possible, but put it down to either his speculation or some device he was using in his teaching. Little did I realize that one day I would put some of these ideas in a book, and astonishingly ideas that seemed to be a threat to my girlfriend's family.

Lisa and Carlo prepared themselves for leaving the monastery. Again, they had a monk to guide them out of a tunnel that brought them to a trail far around the other side of the mountain. It seemed safe enough from whomever was waiting for them in the front of the monastery.

They trekked on a winding trail heading toward their next destination even higher up in the Himalayas. It was very cold, and the pace was slow.

Marco had traversed along the mountain until he was in sight of the area in which he knew his adversary to be hiding. Sure enough, he was still there, and was still scanning the trail below him. Unfortunately, his cover was very good and even at this height his target was small because whoever was there was protected on all sides. The sniper must be a professional which would make this more difficult to finish.

Still, with a good shot he could do it. If he only had a scope, it would be a done deal, but he had nothing but his rifle's sighting. He better not miss this chance.

Marco was always a great shot. Taking aim, he took a deep slow breath as he was taught many years ago and proceeded to pull the trigger on the small view of his target's heart. The man went down like a rock.

He got up quickly to chase after his real targets. As he stood up a shot rang out and he simultaneously felt a sting in his left shoulder. He went down. "Shit," he thought, "I'm hit." He crawled to the opening to view his enemy. There was blood around the sight where the guy was hiding, but he must have only wounded him, and damn now he was hit himself.

It was now impossible for him to get his assailant, since he had to take care of his own wound and not lose sight of the Italians. Luckily, his wound was not that bad as the bullet went right through his shoulder. He had medical supplies to deal with his situation adequately, but he didn't have the time for all this.

Hopefully, he had hurt his sniper enough to eliminate him as a threat. He could not wait to find out.

After bandaging his wound, he started down toward the back of the mountain. The organization had told him about the secret exit the monks used whenever they needed to leave unnoticed.

He had given himself a shot for the pain and proceeded along a path to find the back trail. The only question was, did they leave already, or were they still in the temple?

"How is it possible that I am writing something that mimics your ancient secret, Claudia? I am telling you that Maria told me nothing. Nothing at all."

"It doesn't matter. You're both still in trouble over this. My father will not allow you to proceed and will stop Maria, his own niece, if he must," Claudia answered. "Please go no further."

Maria was biting her lower lip as she listened to her cousin. "Perhaps, Prem, you should stop," she said.

"I cannot," was the answer.

It had been half a day since the couple left the monastery before Marco got to the secret exit. He began watching it from afar, not sure what to do. He decided to wait for the rest of the day to see if they would exit, but after several hours observing he noticed a saffron colored scarf blowing from behind a bush near the exit. It had been concealed prior to this because the wind had been nonexistent until the moment a strong breeze arose. It was a sign that they had already left. He proceeded to follow.

The monk told them that the next monastery would be reached in the morning. Considering the cold, they had been traveling at a fair pace the whole day and were happy that they only needed to spend one night more on the peaks.

They had stopped to eat a cold dinner and settled in their solo sleeping bags thereafter. It was comforting for the couple to think that the next day it would be just a short stretch before arriving at their next and final destination. With that thought in mind they both fell asleep under the spectacle of a magnificent night sky.

Lisa woke up to the Milky Way shining brightly – so beautiful. It was only for a second that she felt a warm appreciation for it before hearing a foot fall on stone near Carlo. She screamed in surprise.

This startled the monk creeping toward Carlo with a knife in hand. At the same time Carlo woke and managed to roll over just before the knife laced through the side of his sleeping bag and through his heart if he had not moved. By this time Lisa was out of her bag lunging at the monk who turned toward her.

She grabbed his hand with her own and in the process received a grazing cut on her middle finger. The monk took hold of her other hand and began wrestling out of her hold. "You must not leave here with the knowledge," he shouted as he freed the knife and plunged it toward his victim.

"Stop!" Carlo grabbed the monk's arm just in time. He managed to throw the monk to the ground, but the monk quickly escaped his loose hold and came up weapon ready. Stalking slowly toward the Italians they looked around for a place to exit, but only a sheer drop of hundreds of feet was behind them.

Occasionally in life, call it luck, call it destiny, the unusual fosters a second chance. This was one such event, for as the usually sure-footed monk came first at Carlo, he tripped over a rise in the stone flooring falling flat on his face, the knife leaving his open fist. Carlo reacted more swiftly than he ever had in his life and grabbed the monk's robe by the back and dragged him a short distance to the edge of the cliff and then over it.

Stunned, he sat by the precipice staring into oblivion. He was not a violent man, except now in horror he knew he could be.

<h1 style="text-align:center">60</h1>

"Are you threatening us?" I was incredulous.

"I am only telling you the truth. My father is charged with protecting information that has been handed down from father to the eldest son for generation after generation. He will stop at nothing to keep that secret from being leaked, including harming members of his own family. Lisa, you know what I am saying to be true." Claudia was clear.

I just couldn't believe that my claim of aliens having been around for thousands of years is important enough to warrant the lengths Claudia is suggesting just to keep it hidden. There must be more. Maybe 'the more' was concerned with where I was going with the info in my story. After all, Lisa's uncle was not yet at the point of forcefully stopping me.

"Let me consider it," I acquiesced. Perhaps I needed to buy more time, and I didn't want to upset Maria more than she already seemed to be.

With that both women seemed to relax, and our conversation turned to other more pleasant events.

Claudia wanted to visit Boston's sights during the short time she would be here. Maria promised to take her on the Duck Tour after which she would treat her to a walking tour of the Freedom Trail that ended in the North End of Boston with its famous neighborhood of Italian immigrants and descendants.

When the knife flew out of the monk's grasp it hit Carlo's leg and gave it a shallow cut that bled. The couple had no first aid supplies as those went over the cliff with the unholy holy man, and although the wound was not deep it was concerning. Lisa helped her lover bind it as best they could, using a portion of a t-shirt to do so, and with that they thought that all they could do was continue the path to the next sanctuary.

The mountain sky had been clear the morning of the incident, but as most afternoons arrived clouds began gathering and the weather became menacing. Their pace was significantly slower than when they were led by a guide. By late afternoon they wondered why they had not reached their next destination.

Perhaps the fallen monk had lied to them when he said that they should be at the monastery by late morning of that day. Maybe they were just going so much slower because Carlo's leg was painfully slowing their progress. Whatever, the sun was going down and they could not see a monastery in the foggy distance.

"We will have to camp one more night in the mountains," Lisa said, not looking at Carlo. Her fear was growing, and she did not want him to see.

"We must be close," returned Carlo. "I am sure that we will see it early tomorrow. Unfortunately, we have no food, but we have enough water to cover us."

With that they camped on an exceptionally wide part of the trail and decided that one of them should be awake and on watch all the time. Sleeping would happen in two-hour shifts.

Marco had been making good time along the path despite his wound and was past the point where the Italians and monk had their scuffle. There was nothing to indicate to him what had occurred, but he was keen eyed enough to see the small amount of blood left by the trail's edge. Someone was hurt.

He realized that if the couple had been taken out by the cabal's temple operative, he would have known it by now. He was left with the implausible assumption that somehow, they were still alive. The blood suggested that the monk had attempted to kill them, but he should not rush to conclusions. Although his wound was getting more painful with each mile, he had to try to increase his pace.

Night came. Unknown to Marco was the fact that he was less than two hundred yards away from Carlo and Lisa. It was foolhardy to continue to walk on a moonless night. However, his only hope was to get an early start and reach them before they could get to the safety that was less than a quarter mile away.

Sitting in my living room sometime after I stopped writing, I had an epiphany about those twelve other worldy masters supporting the one living master. Bhagwan suggested that these thirteen beings represented a concerted effort to enlighten the world.

It had never occurred to me before to think that these off-world masters might just be extraterrestrials or other dimensional entities. Perhaps, Bhagwan was a being from another planet or another plane of existence. How else could he be in contact with these supposed non-earthly essences?

Am I a product of alien intervention? Have I been instructed by a human alien, and has this something to do with my spinning a tale wanting to disclose all this?

Racing a thousand miles a second my mind was rapidly coming to that conclusion.

61

At the first hint of dawn Lisa woke Carlo. She was excited to get a glimpse of a monastery that was hidden in the fog close to their location. The path wound down to it, and they might not be more than an hour away.

Unknown to either of them, Marco had already come upon their position and before they could gather their gear, he entered onto the large shelf they had camped on.

"Finally, I have you my friends." Marco was gloating.

His pistol was out, and he was smiling. "You have gone as far as you're going to go. Normally killing people is just a job for me. Nothing personal, but I am going to enjoy killing the two of you. You really deserve it - this is for Dawn."

Directing his gun toward Lisa a shot rang out. She closed her eyes, but felt nothing. When she opened them, she saw Marco standing there looking down at his midsection where a red stain began to spread out through his clothes. An expression of disbelief was on his face as he crumpled to the floor.

The Italians stood shocked. Carlo then ran over to the body lying on the stone floor and checked its pulse. Marco was dead. He looked up toward where the sound seemed to have come from. Saying nothing he grabbed Lisa's arm and tore down the path with her as swiftly as he could leaving all the gear.

They made it to their destination in less than half an hour nearly out of breath. The doors opened and let them in where they both fell to the ground shivering.

The monk who greeted them rushed to find the head monk who came within a few moments. Asking his guest what happened the abbot proceeded to listen to the couple for the next few minutes telling him all that transpired since leaving the last sanctuary.

The head monk had known the errant monk who had attacked them. They were longtime friends. He was hard pressed to believe that his friend could commit such an act, yet anything was possible when it came to the powerful manipulators of this planet.

He instructed his charges to tend to Carlo's wounds as well as bring food and drink to both his visitors. Then, the Italians were taken to one room with two beds in it and told to rest until they were summoned.

It was after midday meditation before they were called. The abbot looked forlorn when meeting the couple.

"I had my people scour the mountains to find anyone out there that could have killed your enemy, and they did indeed find someone. He is very close to death, but is still breathing. We brought him to our infirmary where he lies unconscious. I will bring you down there now to see him."

With that said, the abbot brought them to a small room with a table in the middle. Lying on the table was someone covered in blankets. His or her head was facing away from the entrance. It took a long moment for Lisa to realize that it was Paolo laying there. His breath was very shallow, and his eyes were closed. No awareness came from their friend.

As Lisa and Carlo walked up to their prior companion his eyes opened and with a smile he said, "Told you that you should have picked me." That said, his breathing stopped.

"Your savior had been wounded for quite some time. He must have been in some extraordinary pain for a while as he seemed to have traveled some distance to get to the ledge where

he took his shot. My brothers could see blood staining the trail for quite a distance back."

"How could he possibly be here?" Carlo was speaking to himself more than anyone in the room. "How did he even know where to find us?"

Lisa lay over the body crying. Paolo was always an enigma. He was an enemy that somehow helped them, probably for his own selfish reasons. But still, he died for them. Here was another person to feel guilty about. He died because she wanted to know a family secret - how selfish she was.

After a time, Carlo grabbed Lisa's shoulders and led her away to their room. That night was one of nightmares and sorrow. Tomorrow something new will happen as it always does.

The morrow came and they were led to a larger room which held a table and six chairs. An old monk was sitting on one of them and invited them to take their place around the table.

The monk spoke. "I am to instruct you on the rest of what you need to know before discovering the key you have been looking for."

"Wait." Lisa stopped him. "This is it? You're just going to go on giving us information when our friend just lost his life for us? Are you that insensitive? I can't just do that."

"We are sorry for your loss, but you cannot stay here long and there is much you need to learn. There is no time to grieve. Whether you like it or not you have started this process and must finish it without delay. Please understand that I am not being callous when I say that all has its purpose in life, including the death of your companion. We are in a play and his part was played well and now is finished. To understand this is wisdom possibly beyond your comprehension, but wisdom you are being forced to embrace. Now I need to tell you what is my part to share. This will take days and then you need to go."

"The truths I am about to share have been orally transmitted to me through a line of predecessors that go back thousands of

years to a time before what we normally think of as our recorded history."

"This world has for all that time been ruled and directed by an elite group of people who have been aided by other worldly beings. These elite have sometimes been more benevolent towards their brethren and at other times less benevolent. There have been periods throughout this history where these rulers have been more open and accessible to the general public and periods where they have ruled from behind the scenes."

"Regardless of whether they were known or unknown by the people at large, this group has directed most of the action humanity has been involved in for millennium after millennium. The people have had very little say with directing what they could or could not do as they were told what and how to live either directly or through manipulation. To many outside this planet, the residents of Earth were considered enslaved by this small group of elite individuals who themselves were directed and influenced by entities not human."

"You have been learning much of the how and what happened in the past that brought all this about. What you need to understand now is that in our present time this group still maintains control in a most covert way. Most of humanity is totally unaware of their existence, nor are they aware of how they are being controlled and manipulated to follow the program."

"To begin with, what you would normally think of as advanced civilizations have been on this planet many times before. Atlantis and Lemuria were not myths, but actual advanced societies that arose and then fell. There were others before those two. These societies were much more technologically as well as spiritually knowledgeable than our present one. Some of them were even exploring our solar system and could do things that even today most would consider magical. They all fell because none of them were able to break the elite's control. They allowed themselves to either be seduced, bribed, or were too afraid to

free themselves from the bondage experienced under the yolk of their controllers."

"Our monasteries in Tibet have been an attempt by that part of humanity that remembers this knowledge. We have tried to help raise the consciousness in our population, in order that we are not so easily blinded to the elite's tactics of mass manipulation."

"The key to withstanding their power is to come to understand just who we are." 'Who Am I?' is the most important question for any individual to answer, yet few of us stop to ask it. Most are hypnotized to think that they already know who they are, but what they think they are, is usually only an inconsequential answer consisting of what they do in the world or a parody of what they are told by the authorities around them. To truly answer that question is to open up into a world where you are in touch with an indestructible self, capable of discerning truth from falsehood, being neither a leader nor follower, but a pure awareness of being one with all there is."

"Meditation is the most needed activity to explore oneself, but again due to the elite's influence few in society are willing to sit quietly with themselves, let alone meditate."

"Our monks and initiates spend many years in meditation and study to reach these heights, yet it is accessible to all of humanity. It is our very nature."

"You are being told this because it is necessary for you to explore this question yourself, especially now that you are becoming aware of all this previously hidden knowledge."

At that the monk got up and told them that they were to go with him to share the only meal of the day and spend some time afterwards in their cells pondering what they have been told and ask the all-important question – 'Who Am I?'

"Without at least exploring the question, even superficially what you discover through your quest will give you nothing useful nor will you be able to help anyone else," the abbot concluded his lecture.

Carlo interrupted the head monk with a question. "Why didn't the benevolent beings just come down and show themselves to the mass of humanity and expose the charade?"

"They did try many times to do just that, but each time ended in destructive calamity. They realized that humans endowed with free will would need to discover the truth on their own, otherwise their lower emotions would get triggered in violent defense which was something the self-centered aliens relished," the abbot explained.

"I am wondering if either of us is ready for all this," Carlo said after dinner.

"No need to wonder," was Lisa's response. "We are definitely not ready for any of it, although we are being given all this information for a reason. I am beginning to think that my grandfather and uncle were aware of all that we are being told – maybe even more. Who are we, if not the things we do and the beliefs we hold?"

Carlo responded, "I don't know."

A monk passed them in the hall as they were conversing; stopped, turned, and said: "That is a great place to start finding the answer to that question." He turned again and went on his way.

An hour later they were back sitting with their instructor.

"The elite have had countless millennia to perfect their control over the general population. They have passed down that control to family members and those that they deem amiable to their cause thus creating a long chain of uniquely capable people to continue the agenda of maintaining authority over a clueless populace. Now their power is godlike, as well as completely secret."

"There will soon come a time when this very elite will gain the technology of the aliens who are light years ahead of our relatively primitive race. When that happens, they will attempt to seal their position for countless millennia more by rallying the People to fight a non-existent alien threat. They will do this by *using their coveted secret alien technology that will be magical to the rest of the world. The things they will do to scare the populace into defending themselves against the alien threat will only seem possible if they were coming from an advanced alien species."*

"The vast majority of citizenry does not ever even consider the question 'Who Am I.' They will be led over a cliff to their own slavery and destruction. They have become followers. They have become children, not childlike. From the magnificent celestial beings that they really are they have stooped to become unconscious robots."

"This scenario of other-worldly war will not happen yet, but as we turn into the next century it is all but certain, unless humanity can turn itself around."

"If you are to be given the key you so desire you must understand that you are taking on a grave responsibility to help humanity turn itself around over the next century. Are you both willing to do that?"

"Before you answer that you must consider all that it may entail. Give me your answer in the morning. One way or another you will be leaving these mountains soon, with or without the key."

"But why do we even need the key? You have already told us so much." Carlo asked.

"The key will give you the proof of all I have told you," was the monk's response. "Until tomorrow."

62

"Maria, I need you to read my last chapter," I insisted.

Maria huffed. "You've never asked me to read any of your book. Why would you want me to read it now?"

"Somehow, what I am writing seems to be directly connected to what is truly hidden knowledge that affects our present world. Your cousin and uncle wouldn't be so threatening if it were not so, and what I just finished writing is starting to blow my mind. I'm not sure if this is going to put your uncle over the edge and if we are going to be in imminent danger because of it. Should I go into hiding? Tell me what you think because I am not going to stop."

After reading the last chapter Maria sat for a long time gathering herself, as if she wanted to say something, but did not know what.

Finally, she uttered, "We both need to call my uncle and tell him that you will not stop and that I will not ask you to stop. If he thinks that this compromises his duty we don't care, and if this story is true, we both believe that it is time it sees the light of day. We need to tell him that perhaps he needs to share his secret knowledge with us and the rest of the world now."

"Are you crazy!" I reacted with raised eyebrows.

"No. This must stop here, and if you're not willing to stop then we need to do this and provide some leverage for ourselves as well. You need to make many copies of everything you have written up to now and put them in packets ready to be sent to as many news outlets (both mainstream and alternative) as possible. Included with the manuscripts should be a letter explaining that they would be receiving this story only in the event of your death at the hands of my uncle and that everything in the story is true and the reason you were murdered. Is there anyone you can entrust these mailings to who would not be easily discovered?"

I thought of Amrit. He would do it and no one would ever think to link him to me. We were still friends but hadn't connected with each other in years. He would be perfect.

"Are you sure this will work?" I was more than apprehensive.

"No, but if you are not willing to discontinue this is the best option. You will need to prepare everything before we confront Uncle Gino. For now, let's just reassure my cousin by letting her believe that you are thinking of quitting. She will keep my uncle at ease until we confront him.

I was beginning to become convinced that somehow, I was getting everything I was writing about through some mystical connection with Maria. Perhaps that psychic link came because of the training I had with Bhagwan for all those years. My mind kept going back to his declaration that he was preparing his disciples to become the new man.

"The New Man" was a being who carried his own light wisdom and was not trapped by societal rules and directions. The New Man was a being who is open and truthful to himself and others and they in turn to him or her. This is the very being that would be capable of exposing the tyranny of the elite.

It dawned on me that for most of my years with Bhagwan I looked at the spiritual messages he gave us as not really meant for this world, but for some etheric realm beyond death and the physical body. Now, I could see that it was all inclusive. The wisdom was to be just as important in the physical as it was in the astral realms and beyond.

The morning once again came and with it the need to decide whether they were going for the key or not.

Lisa had thought that this decision was always only hers to make, but before falling asleep that night, she realized that it had to be made by her and Carlo together. It was important that he agree to this as he risked his life as much as she had to get to this point.

Just before the new dawn's light she woke Carlo with an urgency to make love that was beyond anything she had previously felt. Their coupling was highlighted by deep penetration while looking forever into each other's eyes, exploding into not only the merging of their two bodies, but the melting of their mutual heart, mind and soul creating a single ecstatic bliss. As they both consumed themselves in sensual ecstasy, they both glimpsed the understanding of who they were beyond their personalities. They both saw the is-ness of their being and indeed of all beings.

After a very long time coming down from their blissful heights, they knew that the only answer they both could give to the monk's query was YES.

'Yes,' was such a freeing answer although it meant taking on responsibility that seemed anything but freeing.

Upon entering the room to inform the monk of their decision they weren't surprised to gleam that he had already known their answer. Before they could say anything, he indicated that now the final trip to get the key was for only one of the two to climb the mountain further where that one would find a cave holding the key they were looking for.

"Which of you will it be?" he asked, smiling.

"Why must it be only one of us?" Lisa grew angry.

"Because the cave you are going to holds many sacred and rare objects and only one person is allowed to go to it to maintain its secrecy. One of you is less likely to be able to locate it again whereas two of you comparing notes might. Regardless, it is our rule that only one may go."

Both Lisa and Carlo said at the same time, "I will go."

The monk smiled. Talk it over and know that this will not be an arduous climb although it has many twists and turns and crossovers to it. You need not worry about making it. It will only take three hours one way so you will be back before sunset. Take a few minutes and choose."

Although Carlo felt it should be he who braves the final leg of the journey, Lisa insisted that it was for herself and her family that this was to be done and that it was her responsibility to do it. In truth, Carlo understood where she was coming from, but didn't want her to put herself at risk. It wasn't very long, however, before Carlo reluctantly agreed with his lover.

The monk then explained that she would be led to the cave by his most trusted monk, himself, and that he would instruct her just what to do when they got there.

The final leg of her quest began by starting on a wide path leading up to a place she was told would be above the tree line.

There was complete silence for the first two hours of the climb. During that time the duo traversed a path that was intersected by many other paths. At times they went up and then down. At times they seemed to be on a level plain. She began to understand how difficult it would be to remember how to reproduce this journey after only one visit.

The heights they eventually reached were dizzying as the breathtaking vistas were beautiful beyond anything Liza had ever seen. The thin air made her feel lightheaded and dizzy. She felt at times beyond the world in some other realm unknown to common men and women. The awesomeness brought tears to her eyes and a sense of smallness to her being.

During one of those particularly intense experiences of awe the monk turned around to her and said, "The feeling you are having is that you are nothing in comparison to what surrounds you. Now, instead of comparing yourself to what you see and feel, let it completely erase any sense of self you have and be who you really are."

After saying this he tapped her head lightly and something exploded inside. She became everything she saw, everything she heard, smelled and felt without separation. Only a sense of oneness was there. It was not even really that because as 'the two' was gone, not even 'the one' existed. JUST IS-NESS.

Lisa had no idea how long she was in this extraordinary space, but it felt like an eternity. However, when she became aware of herself again, it was probably a matter of moments because the sun was still in the same place as she last remembered it and the monk continued onward as if no time had passed. Reflections of her morning coupling with Carlo came to her now. She realized her present epiphany was indeed the same space she shared with her lover.

Shortly thereafter the monk began his discourse.

"There were twelve families entrusted with the truth that your own family has protected over all these many centuries. These families were given their trust to assure that the hidden knowledge would come out when the world needed to hear it. It was understood that the power of the elite would grow so enormous that they would be able to uncover many of these families and stop their ability to share the truth with their fellow man, but it was also believed that they would be unable to discover all of them."

"Your family was one of several that were discovered by the cabal. They became aware of your grandfather somewhere around the turn of the century and at that time they set out to eliminate that threat. First by killing your grandfather in a so-called accident and then by eliminating your Uncle Thomas on the field

of war. A war, by the way, that they orchestrated and controlled from both sides of the conflict."

"Yours was not the first family to have lost their sacred charge, but yours is the first to try to recover the knowledge. Usually, the remaining family members had no sense of what their patriarchs had lost, nor who would be interested in it. You, my dear Lisa, are an anomaly, and one that must have given the cabal quite a reason to be concerned. Through your dogged pursuit several more people know, or will know the truth the elite would prefer hidden."

"The knowledge you have been given these past several days is only a small part of the tale. You will learn much more when you see what it is that your grandfather and uncle hold in their secret space. For you see, they never really did lose what they were entrusted with. The cabal only found a false facsimile, and one that I am sure they are aware of by now."

"Unfortunately, there is nothing you can do with this knowledge other than keep it for the future. Now that the power structure knows you still possess it, they will not allow you to reveal it. Anyway, it is not time to do so."

"One thing you could do however is to share it with as many trusted people as you are able to, and in that way threaten the cabal's dominance. The secret you hold is going to be needed and shared with the masses very soon. In the next century your secret must become common knowledge, or the enslavement of the populace will continue far into the future."

"That being said, it is not practical for you to do all this sharing now. If you were to remain out in the open with this knowledge uncovered you will be eliminated just like your uncle and grandfather. Thus, we have decided that you cannot go back to your life as usual."

"What exactly does that mean?" Lisa queried.

"It means that you and the information you have will not last long out in the open, even if you threaten to tell a thousand *others. It means that we need to create you anew with a new identity and life. It means that for you to continue on with your family's legacy you can never see your family again."*

"I don't understand," she continued.

"Lisa, you must understand that there is no other way for you to continue. I am taking you to meet others in my order who will give you a new life that will hide you from the cabal. You will live in India as a modest Western secretary to a minor Raj. You will pass on your secret knowledge along with the proof of it to your daughter, and she to hers."

"You are crazy, and I will do no such thing. You cannot force me to leave everything. What about Carlo? What do you mean by passing this onto my daughter? I demand that you take me back and tell 'whomever', to go shove it."

With these words they turned a bend on the trail and were in view of a large cave entrance just above their position. Lisa could see that it was only possible to get to the entrance by climbing a rope hanging from the cliff on par with the earth's opening.

"The secret you have been searching for is just above you. Are you ready to seize it?" The monk enticed her.

"NO," she screamed.

63

"Stop this," Lisa shouted. "This secret is a curse and I no longer want it. I just want to go home with Carlo."

"Carlo is no longer at the monastery. By this time he has agreed to go to another of our temples to begin his journey of discovering his true nature. He has shown much potential, and I am sure that although he may be as reluctant as you are to do so he will see the wisdom of this course of action. Carlo will understand that to take any other course would be suicidal, and for nothing else he will submit to save your life."

"We do not intend to be cruel and if we saw that it was possible to let you two be together, we would do so, but the elite will be looking for a couple. This way it will be much harder for them to find you. Perhaps, later after Carlo discovers more fully who he is it would be possible to reunite with him, but for now it is unwise."

"Please understand, Lisa. We cannot force either of you to do what we are proposing, but any other way would not end well for you or Carlo. It is too late for you to turn back now."

Lisa fell onto the ground in shock. She and the monk stood by the extended rope for a long time without any movement.

Finally, Lisa lifted her head shouting, "You are telling me that I must end my life. This is beyond cruel."

"I am ascending the rope now. Stay here or climb up and live your fate. It is your choice. Cruel has nothing to do with it.

Your part in the play is what it is. Either play it or get off the stage." With that said, he climbed up to the ledge and disappeared into the cave.

After only a few minutes with tears in her eyes Lisa grabbed the knotted rope and began pulling herself up. It was not long before she stepped onto the ledge and entered the cave.

I interrupted my flow of writing with the thought that I must tell Maria that we have to get her uncle to reveal what he is hiding. He has to see that his effort to stop us should no longer be his directive. Yet, how are we to get him to see this?

There was darkness inside the cave. The outside light was the only source that illumined her to the monk sitting in the lotus posture waiting just inside the cave entrance.

"Please follow me," was all he said and with that he rose and proceeded deeper into the interior. At first, it narrowed until only one of them could slip through the pressing rock walls. The walls then twisted into many turns that went back and forth in a zigzag pattern. This went on for what seemed dozens of turns until after rounding another corner Lisa entered a larger cavern where the almost complete blackness suddenly turned into a warm glow of light.

The illumination seemed to be coming from the walls themselves. This large cavern appeared to go on forever. They began following a well-worn trail through the stalagmites and stalactites. It took them more than a quarter of an hour to get to the other end of the gigantic room.

Finally, they headed towards what appeared to be a solid wall, but became an opening Lisa could only see after almost being up against it. She saw a passageway on the side that bent around on itself and opened into a much larger tunnel that descended deeper still.

Up to this point neither Lisa, nor the monk had said a word since his initial instruction. Inevitably tired, Lisa asked, "How much longer until we get to wherever we're going?"

The monk looked back and said, "A little further ahead we will come to a hole in the floor. A monk will raise a ladder from below and we will proceed downwards."

After another five minutes progressing through the winding cavern they came to a tiny hole in the cave wall. The monk directed Lisa to squeeze through the entrance. Once inside she became aware of what appeared to be an opening in the floor. Looking into it she saw only a bottomless pit.

Once the monk joined her, he called down into the hole and in less than a minute a ladder appeared to come out of the endless pit.

They both climbed down onto a floor that was only twenty-five feet below. Next to where they landed was another hole that had a rope ladder attached that went down much farther. When they reached the bottom of the second hole two monks appeared. They directed both of them to a stone stairway that led down to a much deeper world.

Descending the stairway, the walls were again lit up by some biofluorescent covering. Lisa had been trembling in terror. Much of the passageways after the big cave room were only lit by a small candle that her escort carried. How he could see enough to direct them to that first hole in the ground and to the stairway was beyond her understanding.

Now the light was brighter than at any time since she left the daytime sky hours ago.

Turning to her companion she uttered, "You told me that this was only a three-hour trip one way."

"I lied," he said smiling.

They traveled further down for another two hours until Lisa was completely exhausted. "I cannot go any further," she exclaimed.

Her guide told her that they had arrived as he gestured to an archway through the cave wall before them.

One of the two men they had picked up along the way moved through the blackness of the archway. The first guide went through followed by Lisa and the last monk.

Upon entering what surely was another black part of the cave Lisa was overwhelmed by a brightness that had no possibility of being there.

She stood aghast at what appeared to be a room that went on forever. Below on the floor of this endless cavern there was the largest temple she had ever seen. It was the center structure in what one could only be termed as a city big enough to hold thousands upon thousands of residents.

64

"What is all this?" Lisa was overwhelmed.

"This is the future, my dear. Unbeknownst to the population above are countless cities held within the honeycombed structure of inner earth."

The ancients that you have been learning about have had advanced technology for tens of thousands of years and this is one of the results of it. From here we will stop in a vault room to look up the secret as to where you can find what your grandfather supposedly lost, and then you will be transported to your next life.

"I am so confused," she uttered. "You're telling me that all that you have told me already is not the information my family has been hiding, but that there is something I actually can find."

"Yes and no, dearest. The information is the key to be disclosed, but your family has an actual artifact that will be proof of all that you have learned. This artifact will be brought to you when you become settled in your new home. The hint as to where it is located is sitting in our vault under your family's surname. Now, all we need to do is look in the vault."

While sitting on the stoop with Maria and her cousin a day after I wrote those last words, she and I began pleading with Claudia to reach out to her father to get him to reveal the secret himself.

I told her that now must be close to the time for disclosure to happen. Maria supported my statement and, to my surprise, stated that somehow I was channeling information from her and her family.

"What more proof will he need to see that it is necessary to disclose everything now?" I said.

"Anyway," I went on, "Why is he so worried about my book being written? After all, it is only a book of fiction as far as the general public is concerned. I can't be accused of disclosing anything since I have just made up this story. Your father is being paranoid."

Claudia explained that her father was not so worried about publishing the book as a work of fiction but more concerned with the link between myself and Maria that was somehow allowing me to write the truth that has been kept from humanity forever. She further explained his fear that the connection between Maria and I could become so strong that I could learn where to access the proof of all that I had written.

Claudia advised, "My father knows that his information will be thrust upon the world soon, but he told me that he has to wait for certain telltale signs before doing so."

"What signs?" Maria asked.

"He didn't tell me. I will contact him and share what you told me." Claudia feared the worst. "Please let go of this," she pleaded. "I fear for your safety."

Maria and I looked at each other and I could see something that was incredulous in her eyes. I could see her adamant support of me whatever I was to decide, despite the consequences.

Later, I told Maria that I never had anyone support me so unconditionally the way I felt her supporting me.

She explained that she didn't believe that her uncle would do her any harm, although he might try punishing her in some way. She was not so sure about what he would do with me. "Regardless, I know that you must do what you must do," she told me.

"When you say it that way," I told her. "It doesn't seem like it is such a glorious support as I thought it to be."

"Please don't put this on me. Just do what you need to do," Maria said adamantly.

"Okay. Let's wait to see if your uncle will honor our request or not."

"Before we go to this vault," Lisa questioned the abbot, "I need you to explain something to me. Earlier before we began our deep descent into the cave, you said something about that I would pass on this information to my daughter and she to hers. How do you know I will have a daughter, or any child for that matter?"

"I know because you are pregnant already with her," was his response.

"That cannot be," Lisa insisted.

"My dear, more important than any of the truths you learned about this world is the truth you need to learn about allowing and letting go. These two abilities fostered in yourself will serve you better than any secret you can discover. Let go of what you think you know and accept what is right in front of you. I will repeat that you are pregnant with your daughter as we speak. If you trust anything, trust that."

"Oh, my god. I can't bring up a baby by myself. I need to talk to Carlo. He is the only one who could be the father."

"Of course, he is the father as he was always fated to be. I have explained to you before just why you cannot be with him now. You will be surprised what a wonderful single mother you will be and what a lovely child you will raise. Anyway, she may yet meet her father, at some later time. We must go to the vault, now."

The vault room was very small. Inside were twelve sealed enclosures, each four feet above the floor. Each enclosure held a scroll that could be seen through a wax seal with a name just above it. Lisa immediately spotted her family name above one of the enclosures.

None of the twelve seals appeared broken. She remembered the monk telling her that she was the only family member to ever come this far in seeking the lost knowledge. It seemed only her family seal would be broken.

She was told that she must break the seal and that whatever message was on the scroll would be only meant for her to decipher.

Breaking the seal turned out to be more difficult than she had imagined, but after several attempts and the use of a borrowed knife she succeeded. Once opened the scroll was carefully extracted. She unraveled it, expecting to read it; but the scroll held written words in a language she had never seen before.

At first glance, she was astonished to see her name in the header of the manuscript. Lisa Abrasi were the only words she could read and reading them frightened her more than any other moment in her recent journey.

"How am I supposed to read this?" She had turned to the monk standing next to her.

"You cannot, but I can. The writing is similar to Egyptian hieroglyphs. The heading says, 'For Lisa Abrasi, From Her Family.'"

Greetings from all who came before you and especially from your grandfather. What you are seeking has never been lost. It is found within the guardians of that which appears to be lost. Search there and carry on the legacy.

"How could whoever has written this know of me or my grandfather? Please don't do this to me. Please tell me that you are playing some trick on me. I just can't believe that this is not coming from you. Again, you are being so cruel." Lisa ran out of the vault, but once outside she realized that she had nowhere to run to.

Carrying the scroll in both hands the monk followed Lisa outside where she was on a rocky path overlooking the miraculous city below. "Please follow me," he said. Realizing she had no choice she walked behind him.

They wound down to the floor and landed on a street at the edge of the inner world metropolis. Soon the streets began bustling with people walking here and there. They came upon a tea stall where the monk stopped at a table. He motioned to Lisa to sit and proceeded to order two buttered teas.

When the tea arrived, he began to speak. "I know that this is more than is possible for you to understand, but you must believe me that I had nothing to do with what was written on that scroll. It may be impossible but your ancestors so many years ago wrote those words specifically knowing that one day you would search for them. Except for getting the relic you seek to find, this is the final piece I need to share with you before sending you on your way. The other worldly beings visiting Earth had an intimate relationship with the humans wandering the planet so many thousands of years ago as to be beyond comprehension. Those travelers from the stars and beyond understood that time is not linear. In fact, there is no time as we know it. You can also say that everything that ever was or ever will be is happening at the same time. They shared this knowledge with all our ancestors. Within this knowledge is the secret of how to travel in linear time. One or more of your family members has seen you open that scroll in what you term your past, but was their future. It is beyond your comprehension to even believe this, but I assure you that it is the truth. Believe it or not I must ask you if you know where they are indicating you will find that which you seek."

"I do, but I am not telling you," was Lisa's response.

65

aria and I anxiously waited for her uncle to respond to our request. We were still waiting when the next chapter screamed within me to be written.

Lisa spent that night sleeping in what was the equivalent of a tiny hotel room. It was little more than one of the cells she had spent the past few days in the monasteries she had previously visited.

In her mind, she was fixated on the clue given to her on the scroll. In truth, despite what she had told her guide she had no idea where the cryptic message was trying to direct her.

Who are the guardians of the box? Why does it say that it appears to be lost when the box is actually missing? Perhaps, the box did not contain that which she thought needed to be recovered. Maybe that's the answer.

Lisa lamented to herself that after all her trials she had come to another mystery. Maybe she was never meant to find out her family's secret, although she had found out some very bizarre ideas that were beyond her comprehension and ability to process. If only she had Carlo here to discuss this puzzle.

These thoughts led to sadder reflections on just how much she missed her lover. Why did it take so much time to recognize how much she needed him?

The monk told her that tomorrow she would be sent to a small Indian village where she was expected to make a home for herself and her prophesied daughter. This was to be done whether she told him where he could find the artifact or not. He seemed content to allow her to withhold the information for as long as she wanted.

"Several nuns live in the village you are being sent to in order to watch over your needs," he told her.

Hearing this, she understood that she would be a prisoner in the village unable to wander back to Italy, or anywhere else for that matter. It seemed her quest would end up in the worst way possible.

The only bright spot Lisa could see was that the village she was being sent to was at the foothills of the Himalayas and was a place she had heard about before. She was certain the village was the place Anand and Sita often traveled through on their way to do their research in the Himalayan monasteries.

Uncle Gino got out of the sedan that just parked right in front of Maria's stoop where I was sitting and talking to Maria. He was followed by Claudia who had told us nothing of his arrival. Maria and I both jumped up in shock.

I wondered if he was there to kill us. There appeared to be no malice in Uncle Gino's eyes, and this shocked me even more. A smile was on his face as he came up the stairs to where we were. To my great surprise he gave both of us a huge hug.

"You have passed the test and shown me the first sign of disclosing our message to the world," Gino announced.

Although the monk had spent several days trying to persuade Lisa to tell him the meaning of the scroll's message, she would not budge.

"Send me to wherever you think appropriate, I will get the object myself. I do not trust you and I will never disclose its hiding place to you."

The monk knew that he was at an impasse with her. In acceptance he stopped pressuring her, but rather turned his attention to insisting that Lisa was never to visit her old home again. Whatever way she found to get that which was hidden she needed to do so without the cabal knowing that she retrieved it, nor the fact that she was alive and living in India.

"I understand," was all that she would say before being led to her new abode.

After spending many days in the underground city Lisa was accompanied by two monks who escorted her through wondrously lush gardens with rushing rivers and a towering waterfall. Behind the waterfall was a cave that led further down for many hours until they came to another smaller city still deeper under the Earth's surface.

In this city she saw what looked to be a train, although it was not resting on tracks, but rather seemed to float over a fine gold colored metal strip.

Lisa was directed to the front car. She was asked to enter it but became confused because there were no open doors to enter. Her companions kept indicating for her to walk straight through what looked to be the windowed wall of the car in front of her. She reached out with her arm expecting to feel the vehicle, but found that her hand and arm went right through what she thought was a solid metal and glass exterior.

"Please go all the way through," one of her escorts requested. She did so and found herself in a comfortable, but unfamiliar interior. Everything was ultra-sleek with cushioned chairs that swiveled, and moved up and down with just the mere thought of doing so.

"We will be at our destination in a few minutes. Our master wished for us to tell you that more important than all the information you received about extraterrestrials and the true history of our planet is the understanding that your existence as a separate being on an isolated planet is an illusion and that this illusion has fostered fear and greed in many on the planet. The illusion also gives those same people an opportunity to experience

a profound sense of love and unity. It is every person's choice how they use it. He suggests that you use it wisely."

After sharing their message her companions told Lisa that she had arrived at what was to be her new home. Even though the train-like vehicle had not appeared to move she somehow knew that they had traveled a great distance and stood up to leave.

Traveling in this bizarre fashion finally convinced her to believe all that the Tibetans had told her.

Walking through the vehicle's wall she came to a platform area with a door embedded in the rock wall at one end. The door opened on its own and revealed an elevator which she entered without being asked. The door closed leaving her alone for a short time. Later it opened to the view of a beautiful woman, obviously of East Indian origin. Smiling, her new keeper gave her an intimate hug and welcomed her home.

After their greeting, they traveled through a cave for no more than five minutes and exited onto an overlook situated on the side of a hill. Below, was a small village that looked to be a place that had not changed much in many hundreds of years.

Lisa was then directed to a door behind which she was told was to be her new home. Walking through what looked like a small rather unassuming entry. Lisa found herself looking at a spacious courtyard open to the sky. The edges were bordered by rooms for living in and rooms for housing farm animals for eggs, milk and cheese.

That night at Maria's house we had dinner with the whole family that included Uncle Gina, Claudia, Maria's mother, Joey, Maria, and myself.

While eating we spoke of nothing but present family matters and niceties. It wasn't until after clearing the table to have coffee when Maria confronted her uncle by asking him if he would disclose his secret to the world.

"It is still not quite time yet to do that," he told us. "The fact that you have insisted on publishing this book along with all the chaos currently in the world tells me that it is very, very, close to the time when this will happen. But, there is still one more thing to happen before disclosure.

"So, what more do you need to happen?" This came from Claudia.

"It is time that I become honest with all of you," he responded. "I don't really know what also has to happen for the world to know our secret, because I don't know or have the secret to disclose."

"You see," he continued, "I only know of the secret. It was taken away from my great, great grandfather, and the only knowledge I have is that it was passed into the keeping of my great aunt who I assume still lives in India since the 1930's. I don't even know if she obtained access to the knowledge, although I was told by my father that she most probably had."

"I was also given clues of when it would be time for the world to know of the truth of its history by my father. He is the one who told me that the world would experience great fear, through disease, war, weather and natural disasters, and that someone close to us would reveal most of the information through a fictitious novel before the real disclosure would happen."

"We will have to wait until my great aunt, or one of her female descendants comes forth any time now."

"Do you know anything else about your aunt and her life in India?" I was eager to know.

"The only other information I received, and I have not been able to corroborate it, is that she got married to someone from Italy at some point and had a total of three kids. That's it."

66

Eleanora was feeding the chickens in one of the stalls sur-rounding the open courtyard. It was a very exciting day for her because it was her birthday. She was turning eight-years old and her mother promised her a new dress and new shoes. Life was simple in the village where she lived, but there were a lot of adventures she had playing make-believe with her friends amongst the hilly terrain nearby.

Swimming in the river and exploring caves were also great pleasures for her, but dressing up was also something she loved to do, and her mother promised to get her some beautiful new clothes.

Lisa watched her daughter taking care of the animals. At first, she had found it hard living in the small village, but had grown to love the simplicity of it. She really appreciated all the love showered on her daughter by all her neighbors and friends.

In the beginning, she thought of the nuns and neighbors as her jailers, but it did not take long to see that they genuinely cared for her and her daughter's wellbeing. She no longer viewed them as anything but extended family, even though she was well-aware of the fact that they would not allow her to venture out from the village and its surrounding area.

It had been a few years since she last thought of her quest and the secret that at one time obsessed her. Now, it was but a distant memory. She was satisfied if not completely content to see herself as never succeeding in finding just what her grandfather had so diligently protected.

All this passed through her mind as she looked at her daughter. Lisa smiled at the thought of celebrating with Eleanora and her friends.

As that last thought passed her awareness there came a jingle from the bell she had installed at the front door. She got up to see who wanted to break her morning revelry.

When she opened the door, she gasped. Standing at her doorstep was what she convinced herself could no longer be possible. It was Anand and Sita looking dumbfounded. Lisa broke into tears. Her daughter, with a concerned look, reached for her mother's hand, but Lisa let the hand go and threw her arms around the Indian couple who were also crying.

"We thought you were dead," Sita proclaimed.

"From the first day of living here I told many of my friends to look out for you, but I had lost all hope of that ever happening for some years now. I can't believe it — you're here now." Lisa gushed.

"Several of them told us that a woman here wanted to see us, but we were unsure who that could be. We never made any lasting friends here and only passed through briefly on previous occasions, so we were most suspicious of who would want to see us," Anand chimed in.

"It is more than beautiful to see your lovely face," Sita added. "You must tell us all that has happened, and you must introduce us to this lovely child."

"This is my daughter, Eleanora." With that introduction Lisa made tea and spent the rest of the afternoon describing to her two friends the whole adventure she and Carlo had and the subsequent nine years since they parted.

"I still have no idea where Carlo is," explained Lisa. "I have just about given up hope of ever seeing him again, but then again, I had given up hope of ever seeing you two as well. Now, you have to tell me your story. Did the police ever find

out about the murders? Did they think that you had anything to do with them?"

"Believe it or not, our beloved aiya protected us from anyone ever finding out what happened. She stayed away from the house for a while, but eventually she suspected something amiss and came back to see the gravesites. She never said anything to the police, however, and told the rest of our staff that we were on an extended research trip. Although the police had visited because a friend had been worried about not seeing us for a while, she convinced them that she was in contact with us and that everything was okay."

Sita continued by explaining that when they came back, they explained to the aiya that the graves were for two beloved dogs who died. They said the dogs belonged to a close friend of theirs who had asked the couple to bury them in the backyard. "We knew she thought this explanation strange, but she never questioned our explanation, and although we stayed home for a period much longer than we have in the recent past just to assure ourselves that we would not be in trouble, trouble never did happen."

"So, what will you do now, and while telling your story you never mentioned if you were able to decipher the riddle that the scroll presented to you?" asked Anand.

"I will stay here, because it has become my home and I doubt the nuns would let me leave with good reason. About the riddle, that is where you two come in. I am so glad to see you again for so many reasons; one of which is to help me discover if what I expect is the answer to the scroll's cryptic message is correct or not. If it is correct, I hope you will bring me the family artifact that has gone missing for so long. If not, I will let go of any lingering desire to find it. Either way, I will be free."

Lisa proceeded to tell them what she thought the message was trying to convey. After staying in the village and visiting with her, the two Indians journeyed back to their home to begin pursuit of the mission Lisa had requested of them.

67

*S*ita and Anand had taken some time at their home office to digest all that Lisa had told them about the newfound history she was introduced to. Much of it correlated with their research, yet much of it was beyond anything they had imagined. They used some of her information to edit portions of the book they soon hoped to publish concerning the ancients and their technology.

They were most anxious to investigate Lisa's theory of where her family's artifact was hidden. It would take some effort to be able to verify what she thought was the riddle's answer without being discovered by the cabal.

For some time now, the couple realized that they were being watched, although recently it seemed that this was happening less. The task required them to go to Italy. This meant that the surveillance would become more intense.

Furthermore, the fact that they needed to go into Lisa's childhood home would exponentially confound the problem. The cabal certainly would be still watching that house. Because of all this, they needed to implement Lisa's plan to perfection.

The plan they worked out with Lisa was to go visit her second cousin, Domenic, who lived in Rome and who from time to time visited his first cousin, Juliana. Lisa wrote a letter to him and another to give to her mother and stepfather in which she explained her living situation. She also explained where she thought her mother's father's secret was hidden.

Her mother, Juliana must have thought her dead for over nine years and in this way, she could at least reassure her of the fact that she was very much alive. Her mother would be keen to find out if the artifact was where Lisa thought it to be. After all, it was her mother who had the original passion to find her father's secret.

In the darkness of night Juliana could explore the hiding place and if what was suspected was there, she could spirit it to her cousin and back to Anand and Sita.

The Indian couple would again use a visit to Rome as a research trip as they once previously had done, and later their visit to Milan as an opportunity to connect with their lost friend's parents with the excuse of trying to find out anything of Carlo and Lisa's whereabouts.

Anand and Sita would already have the artifact in their possession safely stashed away before going to see Lisa's parents so nothing would look amiss to the spies surveilling the Indian couple and the parents.

Many months later, the plan unfolded perfectly. Juliana set out on a moonless night to prod around the mantel that once held the box that was believed to have held the family's secret heirloom.

At first, Juliana thought this to be a fruitless effort. She had been living in that house all her life. She would have noticed anything like a button or hidden latch protecting some secret compartment hidden there.

She had been looking for close to an hour and was just about to give up when she discovered that one of the faces on the mantel slid just a bit when she pushed it hard. It appeared to be like one of those European hidden boxes where the panel is so tightly attached that it seems to not be a panel at all. At this point it took her some time to work the panel open only to see a black box.

She took out the box and then proceeded to the other panel and in a short time she recovered another black box. For several hours she examined the boxes but could not see how they were supposed to work.

Several days later Dominic's brother came for a visit and took away the unassuming boxes that were concealed in a large loaf of bread. He took them to Dominic in Rome and Dominic gave them to Sita and Anand.

It was difficult for Juliana to learn of her son's death and her daughter's living situation. She agreed with the letter from her daughter that there was no way that she could ever see Lisa again without jeopardizing her life. The fact that she learned that her daughter was alive and well and that she had a granddaughter was somewhat of a comfort and it would just have to do.

It was some time after all this occurred that Juliana and her husband sold the home that her family had occupied for millennia. This was also the beginning of a new family secret passed down by Juliana's cousin's family line, from father to son that the original hidden knowledge was now in India with her daughter and granddaughter.

Juliana divulged to her family the information that Lisa had written to her that the knowledge would see the light of day when the world was ready to hear it and that would be when the planet was in great crisis. The crisis would be the result of humans not being able to live any longer in the dark as to their place in the universe. They were to become one with the various other occupants in this cosmos.

Much later, Juliana and her husband got a final communication from her daughter explaining that the boxes she had sent to India were discovered to be a product of an advanced technology that would prove the truth to the many manuscripts and hidden history revealed by it.

Hopefully, the cabal would uncover nothing of the switch that happened and her family's truth would be revealed in the proper time.

Incidentally, Lisa told her mother that she was married and that Juliana had three grandchildren, not just one. She never revealed the name of her Italian husband.

"Anytime soon," Gino told his sister at the kitchen table. "I am sure that it will happen anytime soon. The world is going further and further out of control and with that chaos the elite's control of the social order is rapidly disintegrating. Let's hope our cousins in the East will finally share with the world their secret."

The night after the scene that took place at the kitchen table, I had a dream. In the dream Bhagwan came to me as he used to many years before.

"We are all one," he said. "You have done well listening to the inner music presented and it is now time you share this knowledge in your writing before actual events begin to happen. The most important knowledge, however, is that you are that which is. In that is-ness all are one. All that you have learned through meditation and experiences that taught you acceptance and letting go are not only in the service to your greater well-being, but also to fulfill the needs of humanity. The Earth and all its beings are to become an aware and active member of a galactic federation that is composed of all types of intelligent beings; some more and some less advanced technologically, socially, consciously, and energetically than man is now."

"To be able to participate in a membership with these galactic brothers and sisters a new man needs to be born. The sannyas I taught, as well as the teachings of other masters in the later part of the 20th century was to help bring about this new man who is a mature human being, who exhibits the attributes of compassion, awareness of his/her deeper self, acceptance, truthfulness and is in touch with the oneness of everything."

"Separation will be no longer."

Several days after receiving that dream a sannyasin friend sent me a quote by Bhagwan from a book called "Just Like That" Talks on Sufi Stories:

"You are very ancient ones, you are not new ones here. You have trodden the same Earth thousands of times. The Earth is new in comparison to you because you have been to other planets also. You have been eternally here. You have been millions of things. You are not a clean slate, much is written there. Many incomplete systems are alive there."

It is time we come to realize this and get ready for the new man who has always existed, but was only forgotten. It is time to become part of an expanded universe.

THE END

EPILOGUE

While sitting and looking at the trees I am reflecting on my book *Prelude to Disclosure*. I live in a townhouse north of San Francisco. There are no stoops in this townhouse complex and there is no creek with sun sparkling water to view. My backyard is a forest and gladly a place where peace and serenity shower down on me every day.

As for my relationship with Maria, that lasted only a few years after the events of the last chapter took place. Maria still lives in my old neighborhood in the same apartment that is attached to my favorite stoop. Maria's son Joey, is married with a son of his own living near her. Her mother, Isabella, and Uncle Gino are no longer alive.

Thirty years have passed and only now is my story ready to be published. Many expected and not so expected delays have happened, not least of which was due to my own procrastination. Actually, such a long delay in publishing seems weirdly predestined. Events that preclude *Disclosure's* introduction to the world only now seem to be unfolding.

For as long as I can remember, I believed that at the turn of the century Earth would go through catastrophic changes that would usher in a whole new way of how humanity needs to live on this planet. It never occurred in any way that I had imagined it would. Nothing major happened to Earth at the turn of the century, unless you consider September 11, 2001.

That was just one small event, however, and did not merit the kind of multiple calamities I expected.

Now in 2023, it appears to be the time that is more akin to what I believed would culminate into drastic changes on Earth: climate change, disease, social division, confusion, war, and the sense of overwhelming fear. These factors appear to be the catalysts that can catapult society to bring about a new vision for humanity. This new vision is needed for us to enter into a universe that includes many other conscious beings. The truth of our undisclosed history when revealed to the world will aid us in becoming knowledgeable members of this broader universe.

Being a channel to receive a transmission from God knows where, is almost impossible for me to believe. The message that the world has been ruled since time immemorial by an elite class who themselves are directed by other worldly beings using levels of consciousness and technology only the mystics of old possessed, is beyond anything I could have imagined.

The fact that I was somehow given this knowledge through unconsciously tapping into someone else's consciousness has been miraculous. Yet, who is going to believe this story anyway? Most people reading this will interpret my manuscript as a fairytale and its revelation as just a technique to enhance it. How am I to convey that this is all true and that Maria's family is a holder of this truth? Without Maria's great aunt or one of her female descendants coming forward this will only appear to be my imagination.

In any event, we shall soon see.

Who am I? I AM.

BIO

Nirvan, the grandson of Italian immigrants was born and raised in East Boston in the middle part of the 20th century. Over the years he has had many occupations including: property manager, accountant, therapist, astrologer and tarot card-reader, as well as being an entrepreneur participating in a variety of businesses.

Throughout his life his constant interest in metaphysics and spirituality eventually led him to the spiritual teacher named Bhagwan Shree Rajneesh, now known only as Osho. Over a period of 12 years, he lived at Osho's ashrams in India, California, and Oregon where he had many life-changing experiences.

His debut novel, *Prelude to Disclosure,* reflects his keen sense of adventure, storytelling ability and his heartfelt trust in the power of love to help heal and bring light into our world. His multi-faceted prism of insights that are incorporated into the novel about love remind the reader that we are not separate, but are seamlessly connected to all beings as part of a greater consciousness beyond the sense of separateness that we identify with from our earliest memories.

Nirvan currently lives in Marin County, CA with his wife and cat. He communes daily with his many neighbors that include: deer, racoons, turkeys, skunks, coyotes, and the humans living around him.

ABOUT
BHAGWAN SHREE RAJNEESH
NOW KNOWN AS
OSHO

An enlightened man currently referred to as "Osho", was born December 11, 1931. He has been known by many names throughout his life: Raja, Chandra Mohan Jain, Rajneesh Chandra Mohan, Rajneesh, Rajneesh Acharya, and most notably as Bhagwan Shree Rajneesh, "the blessed one". His teachings and efforts to unify the best insights and teachings of the east and the west with the intention of evolving a new and more conscious humanity earned him the recognition of being one of the most influential people of the 20th century. Known for brilliant, insightful, and controversial discourses and approaches to meditation his work continues to touch the lives of countless people; liberating them from social norms, oppressive social conditioning and traditions that often function as obstacles to personal and spiritual growth. Dedicated to waking people up with the means of self-discovery through his Neo-Sannyas movement, his wish was to create a more peaceful world, free from destructive patterns, and the age-old sense of separateness that is the root of so much suffering. He is one of the first gurus to use many varieties of media to spread his message to millions of followers and non-initiated fans around the world. In December 1989, he dropped his title of Bhagwan Shree Rajneesh and requested that he be called "Osho" (meaning=-friend) and left this world on January 19, 1990.

Visit resources below to learn more about Osho, his teachings, social media sites, helpful links to communities, or to visit the Osho International Meditation Resort:

OSHO VIHA BOOK DISTRIBUTOR & INFORMATION CENTER
HTTP://WWW.OSHOVIHA.ORG
PO Box 352, Mill Valley. CA 94942
Tel: 415-472-5381   866-856-7019

OSHO INTERNATIONAL MEDITATION RESORT
https://www.osho.com/osho-meditation-resort
Tel: 91 20 6601 9999
17 Koregoan Park 17, 1ˢᵗ Lane, Koregoan Park, Pune Maharashtra 411001, India
Facebook https://www.facebook.com/osho.international
Instagram https://www.instagram.com/oshointernational
https://iosho.osho.com (Igniting Individual Intelligence)

OSHO WORLD
HTTP://OSHOWORLD.COM
44 Jhatikra Rd, Pandwala Khurd, near Najafgurh, New Dehli, India 11043
Tel: 91 9717490340   9971992227
Facebook https://www.facebook.com/oshodham.delhiindia
Instagram https://www.instagram.com/oshodham.delhi/